WHISPERS OF THE HEART
Barbara Woster

Cover by Ashley Creative

DEDICATION

For my family, without whose love and support, I could never have written this book. I love you all, dearly.

CHAPTER ONE

March 2059
Covington, Georgia

"I'm coming," Kathryn murmured and then rolled over, nuzzled further beneath the quilt, and drifted back to sleep.

A few moments later, the chimes sounded again, twice in succession, and Kathryn opened her eyes, rubbing the fatigue away. She started to poke her husband, in hopes he would crawl out of bed on this chilly morning, but her elbow met empty space.

She glanced over at where he generally slept, and then at the clock on the nightstand. Seven o'clock, the bright red digital display read. *Odd*, she thought, as she threw the quilt back and slid to a seated position; *Robert is usually home from work by now.*

The musical chimes of their doorbell rang again.

"I'm coming!" She quickly donned her pajamas and darted down the stairs, adding in a whisper, "Keep your drawers on!" A thought settled in her brain that Robert simply forgot his key, but as she approached the front door, she saw a note from him taped there.

"So, he didn't forget his key after all."

She pulled the note down and smiled as she read, the early morning visitor momentarily disregarded.

Kat, have taken the little ones to breakfast. They were up when I came in, and you looked like you could use a little extra sleep. Be home soon. Rob

Rob may not be the most passionate of men, she thought, *but even after five years of marriage, he is very courteous.*

3

He worked third shift, and was undoubtedly fatigued when he came dragging in early in the mornings, yet he still took time to think about her. Well, if she continued on her current road of success, she would repay his kindness by offering him the prospect of early retirement.

The chimes sounded again, accompanied by a shout from the other side of the door. "Mrs. McMurray? Are you there?"

"Wait a minute," she murmured, "if Robert didn't forget his key, who's this then?" Although they lived in a respectable neighborhood, it didn't mean she could safely open the door to strangers. Too many wackos in the world, by her estimation.

Besides, why would the caller ask for her and not Robert? That could only mean the man knew she lived there; yet there was nothing familiar about his voice. If it were a burglar, why call her by her name? Why call out to her at all? Why not just break in? To put her at ease? But that hadn't worked. By calling out her name, he actually set her on her toes. Should she ignore him and dial 911? "And look like a complete idiot," she countered quickly. She sighed heavily. Living with a mistrustful police officer had driven paranoia deep into her own brain. She sighed again and took a deep breath. There was only one way to dispel the suspicion and ease the worry over something that could turn out to be nothing. After all, her daddy had always told her that people feared the unknown, but if it became known, there was no cause for fear.

After another deep breath, she stepped toward the door. "I'm here. What can I do for you?" A quick inventory of the locks, all secure, brought her mental imbalance back on an even keel. There was no way a burglar could get through this fortification.

"Could you open the door, please, ma'am?"

Oh yeah, like I'm that *stupid,* she thought with a shake of her head.

She wondered how many innocent women had simply obeyed an authoritative command to open up, only to have the door smashed inward and . . .

Kat ceased that thought in its tracks, but still shuddered at the possibility it could happen to her. She may not like the paranoia that accompanied being married to a police officer, but she certainly couldn't complain that his directives kept her out of harm's way.

"Since I'm not going to open the door, you can leave now. Unless you're prepared to explain – very quickly – why you're ringing my bell so early in the morning." Kathryn moved to the adjacent living room to see if she could get a view of the man on her porch. She was a little more than curious whether the man would remain or if he would leave. If he left, she could all but conclude that he'd meant to crash in and assault her; however, if he stayed . . .

She couldn't quite ascertain what the implications of that would be. What would a stranger want with her before seven in the morning? She lifted the living room curtain slowly and glanced out, but the glare of the rising sun made the figure barely distinguishable. She really wished Robert would concede to getting a peephole put in the door, but he said he never liked them, because it made it too easy for someone to stab you in the eye when peering out. That was a police officer for you, always obsessed about safety.

She glanced back at the door when she noticed that he'd started speaking again. She wouldn't be able to hear him from here, so she moved back to the foyer.

"I'm sorry, but what did you say?"

"I said, this is the police, Mrs. McMurray. It's Sergeant Kieran O'Sullivan. Do you remember me? Your husband and I work together. Could I please talk to you for a moment?"

5

Kathryn had met Kieran O'Sullivan only twice during her marriage. It was a name familiar to her as her husband's superior. Definitely a good name to use if someone wanted to gain entrance into their home. She shook the suspicion away again and moved back to the window. She lifted the curtain and tried harder to make out anything about the man standing at her front door. It wasn't working. The sun was simply too bright. Well, that was one thing she was going to insist upon Robert installing – an overhanging eave. That way, sun or no, she would be able to see who was ringing her bell. She lowered her head and shook it in frustration. There had to be a way to establish if this was Kieran O'Sullivan.

When she looked up, the man was leaning over and staring at her through the window. It startled her, and she dropped the curtain back into place.

"Mrs. McMurray? Open the curtain. I'm sorry I scared you. I have my badge out so that you can call and verify my identity. Please, I really need to talk to you."

Kathryn took several deep breaths to calm the rapid beating of her heart and moved slowly back toward the window. She reached out, and then pulled her hand back when she noticed how badly it was shaking. She took another calming breath and then reached out again. A little steadier, she noticed. *Apparently,* she thought with another deep, calming breath, *this man isn't a burglar, if he is this intent on speaking with me, and is willing to show me his face – and his badge.* Badge?

He said he was a cop, but she ignored that. Anyone could claim being a policeman, but not everyone had a badge to show as proof. She drew the curtain aside and Kieran smiled. He removed his hat and smiled again, but it was an insincere effort; did not reach the sadness enveloping his gaze. He held his badge against the pane. "Call the squadron if you need too. I'll wait." She felt a shudder pass throughout her body, for though she now had no difficulty identifying her husband's superior, she was suddenly even more loathe to move back to the door, to release the security of the deadbolts.

"Mrs. McMurray? Can I come in now?" Kieran asked, placing his hat back on his head. "If you're more comfortable, I can call my partner from the car."

Kathryn shook her head and lowered the curtain. By the time she retraced her steps to the door, there was no longer any doubt as to why he'd come. Her hands were shaking in despondency by the time she released the final deadbolt, and with a cry of anguish, she wrenched open the door and flung herself into the Sergeant's embrace, tears of distress wracking her body.

"I'm so sorry, Kathryn," Kieran whispered, holding her close.

CHAPTER TWO

March 2059
Wind River, Wyoming

"Mrs. Guthrie!"

"Yes, sir. I'm right here, sir!" The housekeeper bustled into the study, eyeing her boss with wary unease. He was drinking too much today. She understood why well enough, but since he wasn't at all familiar with bourbon, it was having a displeasing effect on his disposition.

"Oh," he said, stumbling toward the chair at his desk. "Get rid of everyone," he said, his words already beginning to slur. "I want them all out of my house now!"

"But, sir," Mrs. Guthrie said gently, "they've only come to pay their respects. Surely you—"

"Get rid of them, Mrs. Guthrie. I can't do it, whatever it is they think I'm supposed to do, I just can't. Not today. I can't." He took another gulp of the fiery liquid, gasped, coughed, and then took another swig. He'd heard that drowning one's sorrows was the best remedy at a time like this, and he fully intended to saturate himself so that he would sink straight to the depths of Hell. His mind was already there, so why not let his body join along. *I'm not thinking straight*, he thought as he missed the chair he was aiming for and landed with a loud thump on the carpet. He looked up in confusion.

"Sir, should you—?"

"Go away, Mrs....Mrs...."

"Guthrie, sir."

"I know, now go away now, Mrs...."

"Guthrie, sir."

"I know! Go away!"

"Certainly, sir, and I'll be happy to take my leave of you, but perhaps I'd best take the bourbon along as well. What little there is left, that is."

"Touch it and you're fired!"

"Drinking yourself into a stupor isn't going to bring–"

"Say it, and I'll kill you!"

"Aye, well, you'll certainly be regretting this behavior come morning, and I will, for certain, be making you."

"Go away!" Dalian said through gritted teeth.

"Aye, sir, and I'll see to the guests for you," she said, backing toward the study door. "And I'll make certain you're not disturbed. Not that anyone would want to be in your company right now."

The door closed softly, leaving Dalian Rivers alone with his drink and his mourning. He pushed himself onto unsteady legs, spotted the chair, and took careful aim, plunking his butt soundly into the seat. The bourbon bottle tipped during his efforts and a small bit spilled onto his pant leg before he could right it. His brow furrowed in confused irritation, as the odor drifted into his nostrils, then he noticed the bottle of amber liquid grasped in his hand. *How did that get there?* He wondered. "Oh well, it doesn't matter." He lifted the decanter and swallowed another substantial gulp, then lowered the crystal container, gasping. The burning subsided in his throat and the warmth enveloping his stomach intensified. His head suddenly felt too heavy for his shoulders, so he let it fall back on the headrest. He stared at the ceiling, but the splatters of paint rapidly began configuring into the shape of his dead wife and unborn baby, so he pulled his head up. It was taking a Herculean effort to keep his skull steady, so he finally gave up and let it collapse onto the desk.

Then the tears started falling.

CHAPTER THREE

September 2060
Covington, Georgia

"Do you think that the resurgence has to do with the upcoming hearing?"

Kathryn was sitting across from her publisher and best friend, Janet Ackers, drinking a mocha cappuccino in the cool fall afternoon. The open-air café was a known haunt for writers, publishers, and agents, which is why Kathryn usually avoided coming, but Janet insisted.

"You need to get outside, Kat," she'd said with her usual mother-hen concern, and then added, with a hint of a threat, "and if you don't come, I won't publish your next book."

Kathryn knew it was a bluff, but consented because her publisher was right about needing to get out more. A look in the mirror this morning as she was getting ready clarified that point. Her normally sun-bronzed complexion was getting a bit pasty, and if she continued behaving as a hermit, writing day in and day out, she would soon start to look like a zombie. After a year-and-a-half, it was time to hang up the clothing of a recluse, and return to civilization.

"It's a distinct possibility that the hearing is to blame," Kat said, lifting her cup and gingerly sipping the hot brew. "If this whole nasty affair doesn't draw to a close soon, I may never get a decent night's sleep."

"Well, I think that once restitution is paid, closure will follow and the nightmares will end. You don't think you'll lose, do you? I mean, they're going to have to pay, right?"

"My attorney thinks so, but to be honest, I don't particularly care," Kat said. "I just want the whole thing over and done with. It's not like I need the money all that much."

"We all need money, love," Janet chided softly. "Don't let them turn you into a sacrificial lamb. After all, your books are only just now gaining momentum, dear, so it will be a few years more before your writing will support you fully. Moreover, your husband's insurance will only last so long. Do you really want to go to work now, and write only part-time? Or would you rather take the money and do what you and Robert always knew you could do – write and become rich and famous."

"Fame means about the same to me as money, Janet," Kat sighed. "You know that. I just love to write. I used to tell Robert that I didn't care if my books ever sold, or if my name ever became known, I just have to write."

"I know, dear, and since writing is your passion, and you need to have an income so that you can fulfill that passion, you need money. When's the hearing?"

"Next month."

"Want me to be there?"

"No, that's okay. Kieran and half the Covington P.D. are going to be there to provide support. You'd only get lost in the fray," Kat quipped in a weak attempt at humor, and Janet's bland expression confirmed its feebleness. Instead, she quirked her brow and sighed.

"If the nightmares get too bad, take a Valium to help you sleep."

"Funny."

"I'm serious, Kat," Janet said. "I know you don't hold to

prescription support, but have you seen how hideous you look? You need some rest and soon, and there's nothing wrong with a little help now and again."

"Not for you, maybe, but I can survive another month without becoming an incessant insomniac. I just wish the nightmares had stayed gone. You know, if it weren't for the stress surrounding this upcoming trial, I'd have continued sleeping just fine. Still, if it gets too bad, I'll pop a Melatonin."

"Well, let me offer just one more bit of advice, okay?"

"Just one more? Certain you can refrain yourself? After all, this "last bit of advice" would make it about the hundredth piece of advice you've offered in the past year-and-a-half. Sounds like you're addicted to advice-giving."

"Now who's being funny? If I didn't care about you, I wouldn't even bother with advising you at all."

"I know, and I really do appreciate it. Besides, as my daddy used to tell me, advice is always welcome. Once given, you can take it or leave it."

"Take this and apply it."

"Aye, aye, Cap'n."

"You're too smart for your own britches. Now, hush up and listen. You are a strong woman, and fate dealt you a really malicious hand, but it's up to you to play that hand to a win."

"You can tell you play cards regularly," Kat grinned. "Have you given me that advice before? It sounds familiar."

"Actually, you wrote that."

"I did? Sounds cheesy. Cliché."

"A very overused cliché, and as with all clichés, it makes us publishers cringe, but fortunately the rest of your writing makes up for a few of your ghastly truisms. Anyway, don't you remember writing it? Your book, Heart Anew. Cherish loses her husband...oh, dear. Sorry, my bad."

"I wrote that book before I lost Robert, Stephanie, and Mitchell. Do you think that perhaps I was writing about my own life and didn't know it?"

"No. I don't believe in that kind of negative karma and neither should you. Still, while I may not believe in negative karma, I do believe that good and bad things happen for a reason."

Kat smiled, "Well, I haven't quite discovered what good could come out of my losing my entire family."

"Maybe you can't see the reasons now; but maybe one day you will. Now, let's get down to business. Hand over your manuscript."

"You're going to like this one."

"Not as depressing as the last, I hope."

"No. In fact, it could easily be categorized as a Romantic Comedy."

"Leave the genre categorization to me, dear," Janet said, placing the envelope in her satchel.

"Aren't you going to look at it?"

"I will," Janet said, standing, "as soon as I return to my office from my next meeting. You're my friend, Kathryn, but you're hardly my only client."

Kat shook her head and smiled.

"I'll send the proofs over for your review next week by courier. In the meantime, try to get some rest. Unless you've already got another book in the works?"

"Actually, I do."

"Ah, that's wonderful. I only wish that all my authors were as predictably prolific."

"I like keeping busy."

"No arguments from me on that point normally, but today I have to object. I have a friend who's a doctor. I'll give him a call. Let him write you a prescription for Valium and sleep through to next week."

"No, thank you, but I promise to get some rest, if you promise to stop harping at me."

"Good. I'll see you at the Grayson's this weekend?"

"No."

"Come on, Kat..."

"No," Kathryn said, adamant. "I'm simply not ready to mingle with people."

"It's been a year-and-a-half–"

"I know how long it's been, Janet. I don't need you to remind me."

"Still too touchy."

"Then stop touching and go meet your other client."

"I am your friend, you know."

15

"I know."

"I'll talk to you later, then. Do try to have a relaxing afternoon," Janet encouraged, and then turned and headed toward an approaching cab.

Kathryn lifted her second cup of cappuccino and took a swallow, then flagged the waiter again, "Thanks for offering to buy lunch," she called sardonically to Janet's taxi, retreating from the curb.

CHAPTER FOUR

September 2060
Wind River, Wyoming

"Do you think that you can manage while I'm away?" Dalian sat at his desk signing the requisition forms brought to him by his foreman. When he didn't receive a reply, he glanced up at Harvey. "Well?"

"Oh, no problem, Dalian," his foreman replied.

"Have you got something to say, Harvey?"

"No, no, I was just thinking is all."

When Harvey paused, no further information forthcoming, Dalian sighed, "Care to share?"

"The men and I, well...," Harvey said, stammering. He'd been Dalian's foreman for nearly ten years, but he'd been his friend much longer, and he'd never had this much difficulty talking to him about anything.

"Just spit it out, will you?" Dalian couldn't recall a time he'd had to bark at his dear friend, and could only surmise that his churlish reaction was due to the inkling he had about from where Harvey's reticence stemmed.

"Sorry. The men and I were just wondering if you were, well, if you'd decided to—"

"Let me help you out, shall I? Especially as I need to be leaving sooner than you seem willing to speak. I'm returning to The People to visit my mother. I'm not turning Indian on you, and yes, I will return with the spring thaw, so you and the men can rest assured that your

17

employment is secure. Is that what you had on your mind?"

That tirade snapped Harvey from his timidity, "You realize how absurd your comment was? Turning Indian? Really, Dalian? In this day and age?" Harvey retorted, unable to stop the color from seeping from beneath his collar and creeping up his neck into his face. "We couldn't care less whether you want to go visit The People. Our concern is...well, it's just that you haven't exactly shown the same diligence and care you used to since...well, you know. It's almost as if you want the place to fold. You've been here since your early twenties, and never returned to the Blackfoot reservation before. I guess I just wanted to make sure you were all right, you know?"

"And you consider returning to my heritage a sign of mental instability, do you? Good heavens, Harvey, now who's making it sound as if we're still living in the eighteen hundreds? Do you really think I'd choose to live on a reservation where the Federal Government dictates my life instead of on the ranch that I built with my own two hands?"

"Well, I didn't quite mean that—"

"Listen, Harvey," Dalian sighed. "You're my friend, but you're way off the mark here. Yes, the loss of Carolyn and my baby took its toll, but I'm better now. It did make me appreciate however, how much family means, and that in turn, made me think of my mother. I haven't seen her in decades."

"That was her wish, not yours. Besides, what if you go all that way, and she doesn't remember you, or worse, doesn't want to see you? She did tell you to stay gone."

"It's a chance I'll take. I have a need to see her."

"Well, do you have to make it an extended trip?"

"By the time I arrive at the reservation and pay my respects, if, as you say, she'll allow me to do so, the winter snows will have started and I'm not of a mind to journey back through fifteen feet of snow, especially not on horseback."

"Horseback! Now who's stuck in the eighteen hundreds? Geez man! A horse! In this day and age! You can take the train, drive, or fly for that matter. Of course, if you take the train or fly, then snow or not, you can return when you like, and we've never had fifteen feet of snow."

"I know that, and no," Dalian said, sighing, "I need to ride. It'll be good for me. A way to clear my head once and for all. I'm ready to let Carolyn go, but the memories are holding on tight. The ride will help."

"Then ride your horse around here. Good gracious, Dalian! You have two hundred acres if you need to clear your head. Riding through the mountains at this time of year is foolish, at best. It'll take you a good month just to get there. And let's say that you do manage to make it to Montana without injury to you or your horse, what good is it going to do you if your mother does refuse to see you? You'll be stuck out there with your horse and no way to get home. Why don't you at least buy a ticket and that way if things go sour, you'll have a way back."

"Why don't I just book a hotel room, and then if my mother refuses to see me, I can just hang out...never mind," Dalian sighed, "Okay, Harvey. I'll ride into town today to purchase passage for me and Swift – just in case."

Harvey smiled, "Smart decision. I'll hold things together here, until you get back."

"I know you will. It should be easy enough since we don't open the dude ranch until spring. The biggest concern you'll face is getting the cattle to market. Placing that burden solely on your shoulders does give me a pang of guilt," Dalian grinned.

"Oh, I'll just bet it does," Harvey quipped. "Still, we have enough hands to see them safely there, and I'd say our timing is decent too. Checked the price per head this morning and it's on the upswing."

"What's our estimate?"

"Three-hundred-fifteen dollars per head."

"Decent, but prices sure haven't gone up much over the last few decades. Twenty years ago it was sitting around one-hundred-eighty-five dollars a head."

"Yeah, well it's better than a poke in the eye."

"True." Dalian handed the requisitions across the desk. Harvey took them, and stood to leave. Dalian noticed a renewed hesitation and spoke before Harvey could. "My mother never had a choice but to let me go. You know that."

"Do *you* know that?" Harvey countered, took his hat and jammed it on his head, then left the house.

"She didn't have a choice," Dalian repeated to the empty room. "I only wish I knew why she didn't have a choice.

CHAPTER FIVE

"Dalian! Wait!"

Dalian pulled Swift to a halt and turned the reins back toward the house. He sought out and found the person calling him, and then wished he hadn't. Marsha Canton was running down the drive toward him. When she reached his side, her breathing was exaggeratedly shallow. He sighed. He knew it was an act, for she was in top physical shape. He also knew why she pretended exhaustion, for the heavy breathing drew his attention to her well-endowed assets; assets that would topple from her low-cut t-shirt if she leaned too far over. For reasons he couldn't fathom, she supposed that drawing attention to her physical attributes would impress him. It didn't. He liked his women to be confident, intelligent, *over* twenty, and beautiful – foremost on the inside. Like Carolyn had been.

"I'm glad I caught you," Martha huffed, placing her hand on her chest, another ploy to divert his gaze. He kept his gaze firmly on hers.

"Marsha," Dalian said, tipping his hat respectfully. "What can I do for you?"

"I came over to see if Mrs. Guthrie could use a hand with the cooking and cleaning," she said, smiling shyly, "and saw you leaving."

"Doesn't your father give you enough chores to occupy your time, Marsha?"

"Oh, but we have plenty of help to take care of things over at our place, and poor Mrs. Guthrie is all alone here."

Dalian sighed again. Would she never stop trying to make him feel discomfited for evidently understaffing his household? Well, he certainly wasn't going to offer her employment, or worse, propose marriage to her. If Mrs. Guthrie felt overwhelmed, she'd say something and he'd hire on additional help, as he did when the dude ranch opened to visitors in the spring. "So why are you glad you caught me, if you came here to see Mrs. Guthrie?"

"Well, I ran into Harvey and he said you were going on vacation."

"And?"

"And I wanted to say goodbye and let you know I'll miss you."

Dalian arched his brow. *Now that was blunt*, he thought. Prior to now, she'd only hinted at her affections. "I'm sure I'll see you when I get back, Marsha."

"Oh, I'll definitely be here. Of course, if you think you'll miss having company, I can always ask my dad to let me go with you."

Uh-oh, more directness. Something is up, and I bet it has to do with her father. "It wouldn't surprise me if he said yes," he muttered.

"Does that mean?"

"No, it doesn't mean. Go on home, Marsha. I'm sure Mrs. Guthrie has everything under control at the house and since I'll be gone for several months..."

"Several months!"

"Yes, several months. Maybe by then your father will find you a decent-aged fellow and you'll be happily wed before I get back."

"That's not funny, Dalian. You know I only have eyes for you."

Oh, Lord. She's really going for broke today. "Listening to your Greatest Hits of the Eighties CD again?"

"You shouldn't make fun of me, Dalian. It isn't right." She placed a faux pout on her too-thin lips, "Especially when you know how I feel about you."

Well, she finally spoke what I always suspected aloud. Her father must be getting desperate. "Listen, Marsha. You may think you know how you feel, but there is a huge difference between lust and love; although I highly doubt you feel either one for me. However, once you've found the right man, you'll see that what you *think* you felt for me was nothing more than hormones run amok."

"That isn't true. I know what love is."

"All teenagers think they know what love is, but they don't. Not really."

"How can you say that, Dalian? You know I'd do anything for you."

"That isn't love, Marsha."

"What makes you think I don't love you, Dalian? You can't see inside my heart."

"Because of how hard you try to get my attention."

"I don't understand."

"And I don't have the time to explain it to you. I need to get going, but do us both a favor, will you?"

"What's that?" Marsha huffed, the exaggerated pout more pronounced.

"Go back to your dad and tell him he'll have to find another way of laying claim to my land and to stop wasting his time, and yours, on trying to snare me. I'm not on the market and neither is my property."

"That's just plain wrong, Dalian." Marsha stomped her tennis shoe lightly on the ground and Dalian shook his head in wonder.

She's such a child, he thought, but refrained from speaking it aloud. He wasn't in the habit of deliberately hurting children. Instead, he just shrugged. "Maybe. Maybe not. But I'll make a deal with you, Marsha. Come see me in ten years. If you still feel the same way after growing up a bit, I'll give you a second look."

"You don't really think I'm going to wait ten years for you, do you, Dalian Rivers? Well, I'm not. In ten years, you'll be kicking yourself in the ass for not catching me when you could. You know what? Go on your stupid vacation, and I hope you never come back. I don't care if I never see your ugly mug again," Marsha huffed, turning and heading back toward the house.

"I only wished it was that easy to get rid of you, Marsha," Dalian whispered to her retreating back, "but something tells me you'll be back the very day I return. Unfortunately, your dad wants my land too much to quit that easily."

CHAPTER SIX

March 2061
Covington, Georgia

"The book signing is set for next week," Janet said, settling in across from Kathryn. Honestly, Kat, I think this is one of your best yet. It's only been out for a month, and already it's receiving rave reviews. Good work!"

"Hello to you too, Janet," Kat said. "I'm glad that the book is being well-received." She pulled out her pocket calendar from her purse and flipped it open. "Days and times on the book signing?"

"Next Tuesday through Thursday at the Reader's Nook bookstore around the corner," Janet said, consulting her own calendar. "Two o'clock to four o'clock each day. I'll have information on your book tour later this afternoon. I'm just waiting to hear back from Covington Today."

"Okay," Kathryn said, slipping her calendar back into her handbag. "Perhaps one day though, you'll see fit to ask me before actually scheduling anything. Just in case."

"Why? It's not as if you ever do anything, anyway. Except write, that is."

"Funny."

"True."

"Well, I may have been that way once, but no longer," Kathryn said. "In fact, I'll be leaving week-after-next on an extended vacation."

"Knowing you, you'll take your laptop and continue pounding

away on whatever idea you come up with while you're away."

"Possibly, or maybe I'll actually put writing behind me for a change and take an honest to goodness holiday," Kathryn quipped.

"Doubt it! Now, when did you say this so-called vacation of yours was going to take place?" Janet asked, pulling her electronic organizer from her briefcase.

"Week after next," Kat said.

"Oh, that's just great! I was hoping to get you on the Covington Today show week-after-next. Perhaps you need to be filling me in on your forays before I start scheduling things. Maybe I can get in touch with Tara; see if she can't squeeze you in next week, or maybe we can do it after you get back. How long will you be gone?"

"Eight weeks."

"Eight weeks! Where are you going? An African safari? Now I'll definitely have to schedule a bulk of your promotional tours next week, so you better prepare to stay busy. Think if I book a few online author chats, you can squeeze them in? It would only be an hour a couple of times during your vacation."

"Certainly, Janet. Just shoot me a text or message me the information. And I promise to try to give you a better heads up the next time I plan a trip."

"Where exactly are you going that has to take eight weeks, anyway?"

"You'll laugh."

"Now, that's an odd thing to say."

"You will."

"Well, fine! Tell me, I'll laugh, then we can finish our conversation like the grown-ups we pretend to be."

"Cute."

"Yes, I know. Peter told me how cute I was last week, but I won't go into details."

"A dude ranch, okay?" Kat blurted out.

"A dude what?"

"There's a ranch out west that caters to extended vacations for people wanting to get away from city-life; to experience the life of a cowhand."

"Out west. Cowhand." Janet shook her head as if it would help the information fall into the correct mental location and thus make sense to her. It wasn't working. Instead, she pinned Kat with a perplexed stare.

"Oh, stop looking at me like I'm the one with no brain. It's just a dude ranch."

"A dude ranch."

"Yes, a dude ranch," Kat sighed, wondering why she'd even bothered telling her friend, especially when that friend also happened to be her publisher. She should have known that Janet would receive her announcement with sarcasm. "I figure the fresh air and sunshine will do me good."

"I thought you were over your loss, Kat," Janet said, leaning back in her chair and eyeing her friend with concern. "Are you saying now that you aren't? I mean, the man that killed your family is serving twenty-five years for vehicular manslaughter, his trucking company paid you a bundle in restitution–"

"And your point is?"

"My point is that all of that, plus time, was supposed to bring you closure. And now you're telling me that you need to get away for, not a normal two-week excursion, but eight, whole, freaking weeks."

"Why is it that you sound upset, Janet? I mean, the last I looked this was still my life, you know."

"Yes, well, when you write a potential best-seller, it becomes my life. At least until I get your book mentioned on every airwave, flying off virtual bookshelves, and as the subject of conversation around every water cooler in every office worldwide; but I can't very well do that if you aren't here to cooperate with my efforts."

"Wow, Janet," Kat said in exaggerated awe, "that would sound extremely egocentric if I didn't know you so well."

"It's not being egotistical to want to see you become the successful writer I know you can be. Now if I added that the more successful you are, then the richer I become, then you could accuse me of being self-centered, selfishly motivated—"

"Oh! Do stop being so melodramatic, Janet, I've been writing nearly non-stop for the last two years. I'm ready for a break, okay? And you're probably right about my taking my computer, so you know that it will in all probability be a working vacation—"

"Are you sleeping well?"

"Of course I am!"

"Then your desire to get away—"

"Hasn't got a damned thing to do with Robert, the children, the murder trial—"

"This is the second anniversary of their death," Janet said softly.

"Ah, hell, Janet," Kat sighed, "you had to bring that up, didn't you?"

"So, you are running from ghosts?"

"If I said yes, would you drop it?" Janet didn't answer immediately and Kat sighed again, "I'm tired, Janet. I'm just tired, is all."

"But eight weeks?"

"Yeah, eight weeks."

"That's tantamount to a publicity death sentence in the world of publishing. Still, if you gotta go, you gotta go."

"Yeah, I gotta go."

Janet sighed, "I'll do all I can to keep your name in the minds of readers everywhere until you get back, but do me a small favor, okay?"

"Which is?"

"Get yourself laid while you're gone."

"You really are a piece of work, you know that?"

"Yeah, Peter told me that too, or did he say I have a nice piece of—"

"Alright, Janet, that's enough."

"Want me to have him write you a prescription—"

"I don't need Valium. The Melatonin is working just fine."

"So you *are* still having trouble sleeping."

"Only a little."

"Well, at least you finally admitted it, but you know kiddo, running from your nightmares won't make them go away. They have a nasty way of showing up no matter where you are, unless you give them the boot. Maybe you should see a shrink. You never did talk things through with anyone. Not really anyway."

"That's because I don't need to. I'll admit that my heart still hurts around this time of year, but I expect that's normal. At least I can talk about it without falling apart like this time last year.

"True enough."

"I just need a vacation, Janet. In eight weeks, I'll return to my writing just as if I never left, I promise. Who knows, the trip may just inspire another best-seller."

"Hmm, music to my ears."

"I figured as much."

"Hey, I have an idea. Before you go, why not get laid by the cute police officer you told me about that's been sniffing 'round your door. What's his name?"

"Kieran O'Sullivan, and no, I'm not interested in him like that. We're just friends. Besides, even if I were, it would simply be too awkward. He was Robert's supervisor."

"Yeah, and if he wasn't his supervisor, he was a drinking buddy, or he was an uncle of one of Robert's childhood friends...there's always an excuse for intimacy avoidance."

"Well, Robert had a lot of friends," Kat said lamely.

"Yes, well, you can't sit there and tell me that strangers haven't hit on you."

"Have you ever thought that perhaps that's all I'll ever want from a man – friendship?"

"Sweetie, you are twenty-seven, sexy as hell, appealing to the eye, and extremely successful."

"Careful, you're making me blush," Kat teased.

"Oh! Do hush! All I'm saying is that for most women, that would be enough, but God designed you to be a part of a twosome. You do well in a relationship."

"So, what you're saying is that I'm not meant to be single."

"Right. That in itself makes you a rare breed, aside from your other attractive qualities."

"You should be my publicist as well as my publisher. Still, have you forgotten that I wasn't single; that I was contentedly married for five years? I didn't ask to be single, and you're right, I didn't want to be single. I liked being married, but just because I am involuntarily single right now, doesn't mean that I'm so horny that I have to jump in bed with every man who looks my way. You, of all people, should now that isn't me."

"You're right. My bad. You shouldn't go to bed with someone you know. It wouldn't work. So while you're out west, find a sexy stranger and release some of that pent-up sexual frustration that has you snapping my head off."

"It's like talking to a stone slab," she deadpanned. "You're a piece of work, you know that?"

"So you've said. Now, while you're gone, I'll get busy lining up some appearances for the couple of weeks after your return, get you set up to do some online interviews – not too many, I promise; and while you're gone, I'll push to get your book noticed. I hope that it'll be enough to keep your name in the limelight until you get back. Then we'll really have to work the media to rekindle the spark of interest. Eight weeks. Damn! You had to make it eight weeks. That's a freaking death sentence in this industry."

"So you've said. I'd apologize, Janet, but it wouldn't be very sincere."

"Well, humor me and do it anyway."

"I'm sorry."

"Oh, shut up!"

CHAPTER SEVEN

March 2061
Wind River, Wyoming

"Welcome home, Dalian!" Marsha shouted, coming around the side of the house.

"Good Lord, girl," Dalian sighed in exasperation, "do you have a built-in radar that lets you know when I'm going to be here?"

"Hardly, silly," Marsha laughed. "One of our ranch hands saw you coming through town and rode out to let us know that you'd arrived back safe and sound."

"How much did you pay him to keep track for you?"

"Ha! Ha! Well, I guess that vacation didn't do much for your disposition, sourpuss."

Dalian let go a heavy sigh and closed his eyes to keep from having to look at this particular insipid twit, "I'm tired, Marsha."

"Yeah, riding a train'll do that to a person." Marsha's comment was an attempt at humor, but her tone said that she was frustrated that Dalian still refused to take notice of her as a woman.

Dalian wasn't having any of it. He simply wasn't in the mood to pander to her ego, "Kept better track than I figured. Old man that desperate to keep tabs on me?"

Marsha's face reddened, "Well, since it's obvious my attempt at being neighborly is not being well-received, I think I'd better head on back home. Just wanted to welcome you back."

"Consider me welcomed."

It was Marsha's turn to sigh heavily, "I'll see you later, Dalian," she said with an annoyed shake of her head, and then started toward the path that would lead to her house.

"What happened to never wanting to see me again?" Dalian called after her.

"I forgave you. I'll always forgive you," she called over her shoulder, although her tone was anything but forgiving.

"Lucky me," Dalian shouted, although he felt anything but lucky. He sincerely wished that his time away would give Marsha and her dad someone else to focus on. Apparently, it was too much to wish for.

"Kid getting to you?" Harvey asked, coming around the corner.

"If hiring a hit man was legal, I'd happily do so," Dalian said, leading his horse toward the stable.

"No, you wouldn't," Harvey laughed. "That's why she'll continue to get on your nerves, because despite the fact you want to strangle the little nuisance – and her dad as well – you haven't got a violent bone in your body."

"I'm sure if I looked hard enough, I could find one or two; especially in the area around my fists."

"I'm sure," Harvey laughed.

"What makes it so blasted annoying is that I know her dad is putting her up to it."

"Think so?"

"Call it a very good hunch, but if she wasn't being pressured by her dad, I don't think she'd give someone nearly twenty years her senior the time of day." Dalian led Swift into his stall and pulled the saddle from his back, and then reached for the brush. It felt good to preoccupy his mind with tending to Swift, but he had to exert effort to prevent brushing too hard in his present state of agitation. Just thinking about Marsha and her dad tended to get him riled. He hated having to throw up the imaginary barriers every time she came close to him, but he had to protect himself and his land from predators – animal and human.

"Well, she's a damn good actress then," Harvey was saying, "because it sure as hell looks as if she has the hots for you."

"You nailed it – she's excellent at acting smitten, but it's a good thing I'm not taken in by her charade, or she'd have snared me by now and her daddy would be moving into the guest bedroom upstairs."

"Not a pleasant thought."

"A nightmarish notion, more like."

"Well, call me Randy Rooster, but I think a man needs to have a woman panting over him. Makes him feel real good about himself. Acting or not, she sure is doing a fine job stroking your ego."

"My ego doesn't need stroking. I feel just fine about myself, but if a woman ever did come panting after me, I'd prefer the feeling be mutual."

"Well, if little miss come-and-take-me doesn't do it for you then maybe one of the guests coming in next month will."

"Sorry, Harvey, but men definitely don't do it for me."

"That's real funny," Harvey laughed, "but accurate enough, because if your radar was tuned into that particular frequency, you'd have noticed how Tom keeps eyeballing you every day."

"Oh, holy crap! Tell me you're pulling my leg, old man."

"Yep, but you have to admit, I had you going." Harvey laughed at the reaction garnered by his twisted sense of humor and then had to duck when Dalian threw the brush at his head.

Dalian went to fetch the brush and resumed tending to Swift, a grin on his lips. He should have known that Harvey was messing with him, as was his habit, but the way in which Tom carried himself did make Dalian wonder sometimes as to which side he buttered his bread. He shook the thought away and refocused on what Harvey had said.

"So, what is so unusual about our guests next month?"

"We actually have two women on the register."

"Women?"

"Yeah, you know – the species that have breasts?"

Dalian laughed. He finished brushing down Swift, hung his gear on the tack near the door, and stepped outside. A cool, evening breeze stroked his face and he closed his eyes for a moment, breathing deeply.

"Missed the place, didn't you?"

"While I was gone, all I could think about was home. It's my life's blood."

"Yeah, I know, but you still managed to stay gone for five months. If it wasn't for the regular updates, I'd have thought you never made it through the mountain pass back in September."

"I never intended to stay gone so long."

"I take it that things went good with your mom then? Your occasional messages only mentioned that you were still alive and well. I really wish you'd have called sometimes. Would have made communication quicker, more efficient, and more informative."

"Sorry about that, but I wanted to make sure the few months that we had together were quality. I didn't want to think about everything that needed doing here, nor was I ready to reveal anything Mom may have told me, which you would have hammered me to do – and don't deny it. I can see curiosity etched all over your features right now, and you've been shadowing me worse than Marsha since I entered the stable."

Harvey laughed. "So, how is your mom? Still sexy as hell?"

"Watch it old man, that's my mom you're talking about."

"Yeah, I know," Harvey grinned mischievously, "but that doesn't mean she wasn't worth looking at to a kid my age way back when."

"You're messed up," Dalian said, moving toward the house.

"So, did you and your mom finally clear the air?" The cautious delivery of the question made Dalian stop and look at his friend, eyeing him questioningly; however, nothing in Harvey's return gaze revealed anything, so he resumed his trek toward the house.

"If by, "clear the air", you're asking if she finally told me why she sent me to live with your folks when I was only twelve, then no."

"Sorry about that, Dalian. I know you've always had unanswered questions about your life, and . . . well, you naturally presumed that your mother would finally answer those questions."

Dalian stopped walking and turned to face Harvey again, his brow furrowed in puzzlement, both by the relief in Harvey's tone and by a comment Harvey made a moment earlier. "Why would you ask if my mother is still sexy as hell? That would imply that you knew my mother, but I thought that only your parents had met her. Are you now telling me that my assumption was incorrect? That you actually did know my mother, but if you did, why didn't I know you did?" Dalian questions became rhetorical as he continued mumbling to himself, as if asking the questions aloud might suddenly provide answers.

"Yeah, I knew her," Harvey said, jarring Dalian from his reflections. "Did you think she brought you to live with us because my folks were saints or something? Or that she just pulled our names out of the phone book? She had to have a reason, and that reason was—"

"You?" Dalian interjected, as if saying it aloud accounted for all of the unknowns, but his triumphant declaration was short-lived, as even more questions poured into his brain. "Why did you never tell me? I thought she just dumped me at the first willing couple she came across." Dalian continued toward the house, his footfalls heavier, and his pace faster.

"Good Lord, man, slow down. Shoot fire, there's no need to go getting all worked up. It's not like there was some huge conspiracy going on. You don't really think she would have dumped your scrawny hide with complete strangers, do you?" Harvey asked, plopping onto the front steps. Dalian was about to go into the house, but stopped. He turned around with a sigh and settled onto the step next to Harvey. His head bent, he sucked in a deep breath, trying desperately to calm his elevated agitation; agitation compounded by his visit with his mom and Marsha's continued pursuit. Harvey placed a hand on his shoulder and said softly, "Obviously, there was a history there before you came along."

"You weren't there when my mom dropped me off. I'd have remembered meeting you, so how did you know my mom was sexy?"

"I could have been there, for all the attention you were paying to your surroundings."

"As I was only twelve at the time, I was hardly thinking about anything but the fact that my mother was kicking me out of my tribe. The whys and wherefores weren't important to me. I was losing my mother and I didn't know why; and now, you're sitting here telling me that the reason she chose your family for me to live with was because you knew her. Why, after all of these years, wouldn't you tell me? Why would you keep something like that from me?"

"Lord, Dalian, you've got a suspicious brain. You make it sound as if your mother and I had some torrid love affair that we were trying to keep hidden from you. Man, did you grill your mom like this?"

"She's my mom for heaven's sake. Of course I didn't grill her. I went to make amends, not open old wounds."

"So you wait until you get back and lay into me, is that it?"

"Ah, hell, Harvey, I'm sorry. I just have a feeling there's something more to my past; something I don't know and can't remember. There's always been this empty void in my childhood – and now that I know you knew my mom as more than just a quick "hello, take my child, goodbye" affair – well, I was hoping you'd be willing to fill in the blanks?"

"Tarnation, Dalian, didn't your mom mention even once about my family or her life before she went to live with the Blackfoot?"

Dalian shook his head, "Her life before? What life are you talking about?"

Harvey sighed heavily. "Good Lord above, what exactly did you two spend five months yammering about if not about your past? Sounds to me like she didn't tell you a damn thing," Harvey said. "Damn it all to Hell, I can't believe she didn't tell you."

"Harvey, I've always loved you like a brother, and you may not think I'm capable of killing, but I'll do just that if you don't start talking."

"Okay, Dalian," Harvey said. "Keep your britches on. I'll tell you, but I still think it should be your mother doing the telling. Not me. She's kept your past from you for far too long and it isn't right that the burden should fall on my shoulders."

"Had I known that you knew about my past, I'd have pounded the answers out of you decades ago, but I didn't, and if I could, I'd ask my mom about it all, but I can't. She's dead."

CHAPTER EIGHT

"What did you just say?"

"I said she's dead. That's why I was held over," Dalian said softly. "She was ill when I arrived," he whispered, running fingers through his shoulder-length, black hair, "and getting worse by the day, so I decided to stay with her until the end. That's also why I didn't keep in touch."

"Damn! I'm so sorry, Dalian. She was one of the sweetest girls I've ever met. I hadn't seen her in decades, but I'll never forget her smile."

Dalian looked at his long-time friend as if seeing him for the first time, "Well, now that we know that she can't tell me – I'm listening, Harvey," Dalian said softly.

"Yeah, okay. I guess since your mom can't tell you, there's no reason why I shouldn't." Harvey propped his elbows on his knees and quietly began recounting what he remembered.

"What I don't get is why you couldn't when I first met you."

"It wasn't my place and, well . . . let me see if I can't rectify that now. When I met your mom, she was barely fourteen, and married to a man in his fifties."

"Wait, so you knew my mom for years before I was even born? And what business does a fourteen year old have marrying a man in his fifties?"

"That's the reaction I had, except I think my exact thought was, damn, that's weird. I thought he was her granddaddy, you know? I do know that back then, some states didn't have a legal age limit for marriage, like we do now, and as long as the girl had parental consent–"

"But fourteen?"

"I don't know all about how it happened, man. I just know that when they bought the place next door to us, they did so as man and wife."

"Why'd she marry him? Why didn't she ever mention him to me?"

"You are asking a lot of questions that I never got the answers to myself, and I can't tell you why she never mentioned him to you. Maybe because he was a part of her life she wanted to forget. As for why she married him – her father made her." Harvey raised his hand to ward off the barrage of questions he saw that Dalian was ready to hurl in his direction, "That's all she ever told me. Now are you going to let me tell this, or are you going to keep interrupting me?"

"Sorry."

"That you are. So anyway–"

"How did she know you, though?"

"So much for letting me talk."

"Sorry."

"Yep, you said that already. Mind if I continue?

"Yeah, sorry."

"You keep saying that, and I'll slug you. Now zip it."

Dalian struggled to keep his mouth closed as Harvey continued relating those things he never knew.

"Anyway, you could tell she was miserable being married to a man older than her father, but she made the best of it. As for me, I was only ten, but we soon became fast friends. Probably because I was the only person within a fifty mile radius that was close to her in age and fun to be around."

"But how'd she end up with the Blackfoot?" Harvey sighed again. "Sorry."

"It's okay. I'll answer that one. You don't have to stretch your imagination too far actually. Our ranches bordered the reservation. She met a young Blackfoot man when she was in town and started seeing him on the sly. Fell in love with him."

"So she divorced her first husband?"

"Dadblasted, Dalian! I'll probably get to your questions eventually, so would you just let me talk? All of this happened so long ago that I need to get my thoughts organized, or it'll all come tumbling out of my mouth in a jumbled, incoherent mess."

"Then talk faster!"

"Lord!" Harvey huffed. "Okay. No. She didn't divorce her husband. He died, and don't ask how, because I don't know. I only know it was fortuitous timing, since she discovered she was pregnant with you, and her husband wasn't the father."

"Damn."

"Yeah, well. As soon as possible, she married Jake Twin Rivers and he moved them to the reservation. Unfortunately, the magic didn't last. Of course, we both know what living on a reservation is like, especially since the government stopped permitting the building and operation of casinos on Indian land back in 2035. A lot of Natives depended on those casinos for employment. Your dad was one of 'em. Your mom became severely depressed as Jake bounced from job to job and started drinking more and more. Growing up, you became a source of contention for him. According to your mom, he blamed you for all his woes; and he made you pay for his misery, too. Damned coward!"

"What do you mean?"

"Only a coward beats up on women and children."

"He abused us?"

"You really don't remember, do you?"

"No, nothing."

"Maybe it wouldn't be a good idea for me to tell you then."

"I'm not twelve anymore, Harvey. I'm thirty-six. I think I can handle the truth."

Harvey nodded, "I know. I guess I've just kept it to myself for so long – okay, here it goes. The truth of the matter is . . . well . . . if you must know–"

"Blasted, Harvey. What could possibly be so bad?"

"You killed your old man, that's what."

"What?"

"Yeah, that's right. You heard me. You were just shy of eleven years old at the time. According to your mother, anyway."

"I don't get it. I wouldn't hurt a fly–"

"You would if that fly was five-foot-ten, drunk, and beating your mother half to death."

"Damn. Why can't I remember? I mean, that's not exactly something you forget."

"Actually, I read somewhere that traumatic situations can cause amnesia, especially in children."

"Thank you, Dr. Harvey Psychiatric-know-it-all."

"Well, you asked, smart-ass."

"I didn't go to jail," Dalian said to himself. "I'm certain I'd have remembered going to jail."

"Well, you sure shootin' could have, since they passed that law back in 2030 stating that anyone can be convicted for murder, age notwithstanding. But, in your case, the judge declared it self-defense and dropped the charges. Anyway, after your mother recovered from the beating, she tracked us down and asked if you could come live with us. By then, we owned a nice little parcel of land here in Wyoming, and agreed, but she never showed. We just figured she settled whatever problems she had and moved forward."

"But eventually she decided to get rid of me? Why? Because she couldn't live with me knowing that I killed her husband?"

"I wouldn't put it that way – exactly."

"How would you put it – exactly?"

"Peter."

"Who in hell is Peter?"

"Your stepfather."

"I beg your pardon?"

Harvey knew that the tale was a convoluted one, but did his best to unravel the past without raising too many more questions or confusion, "I said that you had a stepfather, but I didn't find out about him until I was twenty-something myself, and not until your mom showed up on our doorstep – two years after your dad was killed. I was a student at the University of Wyoming at the time, but home for a visit the day your mom showed up with you in tow. You were a scrawny thing. Looked like a strong wind could pick you up and carry you away. Anyway, your mother wasn't alone. Peter – her fiancé then – accompanied her. She wanted you to have a life, but she wanted to be happy as well, and Peter was a good man."

"I don't recall meeting anyone named Peter at the reservation."

"He probably died before she did then, because there isn't a reason why she wouldn't want you to meet him. Fact is, she loved that man, and he loved her. It was good to see her happy for once in her life."

"Damn, I not only killed my abusive father, but I was deserted by my mom so that she could find happiness with another man. Nice to know I was wanted."

"You *were* wanted, but you were also pretty screwed up and your mother felt it was best that you get away from home. Too many bad memories for you there. She was also worried because you were getting older, were already depressed, and the suicide rate for young men confined to reservations is damned high. She didn't want to see you become a statistic. And since Peter is also Blackfoot, and wanted to remain on the reservation–"

"So, my welfare was her primary concern. Is that it? And why can't I remember any of this?"

"Well, the fact that you can't remember probably happened after your mom left you. Whew, were you a handful. A big enough handful that I dropped out of university to help Mom and Dad raise you. One day, you had one of your many major fits, snagged one of the horses, and bolted. The horse threw your bony ass, and you banged your head real good on the fence post on the way to meet the ground. That's how we figured you lost your memory. Damn near lost your life!"

"Good Lord! I didn't know. God, Harvey, I'm so sorry. Why

would your folks ever consent to taking me in? Why did they keep me? Why didn't you kick my ass for making you give up your education? Did I suddenly become my now charming self after nearly cracking my skull open? I thought you said that I lost my memory because of trauma?"

"Smacking your head against a fence post is traumatic," Harvey laughed, and then raised his hand to stop the barrage of questions that Dalian was hurling in his direction. "After your fall, you did change. Maybe losing your memory was a good thing, because you were a lot easier to handle afterward. Downright friendly. Also, I fairly begged Mom and Dad not to dump you at the closest orphanage. You see, I remembered your mom from when we were kids, back when we first met. Remember I told you that she was married to the fifty-year-plus-old grandfather figure? She sure had changed a lot from when she was a kid," Harvey whispered longingly, and then shook his head to get his thoughts back on track. "Anyway, I owed your momma one from back then. A big one. That's why I couldn't kick your butt for being a pain and why I begged my folks to let you stay."

"How could this possibly get any more complicated?" Dalian shook his head, bemused.

Harvey snorted. "Oh, believe-you-me, it can. You see, I wouldn't even have been around to help raise you if it wasn't for your mom. I did something stupid, fell into the river, and would have drowned had a, then, gangly fifteen-year-old girl not jumped in after me."

"My mom."

"Yeah, your mom."

"What stupid thing did you do?"

"I stole into my dad's liquor cabinet. Decided that, at eleven years old, I was man enough to take a swig or two – or ten. Then decided that I could swim – which I couldn't. So, when that same gangly fifteen-year old girl returned over a decade later, son in tow, and asked for their help, I wouldn't let my mom and dad say no. Not that they would have. They felt obligated also – for my life. "A life for a life", they said."

"I guess I owe you one then as well."

"You've already repaid me – a thousand times over."

"I don't see how you figure that? What you did for me and mom–"

"Don't you remember our reunion thirteen years ago?"

"Oh, yeah, that."

"Yeah, that."

"You thought you were man enough to handle a swig or two – or ten – of whiskey, and big enough to take on ten equally drunk cowhands."

"Yeah, losing your wife and kid will make you crazy."

"I know," Dalian concurred, sadness twinging his tone.

"I know you do, but if you hadn't magically showed up that day and kicked ass for me, I probably would have been buried next to my wife. I never did figure out how you knew where I was."

"Your parents told me."

"Ah. Well, you know the rest. You started this spread and asked me to come work for you. Helping you build this place and keep it running, kept me going all these years. You may not have realized it at the time, kid, but if you hadn't brought me here to work with you, I probably would have gotten into another bar room brawl eventually and ended up with my head bashed in."

"What gets me, is that I've known you nearly my entire life and you never mentioned any of this."

"I promised your mom that I wouldn't, and that I'd keep you safe."

"And ignorant?"

"And ignorant. She figured the two went hand-in-hand. Of course I never expected–"

"That I'd go back?" Dalian interrupted. "That's why you seemed so surprised when I told you I was leaving for the reservation. Not because you were concerned that I was abandoning the ranch, but because–"

"I wasn't sure how understanding and forgiving you'd be, once you found out that I'd kept your past from you. Your mom must have had concerns too, because she certainly didn't say anything. So, now that you know, are we okay?"

"The past is past. I only wish you and mom would've trusted me to hold onto my own memories. I may have been a boy, but I was never weak."

"Well, you proved that enough times. I guess if I hadn't promised your mom, I would've 'fessed up long ago."

"You loved her, didn't you?" Dalian asked suddenly, reading more into his friend's body language than his words revealed.

"Yeah, I did. That bother you?"

Dalian shook his head, "Not really, no. None of it bothers me as much as I figured it would. I guess water under the bridge washes away most everything, including revelations that can otherwise make a man bitter."

"Wow, a poet and he didn't even know it."

"You're twisted, old man."

Harvey laughed. "Wouldn't be happy straight."

"Better watch what you say, or someone might misconstrue that statement," Dalian laughed.

"Now who's being twisted? So, are we cool?" Harvey asked, suddenly serious again.

"We're cool."

Harvey sighed, relief flooding through him. He'd carried the burden of Dalian's past for so long, the release made him feel downright giddy. "So what now?"

"We get ready for our guests that are due to arrive next month."

"Yeah, and don't forget that two of those guests–"

"Have breasts," Dalian interjected. "Yes, I know. You really are twisted, old man."

"Nah. I just have a good appreciation for breasts."

CHAPTER NINE

"Welcome to Heart of the Mountain Dude Ranch. My name is Harvey Bennett and I'm the foreman here. I'm usually the one to show you folks a good time during your stay."

"Usually?"

Kat glanced toward the young man that had spoken, and then her gaze slowly moved from person to person, wondering whether they felt as she did. Tired, yet eagerly alert; simultaneously feeling out of place, yet oddly at home.

"Yes, well, unfortunately, I've got a family emergency and am leaving this afternoon, but not to worry none, folks. I'll be leaving you in the capable hands of the owner of this fine establishment. In fact, he should be along shortly so that I can make the intros."

"Doesn't he usually help you anyway?" another guest asked.

"No, he sees to the day-to-day running of the ranch itself. Something I help him with the rest of the year. But come spring, when we open the touristy part of the ranch, he maintains the actual ranch, and I get to spend my time with you fine people."

The sound of an approaching horse reached her ears and she looked over her shoulder. Her eyes widened slightly and she sucked in a deep breath. She heard a sharper intake next to her and glanced to her right. The bombshell blonde, in skin-tight jeans, that had arrived at the ranch at the same time as she had caught sight of the approaching rider as well and was eyeing him with possessiveness. Looking at the man seated in the saddle, Kat understood all too well.

He had a confident bearing that bordered on arrogant, but Kat figured that any man that looked that good had a right to carry himself that way.

"Here he is now, folks," Harvey said, as the rider reined in his horse in front of the line of vacationers. "I'd like to introduce you to Dalian Rivers, owner of the Heart of the Mountain Ranch."

"Welcome folks," Dalian said, tipping his hat. "Everyone, please call me Dalian."

Kat heard a sigh and for a moment thought that it escaped from herself, and then realized that it came from the blonde. She did sigh then, softly and with relief. She'd never make an idiot of herself over a man, even a man as sexy as this one. Obviously, the blonde had no such compunctions, for she was smiling very idiotically, a dreamy expression on her flawless features. "That's a mighty fine specimen," she breathed.

"Which – the horse or the man?" Kat asked humorously.

"What horse?"

Kat rolled her eyes, but had to laugh at the woman's blatant show of lust. Her laugh faded quickly when she looked back to the rider. He was looking at *her*. Surely, he didn't think she was the one drooling over him adolescently. *Keep dreaming, cutie.* She smiled thinly and he grinned. He tipped his hat and turned his attention away.

"Before we let you go and get settled into your rooms, we have something here we like to do; help folks get acquainted better so you don't spend so much time feeling like you're in the company of strangers."

"Oh, but I don't feel that way at all," the blonde said airily, which made Kat wince. "In fact, I'm feeling right at home."

Oh, brother! Kat thought when she caught a glimpse of the batting eyelashes aimed at the ranch's owner. *Laying it on a bit thick aren't you, blondie?*

"Well, that's how we want you to feel, little lady. We hope that you all feel that way before the end of the day. And since you seem to have fewer inhibitions than most folks," Harvey said to the blonde, "we'll start with you." Harvey cast a glance at the boss man. He kind of hoped the boss noticed her, but he didn't. Of course, he'd have been surprised if he had. The boss didn't tend to mix business with pleasure. Still, the signals this girl was sending could be picked up three states away. *Too bad*, he thought, *she'd definitely make a good distraction.* "Why don't you tell us your name, what you do, and what made you decide to visit a dude ranch?"

"Oh, that's easy," the blonde cooed, "I came to meet a real-life cowboy; and for anyone who's interested," she said, eyeing Dalian, "my name's Chloe Harper and I model lingerie. Or, I used to. I'm sort of retired now."

"Well, if I could've retired when I was as young as you, I'd have jumped at the chance," Harvey said, grinning.

"No you wouldn't have, you old coot," Dalian laughed. "Ranching's in your blood and you know it."

"Dalian's got a point," Harvey laughed, and the tourists chuckled politely, "Well, anyway, it's a right nice pleasure to make your acquaintance, Miss Harper."

"Likewise," Dalian said politely.

"Oh, I'm sure," Chloe said, and Kat rolled her eyes again. *This blonde is certainly going to prove the 'blondes have more fun' saying*, she thought, if the glances she was receiving to her 'I'm an available lingerie model' speech were a good indication. *Well, have at it, sister*, she thought.

"And what about you, little lady?" Harvey asked, addressing Kat.

"Oh, well," Kat said. "Um, my name is Kathryn McMurray, but my friends call me Kat, and I'm a writer."

"That's a charming accent you have there, little lady? Where are you from?" Harvey asked and was thrilled to see Dalian's attention perk up.

"Georgia."

"Ah, a real Georgia peach."

Kat smiled politely, but didn't know what else to say, and then Dalian was asking her a question.

"What do you write, Miss McMurray?" Dalian asked. "Or is it Missus?"

"It's Miss," Kat said. "Now," she whispered, and then continued. "I, um, write different things, really. I'm just a novelist."

"Well, Miss Novelist," Dalian grinned, "welcome to my ranch."

"Thank you," Kat replied and wondered why she suddenly felt so flushed. She was glad that Dalian didn't ask any more questions, and would have liked nothing more than for attention to be shifted on to the next person, but then Harvey was asking her yet another question.

"So," Harvey interjected, "what brings you here, Miss McMurray?" He asked, more for Dalian than himself. He'd seen Dalian perk up when she spoke in that lilting southern accent, and smiled. He should have known that he would go for the brunette over the blonde. Especially one with a voice as smooth as honey.

"Call me Kat, please, and I'm just on vacation."

"Ah come on now, little lady," Harvey prodded. "A trip to Europe is a vacation. A dude ranch is fun, yeah, but you can get mighty dirty learning to rope a cow. In fact, we rarely get women vacationers here for that very reason."

"That's okay. A little dirty, hard work never hurt anything, except maybe a manicure."

"Yeah, and don't forget my pedicure," the blonde interjected and everyone again laughed courteously. Kat smiled politely. *Apparently, Miss Blondie has a difficult time sharing the limelight.*

"Well, you're still mighty welcome, and definitely easy on the eyes."

"Thank you."

"That goes for you too, Miss Chloe."

"Oh, without a doubt," Chloe grinned.

Harvey finally moved his attention onto the others standing in line, and Kat determined to pay attention and not allow her mind to dwell on the fact that she could see Dalian Rivers watching her out of the corner of her eye. It was only an occasional glance, but it was still a little unnerving having someone so gorgeous watching you when you weren't all that certain if you wanted the attention. *Of course, your mind could simply be playing tricks on you,* she thought. *He may actually be looking at Chloe, the blonde former lingerie model.* If anyone was out of place on a ranch, it was she, so why didn't either man grill her about her reason for being there? *Because she really is here to find a cowboy, that's why,* she thought.

She glanced around nonchalantly, and her gaze met Dalian's. She felt a small shiver tickle her neck. *Far too sexy,* she thought, smiling slightly, *especially when he smiles.* She turned to look back at Harvey. *Safe territory there,* she thought. *Cute, yes, but too old to be my type. Great! That means I'm admitting that the owner is my type.*

"Well, folks, welcome once again. If you will follow Mrs. Guthrie into the house, she'll see that you all get registered, settled, and then fed a hearty meal." The guests turned in unison, talking among themselves. Kat tagged along, thinking to herself.

"Hi, I'm Chloe." The blonde fell into step beside her.

Kat jumped inwardly at the intrusion, but quickly recovered. She looked at the blonde, wondering if the woman was truly as empty-headed as she acted. A glance into her eyes confirmed she wasn't. This was a very shrewd woman, and her gaze revealed that she could be a force to be reckoned with, if crossed. Then again, so was she. She smiled. "Hello."

"You're Kathryn, right?"

"Kat's fine."

"Since your friends call you Kat, does that mean we can be friends?"

What's her motivation? Kat wondered and then silently berated herself for judging this particular book by its cover. She tried never to judge people before getting to know them. *So why should now be any different?* She thought. "I don't see why not, Chloe. It's probably for the best, since we do seem to be outnumbered fifteen-to-two, and that's without adding in the ranch hands."

"And don't forget the owner. Wow, what a looker that one is!"

"Without a doubt. Speaking of which," Kat said, nodding toward the approaching horse.

"Ladies." Dalian reined in his horse next to the two women. The horse snorted and sidestepped, but with only a slight tug on the reins, it quickly quieted.

I wonder if he's that good with women, Kat thought, but immediately slammed the door on the thought.

"Not hungry?" Dalian asked.

Kat looked toward the house and realized that all the other guests had already vanished inside. Hers and Chloe's conversation, though brief, had delayed their progress.

"Actually, I'm starving."

"I could eat," Chloe added, the airy tone returning, much to Kat's amusement.

"Would you like me to escort you ladies inside?" Dalian asked, directing the question to Kat. Chloe noticed the renewed interest and interjected quickly.

"I'd like to talk to Kat a little longer, if that's okay?" The tone in which her request was delivered seemed lost on Dalian, but not on Kat. She was aggravated.

"Sure thing," Dalian said, tipping his hat. "I'll see you inside then. Try to hurry. Wouldn't want your food getting cold."

"We'll be in soon," Chloe smiled, but it didn't reach her eyes. "Interested?" she said the minute Dalian rode away.

Aha! Motivation revealed. I wonder if I should lie, just to see how far she's willing to go to rid herself of the perceived competition. Nah. That would be too much work. "Not really, no."

"Not your type?"

Kat grinned, "Unfortunately for me, yes. But I'm simply not interested in any relationship at the moment."

"Just wanted to make certain the field was clear."

Kat laughed, "Wide open. Is that the only reason for the offer of friendship? Or was that a genuine gesture?"

The shrewdness vanished from Chloe's eyes and a smile appeared. "Genuine enough. Not all blondes are men-hungry cats willing to slice and dice through any competition, you know?"

"Just you."

"Just me – with good reason – but since you aren't interested in the same guy, I can sheath my claws."

Kat laughed, "Would you really have clawed my eyes out over the ranch owner?"

"You aren't interested, remember?"

"No, I'm not, but I think I understand where you're coming from. I'd probably show my claws too if I were interested."

"Most women back down and don't go after the same guy as me to begin with," Chloe admitted confidently, and Kat perceived a slight menace behind the words.

"That's because most women see you as a threat," Kat said, equally self-assured.

"But not you," Chloe said, the shrewd gaze returning.

"You're beautiful, without a doubt," Kat shrugged. She stopped walking and turned to face the much taller woman, "But to feel threatened by you, I'd have to feel little confidence in myself or care about your prey. And since I have an abundance of confidence and we've already determined that I'm not here for the cowboys – one in particular – then we can go about socializing with each other without the added cattiness."

"Direct, aren't you?"

"Always," Kat smiled.

"So," Chloe grinned shrewdly, "want to help me snare the owner?"

"Not on your life," Kat said sincerely. "If you want him, you catch him. I have to admit though, that it's going to be entertaining watching you attempt to wheedle your way into his affections."

"If he can take his eyes off of you long enough to notice me, I might actually have a chance."

"What happened to sheathing the claws?"

"Sorry, old habits die hard."

"Well, since I won't be reciprocating any overtures on his part, the field is still free and clear."

"So you noticed his attentions?"

"I'd hardly call asking me a question and welcoming me to his ranch as justification for concern on your part. As you recall, he welcomed everyone."

"I can't see you as naive."

"I'm not, but I'm also not interested – whether he is or not."

"Well, glad to hear it. The life of a lingerie model is a short one, which is why I had to retire so early, so if I can entrap a rich husband –

especially one as sexy as me – I'll do it."

"So you weren't kidding about coming here for the cowboys."

"In truth? Cowboys, no. Ranch owners, yes," Chloe smiled.

"What were you going to do, make a circuit of the dude ranches until you found an unclaimed owner as sexy as you?"

"Something like that," Chloe laughed. "I managed to land a couple of rich husbands back home – when I was younger – but those ended badly when I got older. Anyway, I decided to go elsewhere to look, maybe find someone that liked my looks but wasn't necessarily interested only in youth. As far as I'm concerned, I think I was fortunate enough to hit the jackpot on the first stop. I can't see Dalian caring more about a woman's age over the woman. Anyway, I'm getting too old to keep looking for the perfect Mr. Right – one as gorgeous as I am, as you so eloquently put it. I am just ready to settle down permanently with an average Joe Blow, who'll still think I'm pretty when I'm eighty. Besides, the fun has gone out of the chase, since I can't compete with the younger women anymore."

"No offense, Chloe, especially since I don't know jack-squat about you, but I can't see you living here, or anywhere but in a Penthouse on one of those expensive avenues in New York. And before you say you're going to convince the new love of your life to move to the city or commute a hell of a long way, I can't see a true cowboy uprooting to New York, or anywhere remotely citified."

"You know something? You're all right. It's rare to meet someone so straightforward nowadays, but my reasons are simple. Back east, women like me are a dime a dozen, and finding a rich man, not so easy. Too few, too much competition for those few. Out here, well, let's just say, I stand out a lot more."

"Oh, without a doubt," Kat laughed, and Chloe turned a lovely shade of pink, unused to women agreeing with her on how attractive she is.

"Anyway, if that means I need to adapt to ranch life, I may just do that. You'll let me know if you change your mind about pursuing our gorgeous ranch owner, won't you?"

Kat laughed, "Most assuredly."

"So, Miss Novelist, what kind of books do you write?" Chloe asked, finally heading toward their meal, no doubt very cold by now.

CHAPTER TEN

"We've been here four years already!" Jethro Canton snapped. "In that time, our elusive neighbor has seen you sprout from a weed into a full-fledged flower, and you still can't get him to pluck you? What exactly are you doing that will entice him into doing more than smelling your petals, huh, girl? And now there's two drop-dead gorgeous women staying at that place for the next two months!"

"Dad, your analogy stinks."

"Watch your tongue, girl!"

"And when are you going to stop calling me a girl and realize that I'm eighteen. Eighteen, Dad! And sick and tired of playing a love-sick fool for a thirty-six-year-old man that only knows I exist when I throw myself in his face."

"You should be sleeping in his bed by now."

"Prostituting myself isn't going to win his affection or make him propose to me. Can't you see that he doesn't like me or want me?"

"Then you need to change your powers of persuasion. If he doesn't like what you're doing, change it. Make him like you. Make him want you so much that he'll marry you. Cause I'll be damned if I'm going to let one of those sexy guests catch his eye."

"He's onto your game, Dad, so I could turn into his dream girl, or one of those sexy guests, and he still wouldn't get anywhere near me."

"You told him…and not now, Rosalinda, get out!"

Marsha placed a hand on their housekeeper's arm as she passed, and whispered, "Just remember his bark is worse than his bite, especially when he's drunk. Tell Phillip and Cara to stay out of the kitchen for now. I'll come get you when it's time to start dinner."

"You apologizing for me, girl?"

Marsha shooed their housekeeper from the kitchen before turning back to her dad, "I'm trying to keep our help from up and quitting; that's what I'm doing. As for Dalian Rivers, I didn't tell him anything, he told me. Despite what you may think, the guy isn't stupid. He all but told me to tell you to stop."

"I'll stop when I have the deed to that property or access to his grazing land."

"Marrying him isn't going to get that land, Dad, and sleeping with him certainly won't get it, so what purpose could my pursuit do? Besides, we've got a nice spread here. Why do you need his land?"

"Because its two-hundred acres of the finest grazing in the state, that's why. If I can get you married off to him, that will join our two plots and I can share that land. Then later on down the road, when he ends up dead – by natural causes, of course – that two-hundred acres of plum grazing land will rightfully revert to you – and by way of me being your daddy, to me."

"Well he isn't of a mind to marry. He said so, and sleeping with him isn't likely to change his mind."

"If you sleep with him, I can force him into marrying you; play the offended daddy and all that crap."

"You act as if men and women still care about honor anymore. I sleep with him; you can act like a doting daddy all you want. He doesn't have to consent. Thinking like that went out decades ago."

"Well, there are still laws about a man sleeping with underage girls."

"But I'm not underage–"

"Yet, but documents can be forged, but I'd prefer he just married you."

"I had to be your only daughter, didn't I?"

"Yeah, which means that it falls to you to turn that man's head enough to get his ring on your finger."

"You know what? When you first asked me to do this, I took it as a game; thought it would be fun to try to catch his eye, but now the game's up and it's getting way too serious. We don't need Dalian's land. We're doing just fine without it, but doing good isn't good enough. You have to do better than your neighbor, and if you don't then you have to find a way to beat him. Well, you know what, Dad? I'm done. Finished. I'm a legal adult now, so I don't have to keep doing this crap any more. I'm leaving. Moving out."

"Really? Where you gonna go without my money to take care of you?"

"I can get a job. I'm not stupid."

"Yeah, well you're not smart enough to figure out how to get a man into bed, and that's the only real talent a woman's got, so what makes you think you can do anything requiring real brain work."

"Did you insult Mom like this? Is that why she left you?"

The hand that snaked out and connected with her cheek surprised her. Her head snapped sideways and she nearly lost her balance. Her shoulder landed hard against the doorjamb, followed by the side of her head. She grunted and tried to shake off the pain, but it was shooting through every nerve. She stood with her eyes closed and tried to will her brain to shut down, but it refused. After another minute, she cracked her eyes open and glared at her father. He was standing nearby, watching her with a 'wanna open your mouth again?' look. She didn't.

"You done sassing?" He asked when he saw that he had her attention again.

"Yeah," she whispered.

"Still planning on moving out? Or you gonna do what your old man tells you to."

Marsha slowly pushed away from the wall, wiping the blood from her cracked lip, "And what if all the charm in the world doesn't work? What if I sleep with him and he still won't marry me? What if you go to all the trouble of making me whore with the man and you don't get what you want? What then, Dad? I'm trying to tell you that if you have a plan B, it might be a good idea to go to it. He's simply not interested."

"Do you really want to see him dead? 'Cause that's the only plan B there is."

Marsha looked at him incredulously, "You can't possibly be serious. You'd kill him? Just to get hold of his land?"

"You wanna find out?"

Marsha sank onto a nearby chair, shaking her head. "No, I don't," she whispered, and then looked up at her dad, her gaze questioning. "I don't get it. How did you manage to get your hands on all those other parcels of land, without me there to whore for you? And why can't you follow that method instead of pimping me out or murdering the man?"

"Because your mom ain't here no more. That means you get to take her place."

"What?"

"You heard me, girl." Jethro plopped onto a chair. "I told you there was only one use for a female, and your mom was an expert in using her God-given talents. As long as she worked her magic, I had a way of softening up landowners; blackmailing them into parting with their property. Buy it up for a song, then turn around and sell it for nice, tidy bit of profit. Sometimes to the man who sold it to me. Ironic really. Of course, your ma, she didn't have any problem lifting her skirt to keep our profitable venture going. Wasn't a prude like you are. Of course, now that I'm getting on in years, I'm ready to settle down on my own land. Or, in this case, Dalian Rivers' land."

"No...I can't...it isn't possible. I would have known something."

"She didn't want you to know nothing."

"No! I don't believe you! I can't believe you! She wouldn't–"

"Why? Because she acted so squeaky clean around you?"

"No...I just can't...If she was so blasted happy whoring for you, why did she leave then? Huh?" Marsha snapped. "If she was so gall-darned happy with her life, why'd she leave you? Why? I'll tell you why," Marsha continued angrily, "because you're full of it, that's why! She wasn't a whore. You're just saying that to make me feel bad. To make me feel dirty somehow. No, she left you because...because," Marsha stumbled.

"Because why, girl? Go on, tell me, miss know-it-all. Finish your sentence, since you seem to know so damned much. No? What's the matter? Cat got your tongue? Well, why don't I help you out a bit? She left 'cause she fancied herself in love with one of our marks, that's why. Why did I let her go? Because she threatened to rat me out to the law if'n I didn't. Now, go ahead and ask the other question that's been gnawing at you all these years? Let's clear the air so we can get back to focusing on business, shall we? After all, these father-daughter conversations happen so infrequently."

"No, I don't want to know anything else." Marsha's head was suddenly pounding.

"Sure you do, kid."

"No. No, I don't."

"Ah, come on, now," Jethro antagonized. "Every kid wants to know why their mama abandoned them. After all, she's off somewhere living a life of ease with her new rich husband, so why couldn't she take her darling teenage daughter with her instead of leaving her with her reprehensible daddy. Come on, ask!"

"Shut up! I don't...just leave me alone."

"Because you were part of the bargain," Jethro continued relentlessly. "That's why. I leave her be, she leaves me be. I let her live happily ever after with her new man and keep your young body out of his line of sight, and you take over her job. She even suggested letting you go live at the whorehouse where I found her, to help break you into it faster. So, what do you think of your mama now, girl? Huh?"

"Shut up, you pig!" Marsha shouted, jumping up and storming from the house.

"Hell," Jethro whispered to her retreating back, "your mama raised her skirts for so many men, I don't even know if you are my flesh and blood. Damn nuisance, though," he continued his one- sided conversation, moving to the liquor cabinet. "Just like your mama was. A damn nuisance; but I have ways of dealing with nuisances, kid. Just ask your mama. Oh, that's right, you can't," Jethro cackled at his own wit and poured himself a tall glass of whiskey. "Damn nuisance," he whispered again, tipping the glass back and swallowing the contents in one gulp. He coughed and sputtered, then poured another glass. "Just like Rivers. Well, I have ways of dealing with nuisances," he muttered again, then raised his glass in a toast to the empty doorway. "Here's to nuisances. May they rest in peace. Just like that pregnant wife of his."

CHAPTER ELEVEN

"For a city girl, you seem to have a knack for roping things," Dalian observed playfully, stopping by Kat's side.

"That's very kind of you to say, considering the only things I've managed to rope around here are three fence posts and a cowhand passing by."

"I didn't hear him complain none," Dalian laughed.

"No, he didn't," Kat said, color seeping into her cheeks. "He did very kindly point out the direction of my wooden cow and brazenly suggested I might have a directional disorder."

"Oh, did he now?"

"Excuse me, Dalian," Chloe called from across the corral, "I'm not sure exactly how this goes. Could you show me again, please?"

Dalian sighed loudly, "You may have a directional disability, but at least you haven't a learning disability. Excuse me, please."

"Certainly," Kat laughed, eyeing Chloe with a bemused shake of her head. Gone was the shrewd woman she'd met the day of their arrival, and in her stead was a reticent woman who sincerely appeared to be lacking much mass between the ears. She shook her head again and then refocused on the four-legged wood bovine standing a few feet in front of her. "I'm just as determined to rope you," she said softly to her target, "as Chloe is to rope Mr. Dalian Rivers."

She twirled the stiff loop in a circle over her head as she'd been instructed. The rope drooped, and Kat sighed. She found this activity fascinating, but would find it more so, if the rope would cooperate with her efforts. She began to twirl it out in front of her again, picking up the momentum. She grinned, feeling as if she was going to get it this time, as the rope and loop remained taut. Slowly, she lifted her quickly tiring arm, until the lasso was spinning rapidly above her head.

"Now concentrate," A voice whispered near her ear. She squealed and the lasso dropped over her head. Dalian laughed softly. "Now you can add yourself to those items successfully roped today."

"You, Dalian Rivers, are an impish man," Kat turned and glared in mock displeasure at Dalian, who was gazing innocently in return; a grin on his lips that he tried desperately to control.

"What? All I did was offer a suggestion that might possibly help you overcome your handicap."

"Sneaking up on me and breaking my concentration is helpful?" Kat said. "All you managed to do was startle the tar out of me." She pulled at the lasso, but instead of coming up over her head, it tightened slightly and she sighed, suddenly frustrated – at the man, the rope, and her ineptness.

"Would you like some assistance?" Dalian grinned.

"Are you going to tell me to concentrate again? Because by my estimation, your prior assistance is what got me all tangled to begin with."

"Uh, Dalian?" Chloe called from her side of the corral again. Dalian turned and snorted. Kat followed his gaze and couldn't stop the laughter that escaped.

"It would appear that I'm not the only one who's managed to get entangled."

"Yes, but you didn't do it on purpose." Dalian swallowed his exasperation. "It's a good thing our male guests have a propensity for roping or they might think they aren't getting their money's worth of my time."

"I hardly doubt that they are going to take offense at the consideration you are showing to a woman who obviously requires quite a bit of your attention."

"Careful. You're sounding just a tiny bit jealous."

"Hardly, Dalian. I'm merely observing that your male guests are probably envious. I'd wager that each man was wishing he was in your boots and Chloe was calling out his name."

"If even one speaks up, I'll gladly turn over my size twelves. Anything to get that woman's focus off of me."

"Ever run across a Pit Bull with a purpose, Dalian?"

"Yeah. That one makes the second," he grinned, nodding toward Chloe.

Kat laughed, "Then you know to watch out for her powerful jaws. She gets 'em latched onto you—"

"Dear Lord above, don't even say it. Here, let me get that lasso from around you so that I can go assist Miss Harper. I'm fairly certain that you are in far more genuine need than her." Dalian reached for the rope, but Kat moved back a step.

"That's okay," she said. "I can manage just fine."

Dalian eyed the rope with doubt, "I'm not sure you can. You truly do have a roping disorder, Kat." He reached for the lasso again only to have her retreat further.

"No, I can get it off," Kat said nearly breathless, frantically tugging on the ever-tightening rope.

"I've a good mind to let you try, but seeing as how the lasso is designed to tighten with exertion, not loosen, you're going to end with your arms completely pinioned. Now would you please stand still?"

"Since I got myself into this mess, Dalian, I'd rather get myself out," Kat whispered, taking another step back.

"I thought I just explained that it would be nearly impossible, and from our conversation not two seconds ago, you blamed me for this debacle, so the least that–" Dalian stopped when his gaze met hers. Immediately he noticed her dilated pupils. His gaze moved slowly over her flushed features and his eyebrow arched – *so that's it,* he thought. He grinned, and laughed softly when his knowledge registered with Kat. She'd been found out; her secret revealed. Not that she wanted it revealed, he realized. Still–

He stepped closer and she stepped back. His grin widened. He took another step and she bumped into the fence post. He leaned in toward her, "I haven't encountered too many Pit Bulls, Miss McMurray, but I have come across my share of rabbits."

Kat's brow quirked with confusion, but then his words sank in, "Are you actually calling me a scaredy-cat, Dalian?"

"No, I called you a rabbit, although there isn't much difference between the two. Both are skittish as a colt; and would dart away faster than lightening at a perceived threat. You would scamper too, if you weren't tangled up at the moment."

Kat huffed at his declaration, "I startle easily not scare easily."

"You're scared of me."

"Hardly," Kat raised her chin haughtily, but her body refused to stop quivering.

"Dalian!" The two female voices, raised shrilly, snapped Dalian out of his concentrated focus. He turned sharply and Kat felt relief flood through her.

"Ladies," Dalian said tightly and heard Kat mutter behind him, "Enter the other Pit Bull, stage left."

Very funny, Dalian thought. "I'm pleased to see that you managed to disentangle yourself, Miss Chloe; so what can I do for you ladies?"

"Well," Marsha started, "Mrs. McDonald sent me to let you know that lunch is ready and told me to ask you to bring the guests in. And since you were otherwise preoccupied with this one particular guest," she continued, eyeing Kat with open hostility, "I went ahead and sent the others on ahead. Then I tried to get y'alls attention, but neither of you seemed capable of hearing–"

"I wasn't aware you'd come visiting today, Marsha," Dalian interrupted, trying to maintain a polite tone.

"I haven't," Marsha said. "Mrs. McDonald offered me a job this season and I took it." *I'll show my dad how useless I am at doing actual work,* she thought angrily.

"Oh, dear Lord above!" Dalian muttered softly and heard Kat giggle softly from behind him.

"And since you seemed to have Kat cornered," Chloe interjected, her own gaze less-than-friendly, "I thought I might see if she needed any assistance. Do you corner all of your guests this way, Dalian?"

Kat had a difficult time controlling her mirth when she noticed that the cunning Chloe was back. It was easy to see that she wasn't pleased that Dalian's attention refused to focus away from her. Chloe shot Kat a disgruntled look that all but shouted, 'I'm prettier than you so why doesn't he like me?', but Kat merely shrugged.

"I think maybe I'll head on inside and see to our other guests. You ladies come along at your leisure."

"That's a nice way of saying that he doesn't care to see us any more today, ladies," Kat said. Dalian heard the smile behind the words and turned to face her again. Kat's breathing stopped.

"You won't be going anywhere, Kat," Dalian whispered softly, "until I release you."

Kat's mind took his words and twisted them about, leaving her feeling even more breathless and less than steady on her legs. When he reached for the rope, her eyes widened again and then she felt the lasso loosen. He hadn't even touched her. Suddenly she felt foolish. Of course, he meant to release her from her lasso. Certainly not what her mind conjured at his words. Still, his parting gaze left her feeling doubtful.

He tossed the rope over the fence post, tossed Kat a look that promised their conversation wasn't over, and then turned and headed toward the house; Marsha trailing behind trying desperately to get his attention.

"So, what was that all about?" Chloe asked as soon as they were alone. She leaned against the railing with her arms crossed over her chest.

"Just a little roping disability," Kat said softly, and then turned and started toward the house.

"Roping disability, my eye," Chloe called after her. "You promised to give me a heads up, Kat."

"And I will, Chloe," Kat called over her shoulder.

"When," Chloe said, running to catch up, "after you've slept with him?"

Kat stopped dead in her tracks and turned sharply, "Your claws are showing, Chloe," she said softly.

"With reason. Now why should I sheath them instead of clawing your eyes out?" Chloe said, equally soft.

"I'm not interested."

"But he is."

"And that isn't my fault in the slightest." Kat closed her eyes and took a deep breath. She released it slowly before opening her eyes again. "Whether Dalian is interested in me or not, I can only assure you that I haven't done anything knowingly to encourage it."

Chloe sighed and when she looked back up at Kat, the reserved woman was back. She grinned. "Sometimes you don't have to. You know what; I don't think I stand a snowball's chance in Hell with our foxy Mr. Rivers."

"And as far as I'm concerned, he doesn't stand a chance in Hell with me. So what now?"

"I guess I should shift directions and you watch out for little Miss Marsha," Chloe said, starting toward the house again.

"What do you mean?"

"You don't have too much in the way of experience with men, do you, Kat?"

"I was married, you know."

"To your high school sweetheart, I'd wager."

"My college sweetheart, actually."

"Didn't date much?"

"Didn't need to, but what's my dating history have to do with Marsha?"

"She seems to have her sights set on our Mr. Rivers, and she's been after him a sight bit longer than I have, if I'm any judge."

"So?"

"So, it's obvious she hasn't caught him and that, my dear Kat, makes her a desperate woman. And when a woman gets desperate for a man, they get stupid."

"And they tend to do stupid things?"

"Not necessarily stupid, but mean."

"You sound as if you speak from experience."

"Firsthand."

"Why didn't she come after you then? You were actually chasing her interest," Kat countered.

"Because she knows, just like I do now, that Dalian isn't the least bit interested in me, which is why I didn't claw her eyes out. However, she probably has figured out that he's definitely interested in you."

"Well, hopefully, Dalian will catch the hint that I'm not interested and leave me be, then I won't have to worry about Marsha, or any other woman who takes a shine to him. And if the need arises, I'll simply let her know that I'll be leaving in less than two months. Then she can continue her pursuit unfettered."

"Good luck. Wanna grab something to eat? And I'm not talking about our host."

"Funny, Chloe. Real funny."

"I thought so," Chloe laughed. "Come on. We better hurry before the men gobble everything up."

CHAPTER TWELVE

"Before we settle down to eat," Dalian announced the following morning at breakfast, "I just wanted to let everyone know that today we're going to leave the ranch—"

"Where are we going, Dalian?" Chloe raised her hand as a child in a classroom might. Kat shook her head and grinned. She might be done with her pursuit, but she still liked to be noticed.

"Well, part of being a cowboy—

"Uh-hum," Chloe cleared her throat loudly.

"And, cowgirl," Dalian clarified.

"Thank you."

He nodded politely, and then continued, "As I was saying, part of being a *cowhand*, is learning how to live out of doors during a drive. We spent this past week practicing rounding up strays—" Chloe raised her hand again and Kat heard several of the men snicker. "Yes, Miss Chloe?" Dalian asked, trying to keep his patience in check.

"I'm afraid you lost me at the bakery," Chloe smiled. "What do you mean precisely by living out of doors and what's a drive?"

Dalian laughed, "Well, Miss Chloe, when the cattle are taken to market, a lot of times we round them up and drive them cross country. By that I mean, they walk and we ride. During that time, we sleep and take our meals out on the range. It can take a month or more to go and come back."

"Why not just load them up on a truck and drive them that way?" Chloe asked.

"Fuel efficiency," Dalian said. "Even in this day and age of economic fuel sources, transporting cattle can prove costly, which would eat into our profit margin. Moving them via truck is fine if you have only a couple hundred head, but when you're taking several thousand head at once...well, you can only imagine the cost of fuel and the number of cattle trucks required. Not very economical. We did work with cattle trucks several years ago, but went back to driving them cross-country on foot since we aren't but a few hundred miles from the nearest railway terminal. Also, we generally use All Terrain Vehicles these days for a cattle drive, since it's easier, but for the purposes of our week-long foray, we'll ride horses. I found out long, long ago, that most people associate cowboys with horses, and so prefer to ride them when they come out here on vacation."

"We're not going to drive your cows to market, are we?" Chloe asked, her eyes widening in distress.

"No, you're not. We won't take them for a few months yet," Dalian responded. "But, as part of the ranching experience, we like to take our guests out on the range for a week with about fifty head, just to let them experience rounding 'em up, roping 'em in, and sleeping under the stars. That's why we had you fine folks practicing on the wooden steers in the corral." Dalian looked over at Kat and laughed when her face tinted crimson.

"It's not required, is it? I mean, we don't have to go if we don't want to, right?"

"Absolutely not, Miss Chloe," Dalian said, "however for those who do want to go, we'll be leaving later this morning, so after breakfast, we'll meet up and go over the preparations needed for an extended stay away from the ranch. If you don't have what you need, don't fret overly much. I'll see to it that you get it. Okay?"

Everyone nodded in unison. "Good. Anyone besides Miss Chloe planning to stay behind?" Dalian held his breath in hopes that Kat didn't raise her hand. He let it go when she didn't; however, he was surprised to see two men raise their hands. In all his years running the dude ranch, he never encountered a man that didn't want to go out on the range. That's why they came to a dude ranch, after all – to play the part of a cowboy.

"Okay, appears most everyone else is going to brave the trip, so for now, enjoy your breakfast; and meet me next to the barn in an hour," Dalian took his place in the breakfast line. He looked over to where Chloe was busily bending Kat's ear about whatever women talked about and again breathed a sigh of thanks that she'd decided to go, and that Chloe decided to remain behind. That meant he could focus his attentions on Kat without all of Chloe's irritating interruptions. He hadn't known Kat but a week, but something about her sent his senses haywire. He knew she was attracted to him as well, but for some reason, expressing herself wasn't something she cared to do. He'd love to know why. He'd also love the time to find a way to break down those barriers he perceived surrounded her.

Marsha came into the room bearing a fresh pot of coffee and he sighed. He was especially thankful that Marsha wouldn't be going. She was even worse than Chloe about her intentions. His eyes widened slightly when he saw that she was heading in his direction.

"Dalian. Good morning," Marsha's tone was just barely pleasant, which meant she hadn't gotten over his perceived snub yesterday. "Mrs. Guthrie said to tell you that everything will be ready in less than an hour."

"Thank you, Marsha," Dalian said. "Please inform her that three of the guests won't be accompanying us, so arrangements will need to be made for their meals while we're gone."

"Oh, well, I was kind of hoping that I could–"

"No!" Dalian interrupted. "Employees don't go on drives, just hands; and since Mrs. Guthrie hired you to work here, that makes you an employee. Sorry."

"No you're not, Dalian," Marsha whispered. "You know something? You're a real jackass," she said, wanting everyone to hear, but knowing that it wouldn't be wise.

Dalian's gaze narrowed and he lowered his head so that only she would hear, "A jackass, Marsha? Why? Because I won't fall into your daddy's trap? No! Don't say another word! You've said quite enough, and I've tolerated your antics long enough, but I will say this," he grasped her by the elbow and led her from the room. She wanted to pull away, but her humiliation would be too great, so she went along meekly. He pulled her far enough into the foyer, so he could be certain the guests wouldn't hear. "I've put up with your pursuit for longer than I should have, young lady, so we're going to put a stop to it once and for all. Understand me?"

"I don't know what you're talking about," Marsha said sullenly. "I can't help it if I love—"

"Stop it, ya hear!" Dalian snapped, his temper threatening to break. "Damn it, girl! I know what's going on. Does your dad really believe I'm some naive school kid without a lick of sense? Don't you think that at my age, I wouldn't know a genuine attraction when I ran across it; that I don't know that your attentions are all just an act? Now, I'm telling you straight – I'm not interested in you that way. To me, you're just a kid, and I don't mess with kids. And if that ain't plain enough, then I'll put it this way – leave me the hell alone and tell your daddy to do the same. If you want to keep working here, I don't give a rat's ass, but I'll fire your ass if you keep acting like a lovesick puppy. Is that plain enough for you, Marsha?"

"It's that Kathryn McMurray isn't it?" Marsha sniffled dramatically. "She's taking you away from me—"

Dalian grabbed her by the shoulders and shook her very briefly, then shoved her away from him. He closed his eyes and counted to ten as his frustration mounted, then took several slow, deep cleansing breaths. When he opened his eyes, Marsha was watching him warily.

"You've been duly warned," he whispered, and then turned and walked back into the dining room.

"I told you, Dad," Marsha whispered, swiping the tears from her eyes. "I made one final attempt to get him to look at me, but he just ain't interested. I only hope you forget about plan B."

CHAPTER THIRTEEN

Why didn't you go on the drive?

"I couldn't." The whispered reply shied away from the rebuke.

It would have been fun, and you know I like to have fun. But you knew I'd pressure you into going, which is why you didn't give me a hint of your intentions until they'd ridden out, you coward! You are weak and I'm sick of having to keep thinking for you, keep taking action for you. You used to enjoy life with me, now you seem to be fighting me every step of the way.

"I'm not weak, and I'm not a coward." It was a feeble attempt at a self-confident rebuttal. "I'm just tired of playing your games, is all, and this time we don't have a chance of winning. You can see that, can't you? We aren't going to ensnare this one."

You should know after all of these years that I get what I want and it's pointless to try to stop me. You have become a weak, pathetic, mewling excuse for a human being, but you'd better be prepared to step up when they get back from the drive, or I may just have to beat you into submission.

"That won't be necessary. I'll be ready, I promise. Just tell me what you need me to do."

I always do.

CHAPTER FOURTEEN

Kat met the pseudo-drive as she did everything else in her life. It didn't matter if she was good at it or not, she enjoyed herself to the fullest and tried her hardest; however, as with the lassoing, she seemed to lack the proficiency, which was just slightly frustrating. And frustration seemed counter to her objective to relax and unwind during her stay here.

Of course relaxing would be a heck of a lot easier if Dalian Rivers didn't make her so tense. Not that he was rude or horribly aggressive in his attentions – *that* she could handle or even possibly ignore. No. Dalian Rivers was kind, generous, charming, witty, and helpful to a fault...and she wished to high-heaven that he wasn't.

He was also laughing at her – again.

"Need help?" he asked, watching her struggle with her equipment. They were supposed to leave soon, and she still hadn't loaded everything onto her horse. Dalian had demonstrated the proper method, and she knew she wasn't a slow learner – she just couldn't fathom why her stuff didn't stay on her horse the way his did.

"Not at all, thank you." Kat shifted away, trying to ignore his closeness.

"Well, we're heading out in ten minutes," Dalian said, grinning, "so..."

"I'll be ready!" Kat interrupted, knitting her brow as she concentrated on tying down her bedroll on the horse's rump.

"Don't forget to tie that like I showed–"

"Do you mind?" She snapped around like a cobra ready to strike.

Dalian grinned at the scorching look she gave him. She was also close enough to him that if he wanted to steal a kiss, he could – with only a slight tilt to his head. He grinned as her gaze widened – as if she'd read his thoughts. Or was it that she only just realized that by turning, she was closer to him than she wanted to be.

Her complexion reddened. His grin turned into a teeth-bearing smile and he leaned in closer, "You're in a whole heap o' trouble, woman," he said, his breath caressing her skin like a lover's touch.

Her eyes fluttered closed, and she tried desperately to steady her runaway pulse, "Please, Dalian," she said softly, keeping her eyes closed.

"Please, what, Kat?" Dalian whispered next to her lips. He literally felt her nerves jump as her eyes flew open.

"Are you two going to sit there making gaga eyes at each other all morning, or are we going to head out soon?" One of the other guests asked, laughing.

Dalian laughed and took a step back from Kat, "Sorry, Jason. I guess I just have a hard time keeping away from Miss McMurray."

"Can't say as I blame you," Jason grinned, and then laughed when Kat muttered something unintelligible beneath her breath. She turned in a huff and started working on her supplies again.

"Sorry, Kat," Dalian said, taking the rope from her hand, "but it's time to head out, so I'm going to have to make these adjustments for you. Watch what I do, and before long you'll be a real pro." Within minutes, Dalian had all of her gear tied down, much to Kat's chagrin. He turned and held out a hand, but Kat merely stood staring at it.

"I'll help you mount, and before you object," he said quickly, "we really need to get going."

"You're enjoying the hell out of this, aren't you?" Kat snapped.

"Yes, ma'am," Dalian said, tenting his fingers for her to use as a stepladder. He hefted her into the saddle and then stood until she glanced down at him. "I'm enjoying this a whole hell of a lot," He laughed, and then turned and quickly mounted his own horse. "The cattle we're going to be herding are waiting for us in the north pasture, so everyone just follow me and we'll get this show on the road."

CHAPTER FIFTEEN

They were into their second evening on the range, when Dalian approached the campsite on horseback. "We have a calf that's gotten separated from its momma. Anyone up to trying to rope it and bring it back into the fold?" What he didn't say was that he had ranch hands following nearby that deliberately removed the calf from its momma and separated it from the herd, specifically as a way of giving the guests the opportunity to test their skills. It was something that they would do many times over the next couple of days until every person had participated in roping. He didn't mention any of that to them though, because he didn't want to ruin the fun, which it would if they knew it was all staged, so to the group he said, "Don't worry if you don't get a chance right now. There will be plenty of cattle that go wandering during this week, so everyone will have at least one chance of bringing home a stray."

Four of the men stood, ready to tackle the challenge, but as soon as Kat stood too they started to sit back down.

"Ladies should have first crack at it," one of them said at her look of confusion. She blushed and murmured a quick thank you, and then headed over to where she'd tied down her horse. She saddled the docile mare, collected her rope, and then used a nearby stump to help her mount. She gave her gear a once-over, and as soon as she was certain she was prepared, she rode over to where Dalian was patiently waiting.

"This will be good for you, since it's just a calf, but if you get into trouble I'll be nearby, okay?" Dalian's tone was professional, which put Kat at ease. She nodded, and then pulled on her reins, turning the horse to follow Dalian out of camp.

It wasn't until after they topped a small rise that she realized that she and Dalian were away from camp, and very much alone. She glanced over at him, half-expecting that he would wriggle his eyebrows absurdly like the villains used to do in 1920's silent movies, but he seemed extremely focused. She realized then that he took his job at protecting the herd very seriously.

"There it is," he said after a moment, pointing to an opening between some bushes. He looked at Kat, but there was none of the desire or teasing that usually filled his gaze. "Think you got this?"

"We'll find out." Kat slid from the saddle, collected her lasso, and slowly walked toward the calf, careful not to startle it into running. She started spinning the rope out in front of her, and as before, felt confident when it didn't droop. She lifted it over her head and almost stopped the momentum when memories flooded of the last time she'd been doing this so close to Dalian. She ended up lassoing herself. She forced herself to concentrate only on the calf. When she was certain she was close enough and her aim was true, she let the lasso go. She held her breath and waited as it soared through the air the short distance to the calf, then let out a whoop and a holler when it landed over his head. With a quick tug, the lasso tightened.

Her shout of victory and the sudden tug on the lasso, startled the calf, and it bolted, nearly yanking Kat from her feet. She took off at a run after it, wrapping the end of the rope around her hand and elbow as she'd been shown, to provide needed leverage. When she was certain she wouldn't lose her grip, she stopped dead and dug in her heels, leaned back, and pulled with all of her might.

She would have toppled onto her face if Dalian hadn't suddenly appeared behind her, leaned around her, and grabbed hold of the rope. "We've got this," he encouraged. "Now lean back with me and pull." Together, they tugged. Dalian slowly wrapped the rope around his arm, as slack permitted, until the calf appeared around a bush. Its struggle lessened, but it still objected to them pulling it in a direction opposite to its will. Kat was leaning so far back, that when the calf started moving toward them, instead of fighting against them, she fell completely against Dalian.

"Whoa, I've got ya," he laughed, releasing one hand from the rope, and wrapping it about her abdomen. He pulled until she was standing upright again – and flush up against him. "There you go. Steady footing again," he said, then returned his hand to the rope; his focus again on the calf. When the baby was standing next to them, Dalian lifted his arm, raised the rope above Kat's head, and stepped around her. He knelt down next to the calf and stroked its neck, "Let's see about getting you back to your momma, shall we, little one?" He murmured soothingly. Kat felt her heart melt over his gentle caring tone.

He stood suddenly, startling her, "Let's get this baby back. Sun's going down and we want to get back to camp before nightfall. It tends to get dark fast around these parts."

Kat nodded and turned to follow him to the horses. He attached the lead rope to his horse's pommel and then mounted. As soon as he was certain that Kat was saddled and ready to go, he tugged on his reins and headed back to camp.

Kat kept her gaze pinned on his back, suddenly intrigued with this version of Dalian Rivers. During the whole episode with the calf, even when she found herself so close in proximity to his body, he hadn't once flirted or pursued. His attention had remained focused on the safety of the calf. Even his tone when assisting her, while playful, was professional. She looked down at the calf, following faithfully alongside Dalian's horse, a feeling sweeping over her that she'd be willing to follow him anywhere, just like this baby. It was a feeling that startled her and angered her slightly, because she'd never once felt that loyal to Robert.

Although she'd enjoyed being married to him – her best friend – he didn't elicit feelings of ardor and devotion. Because of that, she often ruminated, as she was doing now, about their relationship;

however, right now her reflections were questioning why this near stranger stirred feelings within her that Robert never did?

By the time they entered camp fifteen minutes later, she was no closer to solving the riddle of Dalian Rivers' magnetism, but the sound of applause distracted her and she felt relieved to be back among the other guests.

Dalian raised his hands to silent the noise. When all was quiet, he addressed his guests, "Remember, we need to keep our noise down, or we'll be chasing after cattle all night." The guests laughed softly, and then Dalian continued, "Kat did herself proud. Wrangled the calf all by herself – well, for the most part."

"If it weren't for Dalian's timely assistance," Kat interjected, "I would have come back needing a bath. That calf was a mighty strong opponent considering how young it is."

"You still did a fine job for being a petite miss," Dalian said, tipping his hat. "I'll just take this baby over to the herd. You get yourself settled by the fire."

Kat nodded, and then led her horse back to where she'd tied it down earlier. She removed her saddle, gave the animal a quick brush down, and then made her way back to camp. The sun had set rapidly, and everyone was already preparing to bed down for the night. She didn't blame them. Although their task each day was simply to ride alongside the cattle to keep them from straying, it wasn't as easy as it looked. Keeping constant vigil was exhausting. If any one person let their guard down, one of the cows could get away from the herd and end up injured, or a predator could attack it. Moreover, there was the risk of one of the horses stepping in a prairie dog hole or other rut in the ground if the rider didn't remain alert, which could lame the mount. That was why one of the ranch hands followed nearby, a supply of horses at the ready.

Having to remain hyper-alert was more exhausting than Kat ever imagined it could be, so when she finally settled onto her bedroll next to the fire, she was more than ready to go to sleep with the sun.

She lie down and gazed up at the stars, enthralled at the beauty. It was something she rarely witnessed back East, where the pollution generated tended to obliterate sight of the night sky. She hadn't seen the stars in so long that she'd forgotten how beautiful the night sky could be. She recalled her mother telling her that ancient astronomers divided the stars into named groups, like the Big Dipper, but she'd only seen samples of these groupings in her encyclopedia. Now, try as she might, she couldn't distinguish any of the groupings she'd studied long ago, so she rolled over onto her side and thought about her earlier roping experience with the calf.

She was so proud of herself, that she hadn't even minded being the center of Dalian's attention for that short time. The look of pride in his eyes when he recounted her efforts, brought unfamiliar warmth to her body; warmth that didn't occur when the other guests and cowhands commended her quick and efficient work.

"That was good work today," Dalian said, settling down next to her.

Think of the devil, Kat thought, smiling slightly. "Thanks. It felt good to rope something that actually needed roping."

"I'll bet," Dalian laughed softly. "If it will help boost your confidence any, there was a time I couldn't tell one end of a rope from the other."

"Yeah, right," Kat snorted, "You probably left your mother's womb with a lasso clasped firmly in an iron grip."

Dalian laughed. "Nope, and I'm serious." He lifted two fingers in a boy scout's pledge. "Harvey taught me."

Kat laughed. "How did you ever become a rancher then?"

"Well, I could say it runs through my veins, but that wouldn't be the truth…"

"And you cannot tell a lie," Kat quipped.

"Actually I can, but I'd feel real bad about doing it," Dalian smiled, and Kat's heart started thudding in her ears.

"Well, if it wasn't so late, and I wasn't so tired, I'd let you regale me with how you managed to rope your first cow…"

"Regale? And 'lasso clasped firmly in an iron grip'," Dalian smiled. "You are a writer."

Kat smiled in return, nodding. "A very tired writer. It's been a long day." She didn't have the courage to say what she was really feeling – that his nearness unnerved her.

"I can catch a clue, Kat," Dalian said rising. "We have one more partial day of driving the cattle, and then we'll turn and start driving them back toward the ranch. Think you'll be able to stay seated in the saddle for two and a half more days?"

"Yep, and I can then say I lived to tell about it," Kat said, stifling a yawn.

"Goodnight, Kat," Dalian whispered.

"Goodnight, Dalian," Kat murmured, and then her eyes drifted closed. Within a minute, she was fast asleep.

"Bless your heart, you were tired," Dalian whispered, and then he went to retrieve his own bedroll. He spread it out next to hers. If this were the closest he ever came to holding this woman in his arms, he'd take it.

CHAPTER SIXTEEN

At two o'clock the next afternoon, Dalian tugged Swift to a stop, and pulled his Midland GZV5000 long-range two-way radio from its holster to call a halt to the ride. He waited to see that everyone heard and had stopped moving before issuing his next directive, "I need everyone to ride over and meet up with me. We're going to go over the instructions for turning the cattle around."

Without hesitation, all twelve of the guests spurred their horses into a trot and headed in his direction. He searched and quickly located Kat, a grin spreading across his mouth at how easily she'd taken to horseback riding. The grin slipped as he imagined her sitting astride him in much the same manner. "Whew!" He exclaimed, shifting in the saddle. "Watch what you're thinking, Dalian," He reprimanded himself lightly.

"This is going to be the tricky part of our ride," Dalian started, the moment everyone came to a stop next to him. "These cattle have a current mindset, a heading that they are content to stay traveling. Getting them to change that mindset can be interesting. Here's why. Remember when I asked that you not make any loud noises in camp because it could startle the cattle and cause a stampede?" Everyone nodded, and Dalian continued, "Well, in order to get the cattle to turn and change direction, we're going to have to startle them into doing so. That means deliberately causing a stampede – unless these brutes prove amiable and shift their direction with little fuss. Of course, that hasn't always been my experience."

"Won't that be dangerous?" Jason asked.

"Very," Dalian admitted. "And while you folks signed on to act as cowhands, you didn't sign up to place yourself deliberately in harm's way. With that being said, this is what's going to happen next. I radioed ahead to the chuck wagon about a half hour ago, which means that Shaun will have lunch about ready, so we're going to take a break and eat. I also placed a second radio transmission that called for fifteen of my cowboys, who've been trailing behind at a distance, to meet up with us, which they should do before lunch ends."

"Are they going to turn the cattle around?" Kat asked.

"That they are; however, I will give you folks an option before I release you to ride over for lunch. Take time to think about these options while you eat. If you feel you are capable of sitting a saddle at full gallop, and would like to ride close to one of my cowboys, I'll be happy to pair you up. The stipulation being that you allow my boys to do the work. You'd simply be riding along for the experience. If, however, you are not comfortable riding at full speed, but would still like a chance at playing cowboy, I will have four men nearby whose sole purpose will be to watch for and return strays. Those who wish to stay with those four cowhands, can accompany them and assist with round ups. Again, I'll let you think over your choice at lunch, so let's head on over and take a break from these saddles."

Dalian spurred Swift toward the chuck wagon, his guests trailing along behind. He was curious to see who'd attempt to herd and who'd hang back. The faux cattle drive was something he'd ever participated in prior to this week, but that didn't stop him hearing about it each year. Harvey always returned from the week away, full of tales of those who balked at being restrained from full participation, those who wanted to return to the ranch mid-drive because it wasn't their cup of tea; those who invariably ended unseated from their saddle, and those who didn't want to sign the legal release. Uh oh, Dalian thought, as he pulled Swift to a stop and dismounted, Harvey had given him specific instructions for this leg of the drive, and he'd nearly forgotten to recite one of the more basic requisites. "Folks," he called, "there's one thing I failed to mention." He tossed his reins across a tree branch, and then turned to address his guests, some still in the process of dismounting. "The law requires that to participate in this particular part of your vacation, you'll have to sign a liability form. This form releases Heart of the Mountain Dude Ranch and me from any liability should you take a tumble and injure yourself. It also states that you are responsible for your own medical costs should injury occur, so that is another thing to take into consideration before determining whether you want to ride. Those of you who cater to customers can readily empathize with the legal ramifications of being a business owner – I hope."

"Without a doubt," one of his guests replied and he heard mutters of agreement from nearly all of the others. Whew, Dalian thought, thankful that his first few days on the drive had been free of whiners and complainers.

"Excellent! Now, as you collect your meal from Shaun, he'll have a pre-filled form for you to sign."

"What if we decide not to ride with the cattle? Do we still have to sign the form?"

"Unfortunately, yes. I really should have had you sign the form before we left the ranch. Even though not much is likely to happen, other than taking a tumble from your horse, turning the cattle back towards home is when it really becomes essential. Also unfortunate, those of you unwilling to sign, will have to be escorted back to the ranch by one of my boys. I certainly hope that we all get to stay and enjoy the remainder of our time out here."

Jason stepped forward, "I think I'll head on back to the ranch, if that's okay. I like riding well enough, but I'm more ready to lounge by the pool for a couple of days and relax."

"Fair enough," Dalian said, hiding the disappointment from his tone. "I'll have Achak escort you back as soon as he arrives. If anyone else wishes to return, just be ready to go after lunch. In the meantime, let's eat, shall we?"

Dalian collected a plate of food first and settled on a nearby log, his gaze seeking out Kat. She was mingling with the other guests in the chow line. As soon as she had her plate, he planned to wave her over and ask she join him for lunch. Surprisingly, she made her way over to him unbidden.

"Mind if I join you?" She asked.

Dalian grinned and nodded to the log next to his, "I was hoping you would."

She didn't reply, rather dug into her baked chicken and beans hungrily. Dalian allowed her to eat in peace, but he was chomping at the bit to know whether she'd be staying or if she was one who planned to return to the ranch with Achak. He hoped not. That would make his remaining time on the range very dreary. He really loved her company.

When Kat downed the water in her bottle, she finally spoke, "I actually joined you because I wanted to tell you that I am very impressed, but my hunger got the better of me."

Dalian's brow quirked and he grinned again, "Impressed with me or my cook's food?"

Kat laughed, "Both. More with you, I suppose, in the way you run things here. You're very good at your job, and the way in which you soothed that calf was amazing to watch. You really like doing this, don't you?"

"I can't imagine ever doing anything else. It's similar to you and your writing, I'd wager."

Kat nodded, "It's a wager you'd win. I can't imagine not writing. I used to tell Robert that it didn't matter whether my books sold or not, I just have to write."

"Robert?" Dalian asked, hoping that she didn't have a jealous boyfriend back East. Of course, that could explain her barriers, but what it wouldn't explain is her obvious attraction to him — which she's trying to avoid showing, if you recall, he brain supplied.

Kat's gaze dropped and she sighed heavily, "Robert was my husband. He passed away two years ago, and I think maybe I need to go and put my dishes away now." She stood, but Dalian placed a restraining hand on her arm.

"I'm sorry, Kat."

"Thanks." Kat smiled and walked away, stopping by to place her dishes in the portable dishwasher located on the cook's van. She found it amusing that Dalian referred to it as a chuck wagon; an antiquated term that couldn't do justice to this state-of-the-art marvel on wheels, which followed them about on the drive.

Once she'd taken care of her dishes, she decided to take a short walk while the others helped themselves to a second helping of food. She was truthful when she told Janet before coming out here, that she was over her loss, because her heart barely ached now when she thought of Robert, but it still threatened to shatter into a million pieces whenever thoughts surfaced of Mitchell and Stephanie — her precious twins — which always happened when she mentioned Robert. Her twins had been her world and that world stopped spinning for a long while after they were lost to her. Had she been a weaker person, her life as a recluse could very well have become permanent. Instead, she buried herself in her writing, using it as an outlet for her pain and suffering, which is why her first novel after their loss, Dreamer of Destiny[1], contained so much tragedy. It also proved so cathartic that by the time

---

[1] *Dreamer of Destiny* is a real book, written by Barbara Woster

she'd written three-quarters of that book, the tragic text began to transform into a will to survive and concluded triumphantly.

Her hand swept across the top of the tall grass and she sighed, taking in a deep cleansing breath,

"Just breathe, Kat," she whispered to herself. After a while, the pounding pain in her heart returned to a dull ache and she closed her eyes in gratitude. Once the memories receded, thoughts of Dalian intruded again, and she found herself having to take another deep, calming breath. "What is it about that man that makes my body and brain turn to goo?" She asked herself, but of course received no answer. She slowly turned and instantly her gaze found him, standing, and conversing with the other guests. Even the men seemed impressed by him, as if by standing near, some of his manly charm and graciousness would rub off on them and make them as appealing to the opposite sex.

"You okay? You look a little distraught."

Kat jumped and turned to find Cal Withers, another guest at the ranch, standing beside her. She'd seen him staring at her on occasion, but he'd never spoken to her until now. Like Dalian, he was a fine looking man, and well-built, but he simply did not stir things up in her as Dalian did.

"I didn't mean to startle you. I thought you might have seen me approach."

"No, I was focused on . . ."

"Dalian?"

"What? No. I was just thinking about stuff in general," Kat stammered.

"Ah, well, I'm glad for that."

"Hey, wait a minute. You didn't join us on the drive, so how is it you're standing here talking to me?"

"I'm surprised you noticed that I hadn't come along, since you always seemed focused on Dalian. You two appear attached at the hip of late." Kat's brow furrowed at the tone in his voice, but before she could comment, Cal offered an explanation. "I rode out with the cowhands. I had planned to remain behind, but got bored. When the radio call came in, I was talking to Achak — what a name, huh? — and asked if he wouldn't mind my tagging along. Figured I could finish up the drive with the rest of you."

"Ah, well, it's definitely been an experience to remember," Kat said conversationally, and then saw Dalian look her way and wave. "Well, it looks as if we're about to begin turning the cattle around," she said, sending Dalian a return wave. She gave Cal a polite smile and then started heading back to the group. Cal fell into step beside her, so Kat told him about the requirements for joining the drive. "If you're going to want to ride, I believe you'll need to stop by the lunch wagon and get a release form from Shaun. He's the cook. I'm sure Dalian will go over the options again for this afternoon."

True to her word, Dalian reiterated the options the moment that Kat and Cal joined the rest of the group. As soon as he finished speaking, he made his way over to where she and Cal were standing, "Cal, good to see you decided to join us," he said amiably.

"Apparently he got bored just sitting around the ranch," Kat offered.

"Yeah, sitting around doing nothing can make your brain start to get antsy," Cal said with a laugh, but it lacked humor.

"Well, hopefully you'll not get bored out here. Have you stopped by to sign the release form yet?"

"Headed that way now," Cal said and then turned to Kat, "Are you going to hang back and rope in strays? If so, maybe we can keep each other company."

Cal couldn't see Dalian, but she could, and his reaction to that one simple query startled her. He stiffened visibly, and she half expected him to interject with an objection. To his credit, he said nothing, allowing her to decide what she wanted to do. To her, it felt as if each man were awaiting a decision about whom she preferred to spend time with. Still, Dalian couldn't have known that keeping company with Cal wasn't something she wanted to do, although she couldn't quite put her finger on why. It was something to do with the way he looked at her. His stare made her feel as if she were a gazelle and he a cheetah.

Initially, she had planned to hang back because she wasn't certain she'd be comfortable riding near a stampeding herd, but now that she knew Cal was hanging back, she'd risk the herd. Hopefully, she wouldn't regret her impulsive decision, "Actually, the thought of galloping next to the herd seems fun." Both men's gazes widened at her declaration, and she smiled, trying to hide her nervousness.

It looked as if Cal was about to object, but Dalian interjected, "You'll shadow me," He stated simply, and Kat felt relief flood through her. If anyone could keep her out of harm's way, she was certain Dalian could.

"No surprise there," Cal said sharply, and then turned and headed over to where Shaun was busily storing away supplies.

Kat saw Dalian's perplexed look and laughed nervously, color seeping into her face, "He seems to think that you and I are "attached at the hip". His words, not mine."

"Ah, well, being attached at the hip with you is definitely

preferable to being attached to one of the men; so I can't say as I blame Cal wanting to keep company with you, although I'm glad I get to instead." What Dalian didn't say aloud was that he wouldn't have been as focused on the cattle had Kat decided to remain behind with Cal. In fact, he was very pleased that she seemed disinterested in him. Then it registered that she would be shadowing him on the ride and a different tension filled his body.

"Are you sure you want to ride alongside me though?" He asked. "You sit a saddle well, but I'd feel responsible if something were to happen to you."

"Actually I'm not a hundred percent sure, no, but . . ." Kat paused. How could she state her objection to staying behind without it sounding as if she were choosing him over Cal?

"But?" Dalian prodded. Kat hadn't realized that Dalian had taken a step closer to her, until she looked up at him and saw his face was mere inches from hers.

"Oh. Um," was all she could mutter.

Dalian grinned, but before he could say or do anything more, Jason interrupted, "There you go making gaga eyes at each other again."

"They been doing this often?" Achak laughed at the embarrassment that registered on Kat's face and the disgruntled look on his boss's face. Dalian took a step back and then took a deep breath.

"Yep," Jason laughed.

"Hi, I'm Achak Broadwater, assistant foreman. I'm in charge, second to Dalian here, when Harvey isn't around."

"It's nice to meet you," Kat said softly.

"Oh my," Achak declared, "no wonder Dalian is going gaga over you. Not only are you beautiful, but that accent is to die for." Achak laughed when Kat turned a deeper shade of red, and then he turned to address Dalian, "You want to stop your pursuit boss, just let me know. I'll be happy to have her making gaga eyes at me."

"Yeah, you and every other man on this ranch," Dalian snapped, trying to rein in his jealousy. "Are you ready to take Jason back to the house?" He said, deftly changing the subject. He could tell, even if the others could not, that Achak's comments discomfited Kat, and he didn't want her rabbiting away as she'd nearly done her first week here. He liked that she was starting to feel more comfortable in his company; and even with his flirting.

"Yep, we just came by to let you know we're heading out," Achak replied.

"Anyone else calling it quits," Dalian said and then turned to address Jason. "Sorry, didn't mean to make it sound a negative thing."

"Not a problem. I just know when I'm licked," Jason replied in that good-natured manner that Dalian was beginning to appreciate.

"I have one more person," Achak stated, "who said he'd prefer the pool to more time in a saddle, but don't know his name. Sorry."

"That's alright, as long as I have a head count. We started with twelve, are losing two, and gaining one."

"Oooh, I know, I know. That makes eleven people, right?" Achak said, jumping up and down like an excitable school student. Kat couldn't help but laugh at his antics, and Dalian just shook his head.

"Thank you, Mr. Broadwater," Dalian said in mock seriousness. "Radio in as soon as you get back to the house. We should be riding in sometime Friday afternoon."

"Sure thing, boss," Achak said, and then turned back to Kat, "Ma'am," he added with a tip of his hat.

When both men left, Kat suddenly felt ill at ease. There were simply too many people connecting her to Dalian and she wasn't certain if she liked that or not. Before Dalian could take advantage of their being alone again, she started heading back to camp, "I'll just go get saddled up and ready to go," she called over her shoulder.

Dalian sighed heavily. The rabbit was back.

CHAPTER SEVENTEEN

"Well, I do hope you folks have enjoyed your first two weeks here at the ranch," Dalian said, and waited until after the smattering of applause died away before continuing. "I know you've had an interesting time learning to rope, ride, brand, and everything that being a cowboy entails–"

"Uh-hum."

"Sorry, Miss Chloe. I'll get it right eventually," Dalian smiled.

"Thank you," she cooed.

"You're very welcome." He tipped his hat, and then continued addressing the group. "But every now and again, even we hardworking folk need a little breather, so we'll be taking tomorrow night off and having ourselves a little shindig."

"What in heaven's name is a shindig?" Chloe asked, and Kat grinned. Again, the shrewd woman she'd met two weeks prior was gone, replaced by the reticent, dimwitted, airy-voiced girl speaking now. Kat wondered just how she managed to keep those two personalities separated, calling on the right one at the right time. It must take a monumental effort on her part not to get them mixed up. If she needed a career to fall back on in her retirement, she could easily get a job as an actress.

Dalian was responding and Kat refocused on the conversation. "A hoedown?" He asked with a laugh.

"Nope. Never heard of it."

"A barn dance?"

"I've heard of dancing and I've seen a barn since I've been here–"

"Well, that's what we're going to do. We're going to kick up our heels and have a rip-roaring good time inside that barn you've seen here."

"Aren't there animals in there?"

"Not that particular one. We keep our supplies in there, but a few of the ranch hands will stow it all away and make room for us."

"Are there going to be any other women at that party, or are Kat and I expected to dance with everybody?"

"Most times, the ranch hands bring their wives and girlfriends, and I'm sure that Mrs. Guthrie and Marsha will attend; however, if you're concerned...would any of you gentlemen have an objection to keeping Miss Chloe company tomorrow night?"

"Nope," The male guests said in unison.

"And Kat?" Chloe said, eyeing Dalian with a knowing glance. "Who's going to keep her company?"

Kat's face reddened at the implication of the conversation, "Um. Do I get a say—"

"I am," Dalian answered, stopping Kat's protest in its tracks. Everyone was so focused on Dalian and Kat that no one noticed when Cal stormed from the room. Kat wanted to reply, but when her gaze met Dalian's, all she could do was to suck in a deep breath. If he wanted her to know where he stood, that gaze said it all; but she didn't want what his gaze offered. Did she? After all, she'd spent the better part of the last two weeks ignoring his not-so-subtle intimations; however, something had changed since their return from the time away from the ranch. It was if he was tired of doing the two-step around her, and wanted her to join in his dance.

If she knew what Dalian was thinking, she'd know her assumptions were correct. When she'd bolted from him again on the range, and had spent the better part of the remaining two and a half days avoiding his company, he was ready to go for broke. He needed her to know that he was interested. The delicate part was getting her to admit that she was interested too.

Kat finally forced herself to look away, and then wished she hadn't when her gaze encountered Chloe's. Her smug 'you don't stand a chance in Hell of escaping that one' look made her want to scream. Instead, she turned on her heels and headed toward the house – ready to pack up and flee.

Of course, she'd never run from anything in her life, but then again, she'd never been as scared as she was of the desire Dalian Rivers sparked in her. It was like having permanent menopausal hot flashes. He'd told her she was afraid of him, and she'd denied it vehemently; but she really was. Not of him, rather of the desire she felt towards him. It was a feeling no man had ever evoked, not even her husband. Robert had been her best friend, and while they always enjoyed each other's company, sex had rapidly dwindled away to nothing when the twins were born. She could very well claim a return to virginity after their birth, for he didn't once have a desire for sex after that day. He still kissed her, hugged her, and showed his affection in other ways, but there were times she missed the intimacy. The twins had been four when the truck driver crashed into Robert's vehicle, cutting their lives short; which meant she'd been without a sexual partner for more years than she'd been married. She suddenly wondered why she'd allowed it; wondered why she didn't care – until now.

She went to the sideboard and dished up some eggs, bacon, and a biscuit with gravy, and then plopped onto a chair at the long dining table. When she picked up her mug to take a sip of coffee, nothing poured into her mouth. She looked into the interior and huffed, "I'm so discombobulated; I can't even remember to pour a cup of coffee for myself." Returning to the sideboard, she poured a cup of the steaming brew and returned to the table; but instead of eating or drinking anything, her thoughts returned to her confusion over Dalian.

"You're deep in thought."

Kat jumped, thankful that she'd already placed her cup down. "I didn't hear you walk up."

"Like I said," Chloe grinned. "You're deep in thought, and I don't have to take but one guess as to who's on your mind."

"You'd be right," Kat said ruefully. "Where is everyone? Aren't they coming in for breakfast?"

"They'll be along in a minute. I just got a jumpstart on them. Figured you might want to talk. Although from Dalian's expression when you walked off, he would've preferred to be the one chasing after you."

"That's the problem. He is."

"If it were me, I wouldn't consider it a problem – as you know. Have you told him that you aren't interested in him?"

"Not in so many words," Kat said dejectedly.

"And not in your body language, either."

"What do you mean?"

"Your mannerisms fairly shout 'take me, I'm yours'," Chloe said, grinning mischievously.

"You're joking!" Kat said. "Aren't you?"

"Absoposilutely, not."

"Well, no wonder he's getting bolder in his attentions," Kat murmured.

"I did comment on how inexperienced you are," Chloe chided. "Pegged you, but good. But you seemed to think that being married to your high school sweetheart makes you an expert on the opposite sex."

"College sweetheart," Kat muttered distractedly.

"Whatever." Chloe turned toward the door, "Here comes the rest of the group. So, what are you going to do?" She asked, settling onto the chair beside Kat.

"I'm going to try to enjoy the dance and during the time I have left, avoid Mr. Dalian Rivers at all costs so that I don't turn myself into an adolescent-acting whore. Then go home where I belong and resume my life."

"In that order?" Chloe quipped.

"I don't know," Kat responded sincerely. "I really am enjoying myself here. It's so beautiful and serene. So I would prefer not to cut my vacation short, but if he keeps coming after me the way he is, I may not have a choice."

Chloe looked at Kat and winced, "Good heavens, Kat, what happened to you to make you so skittish? Most women would be thrilled to have a man like Dalian Rivers focus his attention on them. Are you a lesbian?" She asked, but then suddenly retracted, "No, you said he was your type, so what is it then?"

"I really don't know," Kat sighed, "well, I think I do, but . . ."

"Well, spit it out then." Chloe placed her elbows on the table and planted her chin on her hands, eyes wide with curiosity, "I'm all ears."

"Promise not to laugh?"

"Oh good Lord, what could possibly be funny about all of this drama?"

"I've never met a man as . . . well . . . for lack of a better word – manly."

Chloe lifted her chin from her hands and her jaw dropped, "You've seriously got it bad for him and it's scaring you."

Kat nodded and then lowered her gaze in embarrassment, "I'm twenty-seven years old," she whispered, "and I've not once met a man that makes me feel all tingly on the outside and all addlepated on the inside. It's very overwhelming."

"I can see that," Chloe grinned, "and I wish I could help you muddle your way through this particular emotional quagmire, but I've never been where you are, so wouldn't even know where to begin advising you."

"Sure you're not just hoping that I'll run home and clear the field for you again?"

"That thought actually didn't cross my mind; however, now that you mention it – if I thought I stood a chance, I'd escort you upstairs, help you pack, and drive you to the airport."

"Oh, I don't doubt it," Kat laughed.

"Well, I'd better grab a plate before the wolves eat everything all gone."

"Apt choice of words," Kat murmured as Dalian entered the room, eyeing her as if she were rabbit stew. "Dear Lord above, what am I going to do?"

"Whatever you do, decide fast, because that man's got it as bad for you as you do for him."

CHAPTER EIGHTEEN

"May I have this dance?"

"You mean you plan to ask?" Kat replied, ignoring his outstretched hand.

Dalian lowered his hand and stood watching her. He wondered for a moment whether he was reading her wrong, but then he glanced up. It was there in her gaze. Desire mingled with barely restrained wary anger.

"Are you aware that since this party started half an hour ago, not one person has asked me to dance because of your rather possessive statement yesterday morning?" Kat was doing her dead level best to keep her tone level. "They all keep eyeing you and me as if we're a couple; as if I belong to you."

I wish, Dalian wanted to say, but as he'd feared, the rabbit was back and he didn't want her bounding away this evening. He wanted to dance, wanted to hold her in his arms. "I'm sorry if I let my desire overrule my tongue," Dalian said softly.

"Please don't say things like that," Kat whispered.

"Don't apologize?"

"Don't say 'desire' and 'tongue' in the same sentence directed at me," Kat replied bluntly.

Dalian grinned, but held back his response. Instead he held a hand back toward her, "May I please have this dance, Miss McMurray. It would honor me a great deal."

"Now I get the impression that you're mocking me."

"That is something I would never do," Dalian said sincerely.

"Well, I guess if I'm going to get to dance this evening, it's going to have to be with you, since no other man in this room seems inclined to come near me."

"Lucky me."

"The evening is still young, Dalian, so there is plenty of time for your luck to expire."

Dalian pulled her into his embrace, laughing. "Are you going to stay angry with me until it does?"

"That might be the safest course of action," Kat replied, trying to maintain some distance between their bodies. Dalian, on the other hand, seemed determined to meld them into a single entity.

"When are you going to stop running?" Dalian whispered in her ear.

"When are you going to stop chasing?" Kat asked, taking a determined step back.

"I'm not sure I can," Dalian replied honestly.

"And I'm not ready to be caught," Kat replied equally candid, "so where does that leave us?"

"At an impasse?"

"At an impasse," Kat replied, pulling free from his embrace. Kat sighed dejectedly, "If you'll excuse me, I'm suddenly very tired. Good night, Mr. Rivers."

"Good night, Kat," Dalian replied. He watched her leave the barn and move toward the house, his brain mulling over their conversation.

He'd only known her two weeks, but a need deep within made him want to get to know her better. Still, he sensed something inside her was preventing him getting closer. Her husband's death, perhaps?

She'd agreed when he'd said they were at an impasse, but what she didn't know was his definition of impasse didn't include inescapable. He'd get through her self-erected barriers, if he had to chisel through them one brick at a time. He only had six weeks until she left though, so he'd have to chisel fast.

CHAPTER NINETEEN

"You really shouldn't be out here alone. Not at night, at least."

Kat jumped. Instead of relaxing when Dalian stepped from the shadows, her heartbeat increased along with her breathing. What was it about this man, she wondered for the hundredth time, that caused her heart to skip a beat whenever he drew near, and made her innards turn to mush? Yes, he was gorgeous, but her husband had been an extremely handsome man as well. Even Cal, who'd shown an interest in her, was a good-looking fellow.

But when Dalian was around, she felt an animal lust that was confusing to her; a lust she admittedly never felt during her marriage. A lust she'd never felt with any man.

"Kat? You shouldn't be out here alone," Dalian repeated softly.

"Why?" She asked, but wasn't just responding to his comment, but was also questioning her own inner turmoil.

"It's not safe," he said, placing a booted foot on the corral railing. He leaned on his elbows, keeping his gaze averted.

"Why? Are there other men on this ranch that can approach a person as stealthily as you and give a guest a lethal heart attack?"

"Nope," Dalian said with a laugh. "Only I can manage that one."

"Your ability can scare the tar out of a body."

"Sorry about that, but I wasn't necessarily referring to scaring someone to death. There are other creatures hereabouts, besides man, whose stealthy approach can do more than scare the tar out of a body."

"Thanks for that disturbing image."

"I'll plant as many of them in your brain as need be, if it'll keep you safe," Dalian said, suddenly serious. His tone, possessively protective, gave Kat pause. It also sounded like he spoke from personal experience, which made her curious. She shook the protective tone off as simply hearing things due to tiredness and smiled slightly.

"Well, I'm sure glad to know you care about the people who patron your ranch. Of course, you have a funny way of putting people at ease while setting them on their toes."

"Just doing my job, Miss," Dalian said, tipping his hat playfully. He shook off the memory of Carolyn standing in this area the night she died. If he'd been more diligent and determined then as now…

"Well, I wouldn't want you to be overly concerned with my well-being, and I certainly don't want to become some nocturnal predator's midnight snack, so I guess I'll turn in. I just…well, it's just so beautiful here, is all. The sky. The stars," she whispered, taking another quick glance upward.

"Nothing like it in the world, as far I'm concerned," Dalian whispered, his gaze turning heavenward as well.

"I'd have to agree. Well, I guess I'll say goodnight then," she whispered, and started to turn.

"If you want to stay, I've got my rifle with me."

Kat looked down, only just realizing that a weapon lay near her feet. *Armed and dangerous,* she thought, *in more ways than one.*

"If you don't mind the company, that is, especially since I seem to have offended you earlier in the evening," Dalian added, and Kat looked up. Her reply caught in her throat when her gaze collided with his. *His eyes are like liquid chocolate,* she thought. *Fiery pools of dark chocolate,* she amended. *Hormones,* she concluded.

Kat tried to speak again, but it was no use. Her mind had reverted to puberty and her tongue had rapidly followed suit. She'd never speak again, she thought, unless both grew up in a hurry. She looked away. After she felt more composed, she tried again. "I appreciate the offer, but it was solitude I was after, not company. Thank you just the same."

"Still angry with me?" Dalian asked, stalling her departure. He liked the sound of her voice, even when her words spoke of her desire to get away from him.

"No. Just frustrated, I guess," Kat said softly.

"Because I won't call off my pursuit?" Dalian asked. He'd never been one to play games or mince words. He only hoped he didn't offend her further, but something said she was of the same mold and would respond equally direct. He wasn't disappointed.

"For one, I suppose," Kat sighed. "I guess I've been out of circulation for so long, I forgot the rules of the game. It seems I remember though that if a woman doesn't return the interest, a man is supposed to turn his attentions elsewhere. You don't seem to be catching the hints."

"To be honest, Kat," Dalian said, "your words are mixing with your signals, which can confuse a body something fierce."

She cringed a little, because Chloe said something along the same lines earlier. "Have you ever thought that your radar might simply be broken and you're reading me all wrong?"

"Not likely," Dalian retorted. "My radar may have been out of service for a couple of years, but it's hardly broken. Besides, our radars help us men locate a mate, so keeping them working is in our best interest."

Kat laughed, preferring this form of conversation to the overly intimate ones of late. A healthy debate was always a good way to control raging hormones. "If men's radars were so accurate, there would be far fewer offended people in the world. I mean, all men have to do is catch the clue when we toss it at them and move on, but do they? No! They take is as a sign to pursue at all costs and then they end up hurt or offended when they realize that the very radar they relied upon was reading all wrong. It would be easier just to accept the fact that the radar is flawed and tune it towards someone else."

"Sometimes our radar is working just fine," Dalian rejoined, "but the woman simply refuses to accept the fact that a mutual attraction exists – for whatever reason."

Kat's hair prickled along the nape of her neck when she realized he'd turned the conversation back into an intimate one. It wasn't in the words, so much as in his tone. She glanced up and quickly berated herself for doing so. *Those damned dark chocolate eyes,* she thought and tried to look away. *I love chocolate,* she thought inanely.

"Isn't that true, Kat?" Dalian whispered, leaning closer.

"I'd better turn in," Kat whispered breathlessly.

"Prove me wrong, Kat," Dalian said quickly, softly, leaning closer still. "Prove to me that my radar is broken, and I'll leave you be for the next six weeks. Not even a sideways glance. You have my word of honor."

"I don't–"

"One kiss," Dalian interrupted, closing the gap between them with each word.

"Kiss?" Kat croaked. Her throat constricted and she felt a strong desire to run, but that desire was overpowered by a deeper yearning that slowly enveloped her.

"You can hide behind words, Kat, but a kiss bears your soul," Dalian whispered, lifting his hand and tenderly stroking her cheek. Kat's eyes instinctively fluttered closed and she leaned toward him.

Dalian smiled at her response, moved his hand beneath her hair, and lightly grasped her nape, pulling her toward him. "Prove me right," he whispered and closed his mouth over hers.

CHAPTER TWENTY

Dalian reluctantly broke the kiss, more shaken than even she appeared to be, although from the sound of her ragged breathing, he doubted it – or was that his breathing that was ragged? It was hard to tell. They both seemed to be panting in unison. He opened his eyes. She was watching him, her gaze clouded with desire. He slid his hand from her nape and stroked her cheek. Once again, she closed her eyes, her lips parting slightly. He was certainly not one to refuse an invitation. The experiment was over, his case was proven, and now he intended to enjoy the victory of being right. His radar wasn't broken.

He pulled his foot from the fence and turned toward her, slid an arm about her waist and pulled her flush against him. The other hand that had been stroking her cheek returned to her nape, tangled in her hair, and tilted her head to meet his need. His mouth captured her gasp and his tongue began that age-old lover's duel, but he wanted his tongue to caress more than hers. He wanted it to light her skin afire with desire; one that she couldn't deny. He broke away from her mouth, slid his tongue along the side of her neck, and then caught her earlobe between his teeth, nibbling softly. Kat's head fell instinctively to the side, and a groan of desire escaped. Her hands clung to his sleeves like a swimmer to a life preserver; but it was no use. She was drowning – fast.

As if sensing her dilemma, Dalian slid his hands down her back and cupped her rear, pulling her in tighter still. She moaned in acquiescence and Dalian felt himself suddenly sinking. He picked her up and moved backward until he felt the fence bump into his hands, and then released his grip from her rear and grabbed hold of the top of the rail, leaning into her. If his shirt was her life preserver, the fence was his.

His mouth made a return voyage and claimed her lips in another breath-stealing kiss. Kat wrapped her arms around his waist and clutched his shirt with what strength she had left. Never had she felt such intense heat pounding through her body. It was as if someone had bound the two of them together and lifted them over a roaring flame of desire.

"I can't..." Kat panted, when his lips finally broke from hers.

Dalian stiffened, lifting his gaze to meet hers, "Can't what?" he asked, his own breathing heavy.

"I can't breathe."

Dalian took a quick, unsteady step back, but Kat's hands were still clutching his shirt and he dragged her with him. She collapsed into him, her legs giving way. He reached down and scooped her into his quivering arms and, on unsteady legs, made his way toward the barn. With a barely balanced sway, he kicked the door open and moved toward an empty stall, carefully laying her down upon the fresh bed of hay. He knelt over her, examining her with his eyes. "Are you okay?" He asked, stroking her face.

"I'm fine," she whispered. "I think."

"You need to explain better than that. You're extremely flushed."

"So are you," Kat whispered.

"But I can breathe."

"It's just that I've never felt anything so intense before and it took my breath away – literally," Kat breathed. "I'm okay now. I think. I'm sorry I worried you."

Comprehension dawned and Dalian grinned, and then stretched out beside her, "I'll admit I was having a hard time too. Damn, but you're the most powerful presence to enter my life, Kat. I've never experienced anything like I did when I kissed you. Guess that means my radar isn't broken."

"No," Kat grinned. "I'd say everything about you is in working order."

"How would you know?" Dalian purred. "You haven't even tried out the whole package yet."

"Yet?"

"Hell yes, yet!" Dalian grinned, planting a quick kiss on her lips. "You don't think I'm going to let you get away, do you?"

"I don't think I'd get far," Kat murmured. "You're like a gigantic magnet, do you know that? I felt drawn to you from the minute I saw you."

"Same here."

"I guess it's time to stop running."

With a suddenness that startled her, Dalian jerked upright and flipped atop her. His legs were spread eagle on either side of hers and his hands were positioned beside her head. His arms, rigid with the exertion, were holding his muscled frame elevated above her. He grinned and she laughed.

"If I wasn't lying here beneath you, I'd say you were preparing to do pushups."

"I am," he said and laughed when her eyes widened. "You shock easily, do you know that?"

"I don't know why I would. It's not like I'm an inexperienced teenager," Kat said. "I guess I'm just not used to someone as flirtatious as you coming onto me so strongly."

"Women flirt, men pursue."

"You've definitely been doing that," Kat said softly. "How much do you weigh?" She asked suddenly in a deliberate change of subject.

"I don't know exactly. About one hundred-eighty-five."

"All muscle, no doubt," Kat murmured in such an admiring tone that Dalian laughed.

"Would you mind not laughing?" She asked, concernedly. "You quiver when you laugh. Exactly how long can you hold yourself upright like that?"

"Afraid I'll squash you?"

"Like a bug," Kat admitted. "I only weigh one-hundred-twenty pounds, and can only bench press forty. If you pass out, I wouldn't be able to get you off of me."

"If my muscles tire, I'll roll away," Dalian said, bending at the elbow and lowering slowly. He stopped a mere inch from her mouth and grinned before dropping the rest of the way and placing a thorough kiss on her lips. "One," he said, when he raised himself.

Kat laughed breathlessly. "How many pushups do you do a day?"

"At least fifty," he said, lowering himself again. "Two," he counted, after another searing kiss; however, instead of extending his arms again, he collapsed – pinning her helplessly beneath his weight against the bed of straw.

CHAPTER TWENTY-ONE

All of Kat's senses were on high alert. She heard the muted thump, saw an indistinguishable figure scurry away, and smelled the concentrated aroma of fuel as it started to permeate the air. Although fear bounded about in her mind, seemingly out of control, her greatest urgency was that a one-hundred-eighty-five pound man lie unconscious atop her, restricting her breathing. No matter how hard she tried, she didn't have the ability to draw air into her compressed lungs. She tried not to panic; tried to form a rational thought as her brain began misfiring from lack of oxygen. Soon, spots began to cloud her vision.

She turned her head to peer beneath the wall of her stall when the horses began whinnying in terror within their confines, her eyes widening in renewed alarm. All attempts to remain calm fled, when she saw the smoke and flames consuming the hay in a stall nearest the doors.

She struggled mightily, managing to free her arms from beneath Dalian's inert body. Her body was weakening fast, and the spots before her eyes were increasing in number as her oxygen-deprived mind continued shutting down. She pushed against his shoulders, but as she'd joked with Dalian less than ten minutes prior, she simply did not have the upper body strength to move one-hundred-eighty pounds of dead weight. She felt the tears well in her eyes as dizziness invaded her head; and numbness crept into her limbs. She was rapidly swimming towards unconsciousness.

"Help," she breathed, wondering if anyone would ever hear such a pitiable cry. The alarm bells ringing in her head, as she saw the flames consume the first stall and move to the next, slowly diminished; and then the darkness overtook her brain and her eyes drifted closed. Her last conscious thought was that she was going to die beneath a man in a blaze of searing heat.

Dalian moaned, but she could no longer lift her arms, could no longer breathe the words that he might hear. His weight was completely compressing her upper body, making it impossible for her to intake air into her lungs. Her body went limp, a lone tear the only escapee from the approaching conflagration. The nerve endings in her brain were firing faster, as if arguing with her lungs to do something before it shut down all together, but there was no answer forthcoming, and soon she felt herself floating away from her body, sadness enshrouding her spirit.

CHAPTER TWENTY-TWO

"Breathe, damn you!" Dalian breathed another round of oxygen into Kat's unresponsive lungs. "Breathe," he yelled when he came up for air.

"I still don't have a pulse, Dalian," Chloe exclaimed softly, her fingers frantically roaming around Kat's wrist, trying to find any sign of life.

Dalian pushed his rigid arms up and down on Kat's chest, keeping a steady pace, a steady count. When he reached thirty, he shifted position, lifted her neck, pinched her nose, and breathed into her mouth, twice in rapid succession. He couldn't really remember if he had the count right, but he didn't care. His only concern was to keep trying until the medics arrived. His head pounded; the ache so strong that his vision blurred from the intensity of trying to revive Kat, but he pushed aside his own discomfort and all offers of help from those standing around.

"Breathe baby, breathe," He whispered, moving his ear beneath her nose. Nothing. He looked at Chloe who was keeping vigil on Kat's other side. "Anything?" He asked, and Chloe quickly felt along Kat's wrist again. She shook her head, tears streaming slowly down her face.

"Don't cry," Dalian whispered harshly. "Crying means we've given up." He moved back to start compressions on Kat's chest again. "We can't give up. Don't give up, darling," he pleaded with Kat's inert form. "Please don't give up."

"Dalian," Chloe whispered.

"No!" Dalian refused to accept what everyone standing around felt was inevitable. "Breathe, Kat. If not for your own sake, then selfishly for mine," he cried, each word punctuated in time with the compressions.

One of the cowhands walked up, "All the horses are safe, rounded up into the exercise corral. How is she?"

"Not so good," Mrs. Guthrie whispered. "We've never had such a horrible accident happen to one of our guests before," she continued, wringing her hands in her nightgown. "It's a sad day."

"I have a pulse," Chloe exclaimed, and then her brow knitted in confusion. "I think. I'm not sure. It's so faint."

Dalian grabbed Kat's wrist away from Chloe, his calloused hand searching, his eyes closed in supplication, "Please be there," he whispered. "Please." When he felt nothing, he laid her arm on his lap and leaned across it, his eyes tightly closed against the pain pounding in his head, and his heart. He placed his fingers on her wrist where a pulse should be, and for the first time, since his wife died, began to pray, "Please, Lord, don't take her away. Let her stay with me. Please. I promise to love and protect her forever, just please let her stay."

A barely perceptible thump tapped against his fingertips, then increased in rhythm and strength, until he felt a steady pulse. His eyes flew open, tears blurring his vision, "She's alive," he whispered, gathering Kat into his embrace. "She's alive," he laughed.

Mrs. Guthrie clasped her hands together, "Thank the good Lord above," she exclaimed.

Chloe closed her own eyes and breathed a sigh of relief, her own tears quickly turning into full-fledged blubbering. She clasped Kat's other hand and kissed her knuckles. "I'm so glad you're going to be okay," she whispered. "You're the last person that should be taken off this earth."

Just then, the sound of approaching sirens reached their ears. "Chloe?" Dalian whispered.

"Yes, Dalian," Chloe sniffled loudly, wiping her arms across her eyes.

"Could you ride with Kat to the hospital?" He asked, reluctant to release Kat into the care of anyone. "I've got to stay to talk to the sheriff."

"I'll make certain that no one gets near her," Chloe said. "You have my word."

Dalian nodded. He leaned down and placed a kiss on Kat's immobile lips. Kat's eyes fluttered open, startling him.

"Kat?"

"Dalian," she breathed, barely audible. "I can't breathe."

"You can now, sweetheart," Dalian whispered, placing another kiss on her forehead. He stroked her hair, "How are you feeling?"

"Squashed."

Dalian groaned, pulling her against him, "I'm so sorry, baby. I'm sorry. I never meant to hurt you. I'd never hurt you."

"Dalian," Kat whispered. "Someone hit you on the head."

"I know, baby," Dalian said, kissing her again. "I've got a rather large goose egg."

"Why?"

"Because someone hit me on the head," Dalian answered.

"Why would someone want us dead?" Kat whispered.

"I don't know, darling," Dalian replied, "but I plan on finding out."

The ambulance pulled to a stop in front of the barn and two paramedics leapt out. "Step aside, please, folks," the elder of the two said, pushing his way toward Kat. Chloe stood and moved aside, making room for him to kneel at Kat's side.

"How are we, little lady?" He asked, noticing Kat staring at him. Kat shook her head, barely perceptible. "What happened here?" He asked, taking Kat's vital signs.

"There was an accident," Chloe answered, pointing toward the burnt-out shell of the barn.

The paramedic looked up and nodded. He pulled his stethoscope and placed it on Kat's chest. "Can you take a deep breath for me, please?"

Kat complied, but it pained her and she coughed.

"Okay. Peter, let's get her loaded into the ambulance."

"Sure thing, Jake."

"Anyone else hurt?" Jake asked, looking around.

"Dalian was clobbered upside the head," Mrs. Guthrie answered, when it didn't look as if Dalian would.

Jake nodded, turning his attention to the ranch's owner, "Let's have a look-see."

"I'm fine," Dalian protested, his gaze following Kat, as she was loaded into the back of the ambulance. "Just take care of her."

"We'll see to it that the lady gets to the hospital safely, but I need to make sure you don't need to join her," Jake said, pulling a flashlight from his belt. "Now look at me. Peter's taking real good care of your woman," he added when Dalian didn't immediately comply.

"Do what he says, Dalian," Sheriff Jonathan Masters said, stepping from his patrol car, "and if you have to go to the hospital, I'll be right behind you."

Dalian did as he requested, silently willing him to hurry. He felt fine, but he knew how quickly concussion could knock a man down, so he didn't argue. He winced when the paramedic felt along the back of his head, encountering the knot forming.

"You're going to have a headache for a few days, but I don't see any signs of concussion. Put some ice on that bump as soon as you possibly can."

"I've got it," Mrs. Guthrie said, scurrying toward the back of the house.

Jake continued, "And if that bump hasn't receded in a few days, you're to take yourself on down to the hospital and have a doctor check you out. Understand?"

"Yeah." Dalian nodded. "Chloe's going to ride with Kat, okay? She needs someone with her."

"Sure," Jake said, and then turned to make his way back to the ambulance. "They're all yours, Sheriff."

"Thanks, Jake."

"No problem."

"Oh, I'd say we have a pretty big problem," the sheriff said. "A familiar problem. Isn't that right, Dalian?"

CHAPTER TWENTY-THREE

"Why don't we go onto the porch and have a seat," the sheriff said, reaching down a hand to help pull Dalian to his feet. "Think you're up to getting there?" He asked, when Dalian swayed slightly. Dalian nodded and together they slowly walked the lengthy distance from burnt-out barn to front porch. They'd barely settled onto the front steps, when the sheriff launched into his investigation. "What do you think happened here, Dalian?"

"Someone conked me on the head and tried to burn the barn down around mine and Kat's head, that's what happened here, Jonathan," Dalian snapped.

"And do you think it's going to help to take my head off?" The sheriff asked, pulling a pad and pen from his coat pocket.

"Sorry, Jonathan," Dalian said, taking a seat on the front porch swing. "It just makes me so damned angry that someone would deliberately try to take my life and harm an innocent woman in the process."

"How did Kat get hurt? Did someone conk her on the head too?" The Sheriff asked, "And what were you two doing in the barn in the middle of the night?"

Dalian chewed on his bottom lip and didn't answer immediately. By the look on the sheriff's face, he didn't need to.

"Okay, so let's just say that you and the lady were seeing each other socially," the sheriff said tactfully.

"Thanks, Jonathan."

"I am a man you know," the sheriff said by way of explanation. "So, who do you think did this, because I'm pretty certain I'm not going to be investigating this as an accident?"

"Damn straight it wasn't," Dalian said, "unless someone just happened to place a shovel above my head and it accidentally fell on it."

"The sarcasm isn't going to get us anywhere, Dalian," the sheriff sighed. "I know you're angry, but try to work with me okay?"

"Sorry, Jonathan, I'll try to curb my tongue," Dalian sighed again.

"Well, my next question isn't going to help your disposition any, that's for damned sure, but I got to ask it just the same," the sheriff said, pushing his hat up and rubbing the back of his hand against his forehead.

"What do you want to know, Jonathan?" Dalian asked, rubbing the sweat and grime from his own brow.

"Do you think this could be related to your wife's death?" the sheriff asked softly.

Dalian clenched his eyes closed, as memories flooded his brain of that horrifying night two years ago; the night fate snatched away his wife and unborn baby boy.

* * * * * * * * * * * * *

Two years prior

"Carolyn?" Dalian called. "Are you out here?"

"I'm over here by the corral, darling," Carolyn called.

Dalian leapt off the front porch and sprinted across the grass. He slowed when he spotted his wife of two years standing against the fence, her light-brown hair reflecting the moonlight. She looked huge in her maternity dress, which made him grin. She always complained about looking like a beached whale, and although he couldn't quite agree with her description, she'd definitely gained a few pounds over the last eight months. Not that he minded. To him, she was the most beautiful woman in the world. More so, now that she carried his child. He glanced down at the enormous mound protruding below her enlarged breasts. Only three more weeks until he could hold his newborn baby boy in his arms.

He still couldn't decide on a name, still couldn't believe she was leaving the honor of naming their firstborn son to him. He already knew the middle name – Harvey, after his foreman and dearest friend – but a first name eluded him. He couldn't name him after his father, and knew of no other male influences upon which to draw. There was always Charles, named after Carolyn's father, but she'd said she didn't want to name their son after a family member. Perhaps Vincent or Dylan, but it needed to…

"Are you going to stand there staring at me," she called, interrupting his musings, "or are you planning to join me?"

Dalian laughed, closing the remaining distance quickly. "Sorry, you just look so angelic," he said, carefully drawing her into his embrace and giving her a thorough kiss, "that, and I was thinking about what to name our son," he finished when he came up for air.

"You still haven't decided?" Carolyn asked, incredulous. "You'd better step up the thinking process a bit or our baby's going to be nameless upon arrival."

"Are you sure you don't want to give me any ideas?" Dalian asked.

"Not on your life," Carolyn laughed. "A boy should have a man's name given to him by his father. Or would you prefer that I come up with something that might have the poor child teased for his entire youth?"

"Oh, come on, Carolyn," Dalian said, "what could you possibly come up with that would emotionally stint our child?"

"Mmm, I don't know," Carolyn teased, "Ashley, perhaps?"

"That's a girl's name!"

"Not in England," Carolyn argued.

"We're not in England. You'd really name our child Ashley?" Dalian asked, looking for any signs that she was teasing him.

"Incentive enough for you to start thinking harder?"

"That's cruel, Carolyn," Dalian said, but he couldn't help the laughter that escaped. "So, what's my beautiful whale of a wife doing out here all alone?"

"Looking at the stars," Carolyn said, her gaze turning heavenward.

"They are beautiful tonight, but it's getting a little chilly. Don't you think you should come inside now?" Dalian asked, taking off his jacket and wrapping it around her shoulders.

"You worry over me too much," Carolyn said, pulling the front of the jacket as far over her abdomen as she could.

"Would you rather I not give a crap?" Dalian asked softly, stroking her face gently.

"I like that you worry over me," Carolyn whispered, turning to kiss his hand, "it's just that I selfishly wanted to spend a little time alone talking to the baby. Would you mind leaving us to ourselves a bit longer, if I promise to come inside soon?"

"Soon, okay?" Dalian said, placing a kiss on her chilled lips. "I don't want you and little what's-his-name to catch pneumonia."

"Just a few more minutes, I promise," Carolyn said, smiling softly, inwardly.

"I love you – both," Dalian said.

"I love you, too, sweetheart."

Dalian reluctantly turned and made his way back to the house. When he reached the porch, he sat down on the swing and turned his gaze toward the corral. He could barely make out her form in the starry shadows, but when he closed his eyes, he could easily imagine her standing there, whispering secrets to the tiny body swimming around in her abdomen.

The sound of a rifle firing startled him. His eyes flew open and for a moment he thought he imagined it, but then another report sounded and he leapt from the swing, his gaze trying to penetrate the night sky, his ears trying to pinpoint the direction.

The sound of a cougar screaming was the next sound to reach his hearing and the hairs on the nape of his neck pricked. The hairs on his arms joined those on his neck when he heard another rifle report – and then his wife's screams.

"Carolyn!" He shouted, jumping from the porch. The corral wasn't that far, but it seemed to be taking him forever to reach it. He skidded to a halt as the cougar he'd heard, ran past him, heading straight for the horses – and his wife.

"Move!" Someone shouted, running past on foot, the rifle aimed and cocked.

"Be careful! My wife is over there!" Dalian screamed at the man, but he didn't appear to hear. It was as if he could care less that his actions might kill an innocent woman and her unborn child – his wife and unborn child.

That thought sent a streak of terror racing through his veins. He turned, racing after the man with the rifle. The man had stopped less than a hundred feet of where Carolyn stood frozen, looking after the cougar which had gone past her, heading for the hills.

She's safe! Was Dalian's first thought, but then he realized that the man was still aiming the rifle, and the cougar was too far away to hit. Didn't the man realize that? And why was he sighting so high? Too high, Dalian realized, increasing his pace. The aim of the rifle was too high. It was as if he wanted to kill his wife and was just using the cougar as an excuse.

"No!" Dalian yelled and tackled the man, but it was too late – he'd already fired.

He tackled the man, but his movements had been too slow; although the entire event had transpired over a period of less than five minutes.

* * * * * * * * * * * * *

April 2061
Wind River, Wyoming

"Dalian?" The sheriff whispered, drawing Dalian from his musing.

"I don't know, Jonathan," Dalian whispered. "Jethro Canton was cleared of the crime. Claimed that he was just trying to kill the cougar that was killing his sheep; was so upset that he wasn't thinking straight and that affected his aim."

"But you never believed it," the sheriff said.

"I was there, Jonathan," Dalian said. "I saw his aim. So either he's the worst damned shot in the world, or he's a liar who got away with murder."

"I know it's taken a lot for you to live beside the man these past two years feeling the way you do. You're definitely a bigger man than I am, but I guess what I want to know is if you think it possible that Canton had a hand in this?"

"If he did, there's no way to prove it, is there?" Dalian sighed in frustration. "After all, any evidence likely burned with the barn. I do know that he's been after my land; been shoving his daughter at me in the hopes that I'll marry her, so whatever children she spawned inherited. But I told Marsha back in the fall to tell her dad to lay off, that my land and I are not on the market. Repeated that just a couple of weeks ago, when she made another play for my attention. I don't know if it's related or not. Just damned funny to me that I just happen to start seeing someone, not his daughter, and shortly thereafter, my new woman and I end up in a deadly situation. I can also tell you that Marsha wasn't thrilled over my rejection. Does any of this add up to motive for murder or point a finger in Canton's direction? You're the sheriff, you tell me?"

"If it does, it would barely reach the level of circumstantial."

"That's what I thought," Dalian said, running his fingers through his hair.

"My deputies are poking around right now along with the team from CSI. We'll see what they turn up. In the meantime, I'll go pay a visit with Canton and his daughter, see what sort of alibi they produce," The sheriff said, standing.

"Marsha's here," Dalian said, a sudden chill running up his spine. "She's been working here since we opened the dude ranch."

"Well, isn't that mighty special," the sheriff said. "Isn't the smartest thing in the world rubbing a new relationship in the face of a rejected female – daily. Might just piss her off, but good."

"Didn't dawn on me at the time," Dalian said.

"What's she doing sleeping here anyway? Her house isn't that far away."

"Yeah, but we prefer to house temporary employees, so that they are on time to help the guests in the morning. Less likely to be late when Mrs. Guthrie is knocking at your door. Speaking of which – Mrs. Guthrie!" Dalian called loudly.

"Oh, there you are," Mrs. Guthrie said, hurrying toward the front of the house. She handed Dalian a baggy full of ice wrapped in a washcloth. "Now put that on your head like the paramedic said to," she ordered.

"Have you seen Marsha this morning?" Dalian asked, slapping the baggy against the back of his head. He winced when the cold seeped through to his skull.

"No," Mrs. Guthrie said, pointing at the baggy when Dalian removed it. "Back on, now!"

Dalian rolled his eyes, but did as she said. "Any idea where she is? She's supposed to be residing here during the week."

"She is, but I haven't seen hide nor hair of her since she went to bed last night."

"Sheriff," Dalian said.

"Already one step ahead of you," the sheriff said. "Mrs. Guthrie, could you tell me which room Miss Canton is occupying."

"Sure, I'll take you on up," Mrs. Guthrie said, pulling the front screen door open.

"I'll take care of things, Dalian, you go on to the hospital and check on your girl."

Dalian smiled, "Thanks, Jonathan, I think I'll do that. You'll take care of whoever's responsible, won't you?"

"Forgot to add 'this time', didn't you, Dalian?" The sheriff asked.

Dalian nodded, "No, what I forgot to add was you might consider taking care of him because if I find him first—"

"Come on, Dalian," the sheriff interjected, "you know I can't listen to you issue threats. Listen, I'm going to do everything in my power to keep you and your new woman safe, I give you my oath as sheriff and friend. As to catching the person responsible," the sheriff shrugged, "I'm sure going to give it my best effort, but we both know that if Canton's responsible, he did a better job this time in covering his tracks than when your wife was killed. I can't even call him a person of interest – legally."

"I know, but I appreciate you doing what you can."

"I always do. Now let me go see about some alibis and you go see about Kat." Dalian nodded again, and the sheriff followed Mrs. Guthrie into the house. "Just point out her room, and I'll take it from there."

"Top of the stairs, third door on the right, but sheriff, I don't see how Marsha could've had a hand in all of this. I've known the girl for four years now, and while she might be a wee bit off in the head sometimes, I can't say as if I'd call her a murderer."

"I'll keep that in mind, but there's been far too much commotion going on for her not to have taken notice. You can't say that isn't a mite bit suspicious."

Mrs. Guthrie nodded in resignation, "Aye, that it is," she whispered. "I'll be in the kitchen if you need me for anything more."

"Thank you." The sheriff turned and headed up the staircase, wondering just how Marsha would be able to explain her conspicuous absence. He knocked on the door to the room indicated by Mrs. Guthrie, and waited. After a minute, he knocked again and pressed his ear against the door panel. He heard muffled noises, and grinned. Someone's rest is being disturbed, he thought. When all became silent inside, he lifted his fist and pounded. *That should let them know that I'm not going away,* he thought.

"Coming!" A man shouted, his tone irritated. Masters cocked his brow. Well, he thought, there is no longer any doubt as to an alibi for the daughter of Dalian's enemy, unless she pulled a man in her room afterward to provide said alibi.

The door jerked open and the anger on the man's face quickly turned to surprise, "Sheriff Masters! What are you doing here?"

"I don't think I need to ask you the same thing, do I, Kenny?" Jonathan asked, grinning when the ranch hand self-consciously tugged the sheet higher onto his hips. "You aren't aware of the hullabaloo going on outside? There's been an awful lot of racket for you to have slept peacefully through it all."

"Heard the sirens, but didn't think they were . . . I mean, I was kind of preoccupied and, um..."

"Didn't think to check on your employer's well-being and the well-being of his property?"

"It's not like he doesn't have enough employees, Sheriff," Kenny defended. "Am I in trouble, or what?"

"Depends on how honestly you answer the next question," Jonathan said, then quirked his brow when Marsha, wrapped in a blanket, stepped up beside her lover.

"Sheriff, is something wrong?" She said shyly.

"I just need Kenny to answer one question," Jonathan said, trying to ignore her disheveled appearance, "and then I'll let you two get back to . . . whatever it is you two were doing."

"So, what's up, Sheriff?" Kenny asked, impatience written all over his face.

"How long have you been up here, Kenny?" Jonathan asked candidly. "And think carefully before you answer. I need you to be as close to accurate as you can get."

"Uh, well, I don't rightly know for certain–"

"I said think carefully," Jonathan snapped, "and answer when you do know for certain, and not before."

"What's going on, Sheriff?" Marsha asked, clutching Kenny's arm.

"I'll answer that as soon as Kenny answers me." Jonathan kept his gaze pinned on Kenny, searching for any sign that his brain was doing anything but searching for an answer to his query. Thus far, he only read perplexity and sincere contemplation. *He knows nothing,* the sheriff concluded tacitly.

"Well, whatever is wrong, Kenny's been here with me–"

"I'd rather Kenny answer my question," Jonathan interrupted. "Thank you just the same."

After a few more minutes of deliberation, Kenny finally answered, "I don't know what this is all about, Sheriff, but if I had to hazard a guess, I'd say I got here sometime after midnight."

"Don't you own a watch, boy?" The Sheriff snapped.

"Wasn't wearing it," Kenny barked back. "I just know that I finished up watching Season One of the newest Law and Order spinoff, grabbed a snack, took a shower, and then..."

"Then, what?"

"Marsha invited me up for some sport," Kenny explained. Marsha looked at the sheriff and her face reddened in embarrassment.

"Couldn't sleep, Miss Canton?" The Sheriff asked, watching as the flush in her cheeks intensified.

"A woman has needs too, Sheriff," Marsha huffed, raising her chin a notch. "Or is participating in sports illegal in this state now?"

"Not at all. Got tired of waiting for Dalian to take notice?" Jonathan said, deliberately provoking. It was time for him to watch her reactions intently, to see if there was anything hiding behind her heated mortification.

"Am I supposed to find that funny, Sheriff?" Marsha replied angrily.

"I guess not," he answered, continuing to watch her reaction carefully. So far, if she was hiding anything, it wasn't showing up on her expression.

"A woman could shrivel up and die waiting for that one to take notice."

"Kathryn McMurray didn't shrivel up," Jonathan said.

"That is not even funny!"

"Got something against Miss McMurray, Marsha?" Jonathan asked.

Marsha rolled her eyes, "What could I have against a woman I barely know?"

"She just happened to catch Dalian's eye. Something you couldn't do, right?"

"Am I on trial for finding the man attractive or something?" Marsha rejoined.

"Wait a minute!" Kenny interjected; watching slack jawed as their conversation intensified. If Marsha wasn't a woman, and the sheriff not wearing a badge, he was certain the two would start beating up on each other in another minute or two. Not that he cared, what his brain latched onto was the conversation about Dalian Rivers. "Let me get this straight. You telling me that I'm only up here because you couldn't snare the boss man?"

"Like you care," Marsha snapped at Kenny. "You're getting what you want."

"Damned straight," Kenny snapped in reply. "And now I'll be getting the sleep I want. I'm outta here."

"Good riddance," Marsha swiped at the tears welling in her eyes as Kenny turned to collect his clothes from the bedroom floor. "Thanks a lot, Sheriff!"

"So, aren't you two interested in why I knocked? Why all the sirens and ruckus so early in the a.m.?" Jonathan asked, watching the emotional display with detached interest.

"Not really," they both answered simultaneously.

"Well, I'll tell you anyway," he said, waiting for Kenny to finish collecting his things. When they both were facing him again, he continued, "but I'll say this first – if I find out that either of you are holding out on me, not imparting information that can help resolve this matter, I'll haul you downtown, throw your hides in jail, and toss the key into Wind River Canyon."

"What case? What in Hell are you talking about?" Kenny snapped at the same time as Marsha exclaimed, "What in Hell matter are we supposed to know about?"

The Sheriff eyed them like a hawk. It was apparent by their reactions that neither of them knew a thing about the early morning activities, and since both had a solid alibi, he'd have to turn the investigation elsewhere. "Someone tried to kill Dalian Rivers and Kathryn McMurray. Nearly burned the barn down on top of them," the sheriff informed them, and then turned and walked away, leaving Kenny standing there with his jaw on the floor and Marsha with fear and worry in her eyes; praying silently that her father hadn't reverted to Plan B.

CHAPTER TWENTY-FOUR

"Hey, you!" Kat awoke to see Dalian sleeping in the chair next to her bed. The sound of her voice jarred him awake, and she giggled as he nearly toppled from the seat. He shook the sleepies away and scooted the chair closer to the bedside.

"How are you feeling?" He whispered, clasping her hand in his.

"You can wipe the worry from your eyes. I'm going to be fine," Kat assured him, and was relieved to see a genuine smile replace the concern in his gaze. "What about you? Goose egg gone?"

Dalian laughed shortly, and leaned up to place a kiss on her lips. When he leaned up to look down at her, the laughter in his gaze was gone, and the concerned look had returned. He didn't answer her question, instead said, "I haven't been this scared about anyone since–" He stopped talking abruptly and returned to his seat, lying his head down atop her hand. This wasn't the first time she'd sensed a tragedy in his life behind the words spoken, and wondered if he would open up to her if she asked. She was all too aware the anguish that talking could generate after heartbreak and could readily empathize should he decide not to share. Still, she needed to try. She couldn't say why, but Dalian had suddenly become very important to her, and knowing all about him an unexpected need.

"What happened, Dalian? Did you lose someone like I did?" She whispered. He lifted his head and sighed.

When he just sat there shaking his head, she didn't think he was going to answer, but then he began to speak in a near whisper, "Two years ago, my next-door neighbor rode his horse onto my land, in apparent pursuit of a cougar that had been slaughtering his sheep. I heard the rifle fire, but the imminent danger didn't register; not until I saw Canton leap from his horse and give chase on foot, firing wildly."

Dalian lowered his head and sighed heavily before continuing. "By the time I realized that the cougar and Canton were headed to where my wife was standing, I was too late. Canton took aim, fired, and killed her. She was carrying my unborn boy."

"Oh my God, Dalian. I'm so sorry." Kat placed a hand in comfort on top of his head.

He raised his head, picked up her hand, and kissed it lightly. "Time does heal the heart, but sometimes having a reminder of our mortality shoved in our faces can make the hurt return with a vengeance."

"I know."

"You do, don't you? You said you'd lost your husband about the same time, apparently, that I lost my wife." Dalian sat stroking her hand with his thumb.

Kat sighed and nodded. "Not just my husband. My twin sons also."

"Oh my God, Kat . . ."

"Just like you," she continued, trying to recite the events without falling to pieces, "I lost my entire family in one fell swoop, two years ago. My husband came in from work – he worked third shift – and saw that our four-year-old twins were awake before me, so gathered them up and took them out for breakfast. A friend of his, from the force – my husband was a cop – woke me early that morning to tell me that a truck driver – a drunk driver – was speeding down Interstate 20; the same highway as my family. He lost control, flipped his rig. It landed on top of our little Prius. They didn't stand a chance. The rig was carrying a full load and the weight crushed . . ." Kat stopped, closing her eyes against the onslaught of pain.

Dalian slid from the chair onto the bed, and pulled her into his embrace; both crying tears of loss, but also of relief over being able to speak to someone who could empathize with their misery. It was more than five minutes before either moved or spoke. Kat sniffled loudly and pulled from Dalian's embrace. She reached over and yanked two Kleenex from the box on the table next to her bed, handing one to Dalian before blowing her nose delicately.

"Oh, I need to get in touch with Janet," Kat sniffled, blowing her nose again. "Let her know what's going on. I saw she called yesterday, and completely forgot to call her back." She knew it was an abrupt change in subject, but she didn't dare dwell on their loss or she'd never stop crying.

"Is Janet a relative?" Dalian asked, blowing his nose.

"No, my publisher."

"Really. I didn't realize that publishers stayed in such close contact with their clients. You must be a mighty important writer."

Kat smiled, "Wishful thinking. Janet is more than just my publisher, she's also my dearest friend. Talking about my loss reminded me of her only because she went through every hellish step with me. I'm not certain I could have made it through without her. Hey, wait a minute! When we were talking a few minutes ago, you mentioned the name Canton. Isn't that Marsha's last name? The girl working at your ranch?"

"Yeah. It's her father," Dalian said.

"Good God. And he's still walking around free?"

"Yeah."

"I don't see how the man isn't in prison for murder. The man who killed my family is in prison for a majority of the rest of his life." Kat shook her head, unable to comprehend how the man was still walking around free. "And how can you allow Marsha Canton to work for you knowing what her dad did? How can you live next to them?"

"I don't blame Marsha. I can't hold someone else responsible for another's actions. Her dad is the one to blame, and though he's been a pain in my backside, trying to shove his daughter down my throat, it isn't something that I can't deal with. I never see him and that's good enough for me. I can't say I felt that way two years ago. Had he or his daughter shown their faces on my land, I'd have likely shot first and asked questions later."

"I still don't see how he got away with it."

"He claimed he never saw my wife; that she was hidden in the shadows. He also said that he was aiming for the cougar, and it was never his intent to harm anyone. He skated on the charge, but lost his license to carry a gun."

Kat shook her head, "Unbelievable!" She whispered. "That's why you brought your rifle out to the barn . . . was it Canton that tried to kill us? But why would he want to? Could Marsha be capable? I know she didn't like that you and I . . . well, you know."

Dalian didn't respond, just sat watching her. Kat's cheeks colored a deep crimson. He smiled, lifted her hand, and placed another kiss on the back. "You and I think alike," he said after a minute, "but I can't think of a justifiable reason for Canton wanting us dead — other than he seems Hell bent on getting his clutches into my property. That's why Marsha hangs around. I think her dad wanted me to marry her, so that any offspring would inherit my 200-acre spread. But is my land enough to kill over? I just don't know."

"Well, something we do know — someone wanted either you or me dead, or both of us, and since we're not—"

"Don't say it, Kat," Dalian interrupted sharply. "Sheriff Masters is looking into what happened. He'll catch whoever's behind this."

"But is it safe to return to the ranch? For either of us?"

Dalian nodded, "Now that we're aware, we'll be safer. But you have to promise me, no more pre-dawn visits outside, ok?"

"Maybe it would be safer for me to return to Georgia," Kat's heart wasn't in the declaration to begin with, but sank further when Dalian didn't immediately respond to her suggestion. "Dalian?"

He shook his head, mumbling curses beneath his breath. The sudden flare of anger emanating from him was almost tangible. After a few minutes more, he lifted his gaze to hers, the intensity boring into her own. "If I thought you would be safer in Georgia, I would put you on the first plane out in the morning, but I can't know for certain that you weren't the target, and if you were, and I send you away, I wouldn't be there to protect you if another attempt is made. I know you won't feel safe at the ranch until this is resolved, so I will fully understand if you want to hightail it back to your home state, but can you see my side of it? My desire to protect you? And you can trust that I'll do so with my life..."

Kat placed her fingers gently onto Dalian's lips. "I trust you. I know you'll protect me, but who'll protect you, Dalian?"

"My Remington shotgun and Ruger 22 Magnum begin double duty, round-the-clock protection beginning the moment we return home."

CHAPTER TWENTY-FIVE

"Dad, where are you?" Marsha called as she pushed through the front door. She was still shaking over the sheriff's visit earlier that morning, and had waited until he left the property to collect her things, mount her mare, and hightail it for home. She wasn't thrilled at doing so, but despite her feelings toward her old man, he was still family and she felt it her duty to warn him that the sheriff would be paying him a visit soon.

She also had to know. Why, she wasn't certain, but her desire to know whether her father had a hand in Dalian's attack was weighing on her as heavily as if a horse sat atop her chest.

"Dad, you in here?" She peered into the kitchen. When she didn't see him, she made her way down the hall toward his bedroom. She pushed open the door and sighed loudly, both with relief and in annoyance. Her dad was sprawled across his bed covers, still fully clothed, the aroma of alcohol permeating the air. With that evidence before her, she knew he couldn't have snuck over to Dalian's property in the wee early hours and assaulted him, or set the barn on fire. Unless he managed to get dead drunk afterward. Her dad simply wasn't a functioning alcoholic; however, there was really only one way to know.

She moved to waken her dad, but a pounding sounded at the front door halting her in her tracks. Instinctively she knew that the sheriff had arrived. She looked over at her dad again, and then made her way back to the front door.

It still stood wide open from when she'd barged in, so when she approached, she could see the sheriff standing on the porch, his fist lifted ready to pound on the screen door jamb again.

The sheriff saw Marsha draw near and his brow quirked, "Didn't take you long to race over here. Come to warn your dad?"

"Yeah," Marsha said with a nod, and then pushed the screen door open to admit the sheriff. "He may be a drunken sod, but he's still my dad, so I felt I owed him a heads up. In fact, I was just about to warn him when you showed up, and when you see what I did when I got here – just a minute ago, by the way – you'll be marking him off of your suspect list."

"You sound mighty confident about that."

"I am." Marsha turned and headed back down the hall toward her dad's room. When she reached the door, she stepped aside and motioned for the sheriff to look inside. "He was like that when I got here. Drunk as a skunk and dead to the world. And from the smell of alcohol lingering in the air, he's been binging for more than a day."

"That a fact," the sheriff asked, making his way across to the bed.

"I'd say so, yeah," Marsha replied, following behind. "I've seen it too many times in the past to know he only gets this way when he's on a binge. Look sheriff, I know you think you've got just cause to suspect my dad – hell, if it were me, I'd put him on my suspect list simply for being a grade A jackass – but I'm telling you right now, there's no way he could've have done what you said happened. Not in this condition."

"While I appreciate you going to bat for him, Marsha, I think I should ascertain for myself whether he's a viable suspect. Fair enough?"

"I have a feeling that nothing about this investigation is likely to be fair," Marsha muttered.

The sheriff chose to ignore her comment, and instead reached down and roughly shook Jethro Canton on the shoulder. Her dad didn't so much as moan at the intrusion. Jonathan tried again, this time calling Canton's name loudly in the man's ear. That elicited a small groan, but Jethro remained out cold, and unaware. The sheriff straightened and shook his head, releasing a loud sigh of frustration.

"Sorry it wasn't him, aren't you, Sheriff?" Marsha asked unable to keep the smugness out of her tone.

"Mighty sorry, yes, because that means there's someone unknown to me that has a motive for doing away with Dalian – a motive other than his land," Jonathan admitted, and then turned to face Canton's daughter. "You are not to return to Dalian's ranch . . . and don't interrupt," he said, when she started shaking her head and opened her mouth to speak. "You and your dad may not have been responsible for this latest attack on Dalian, but I am going to have a tough time convincing him of that. And another thing, get your daddy up and sober a.s.a.p. When you do, deliver a message. Tell him that I want to see him and you in my office first thing tomorrow morning. If you aren't there, I'll issue warrants for your arrests for obstruction. Understand?"

"But I thought we weren't suspects anymore?" Marsha asked, eyes widening with renewed concern.

"You'll be cleared of any wrongdoing as soon as I interview your dad formally about his whereabouts. Not a minute sooner. The same goes for you and your whereabouts." The sheriff walked past Marsha and out of the Canton's ranch house. When he settled behind the steering wheel of his Jeep Comanche, he gripped the wheel tightly and laid his head down on his whitening knuckles. He had to let Dalian know about what he discovered, and didn't relish his reaction. Admittedly, he was as convinced as Dalian was about Jethro's involvement; was certain as could be that he'd found justifiable cause to lock the man away for the rest of his life. Vindication for both this current act and the killing of Carolyn Rivers two years earlier. He'd hoped to give Dalian peace of mind, at last. Now, even his own peace and certainty was shattered because he now had to find another suspect, where there didn't appear to be one.

After another moment, he lifted his head, and reached into his coat pocket to retrieve his cell phone. He dialed Dalian's number and left a message when he got his voice mail.

CHAPTER TWENTY-SIX

Jethro Canton looked on the verge of demise, as if the Angel of Death was only minutes out from coming to claim his soul from this world. Marsha's skin was so pale, that the sheriff was concerned she'd pass out any moment. Despite looking peaked and ill, both still carried a chip on their shoulder the size of a boulder and sat sullenly across from Sheriff Masters. Neither were pleased that the sheriff sat silently observing them – had been doing so since their arrival five minutes earlier.

As if suddenly weary of trying to maintain an affronted facade, Jethro slumped further into his chair, rubbing his temples, but the headache refused to abate. He finally gave up on his head and wrapped his arms about his midriff, hoping to contain what little contents remained in his stomach, as nausea welled and settled repeatedly. He opened his eyes and glared at the sheriff, suddenly filled with an overwhelming animosity at the man who'd made him drag his hide out of bed after visiting too long with alcohol.

After another minute of silence, he determined enough was enough and sprang back to a seated position. The sudden movement was too much for his recovering body and he doubled over, gripping his abdomen tighter, as the acid in his stomach shot up his throat and threatened to fly out of his tightly clamped mouth. He didn't much care whether he threw up all over the sheriff's floor, but he did care about the mortification that would follow over being unable to handle his drink and the subsequent hangover.

When he felt steadier, he slowly righted himself, taking deep steadying breaths. If it were possible, the sheriff thought, he looked even more peaked than before, but his bout with sickness did not prevent his spewing anger in the sheriff's direction, albeit in a near whisper.

"My daughter filled me in in the car on the way over here, so if you don't think we had anything to do with what happened to Rivers, what are we doing here? And why are we just sitting here with you staring at us like we're some sort of reprehensible rodents."

"You sure you don't need to pay a visit to the bathroom before we proceed. You're looking mighty pasty," The sheriff said, deliberately ignoring Canton's questions. He wasn't ready to start the interview, even though he'd determined Jethro was of sound mind to continue. He'd made that determination on the fact that Canton was sober enough to walk into the office this morning under his own impetus. So, despite his still slightly slurred speech and sickly visage, Jonathan judged him capable of giving a statement. An annoyed Canton was just about to reiterate his questions when the front door opened and the sheriff stood suddenly.

"I'll be right back," the sheriff said, "and then we'll begin."

Had Jethro the strength to turn to see who the new arrival was, he'd have sobered quickly and made a beeline for the back door. As it was, he slouched in his seat again and resumed rubbing his temples. Marsha, on the other hand, wasn't ill — until she shifted in her seat and glanced over her shoulder. Immediately wishing she hadn't. Dalian strolled in, his body stiffening when he spied the two people sitting in front of the sheriff's desk. The sheriff made his way over, questioning the wisdom of putting these people in the same room together; however, the way he saw it, Dalian needed to hear the interview to believe Canton was innocent; needed to judge the man's veracity for himself. He hadn't told Dalian in his phone message the day before the purpose for coming into the office this morning because he'd wanted him to show up. Now he only hoped he'd stay.

"Dalian, thanks for coming. I have a seat in the corner for you."

"I don't get it, Jonathan," Dalian hissed, his gaze pinned to the back of Canton's head. "What am I doing here? What are they doing here? Did he confess?"

"Easy, Dalian," the sheriff said, leading Dalian to a chair next to his, behind the desk – away from Canton. When Dalian moved around the desk, into Jethro's line of sight, the man visibly blanched. "I wanted you here during the interview so that there isn't any doubt in your mind as to whether Jethro is innocent or guilty of what happened to you yesterday morning."

"I am innocent," Jethro exclaimed, looking anything but, "but I'll be damned if I'm going to let him and you railroad me because you think I killed his wife."

"You did kill my wife, you son of a bitch," Dalian hissed. "And if that judge had seen the truth of the matter, you'd be rotting in prison now instead of trying to kill me too."

"I didn't mean to, I tell ya," Canton screeched. "I swear I didn't see her."

"Sheriff, you can't have him in here. He's just likely to kill my dad before you get around to interviewing us," Marsha interjected.

"He's here," the sheriff said, addressing all three, "because I believe you both to be innocent of these current charges, and he needs to be certain of it too."

Dalian sat down heavily in the chair when the sheriff made his announcement, his own tanned skin pale. "No," he whispered.

"I'm sorry, Dalian," the sheriff said, settling into his own chair, "but the evidence attesting to his innocence is too overwhelming to ignore. And to Marsha's innocence."

Dalian shook his head, as the sheriff started the video camera sitting on top of the tripod next to his desk. He turned on his laptop, and attached the USB cable from the camera to the side of the laptop, so that the recording would be automatically filed, and, with the press of a key, submitted into evidence at the county courthouse.

"We are here to question two individuals in the assault of Dalian Rivers and of a guest at his ranch, Kathryn McMurray, on April 22nd, 2061 at approximately 0430," He began formally. "Here with me today are Jethro Canton, and his daughter, Marsha Canton, as well as one of the victims of the assault, Dalian Rivers. This interview is a formality in which the intent is to establish the whereabouts of Jethro Canton and Marsha Canton at the time of the incident. Mr. Canton, could you please tell us where you were in the early morning hours of April 22nd? And please remember that my computer is enhanced with the latest voice stress analyzer, which will automatically review your responses as being either truthful or suspect. Do you understand?"

"I understand, but hell, I can barely remember where I am now," Canton muttered, wiping a hand across his unshaven face, "but I can definitely tell you where I wasn't. I wasn't at River's house, or anywhere near his barn. I may not know specifically if I was in my house or not, but I had been visiting with a bottle of Jim Beam for two days straight and when Marsha woke me up late yesterday, I was in my bedroom."

The sheriff looked at his laptop to read the voice analysis, and then over at Dalian, who was watching Canton carefully, murder in his gaze. When Jethro finished, the sheriff saw Dalian's shoulders slump and knew he believed Canton's story, though brief, although he hadn't yet revealed the results of the stress analysis. He sighed heavily, sorry for having to put Dalian through yet another letdown. However, now was not the time to issue condolences or apologies, since he also needed to confirm Marsha's whereabouts for the record.

"I know that you and I have already spoken, Miss Canton, but I need your testimony for the record also, or it won't be official, and I won't be able to mark you off as a person of interest. So, if you would, please repeat to me where you were at 4:30 a.m., on April 22nd."

Marsha blanched and shook her head, her gaze widening in fear. The sheriff realized his mistake immediately. He'd callously asked the question without regard to how her father might react to his daughter whoring with one of Dalian's ranch hands; especially, when it had been made apparent that she was supposed to be chasing after Dalian. He called to his deputy who quickly appeared from a side office, "Could you escort Mr. Canton into the waiting room, Harold?"

Canton stiffened in his seat, "I ain't leaving here so that you can harass my daughter into confessing something she ain't done."

"Your daughter is eighteen, so I can legally question her without a parent present. And since I prefer to do so, you'll wait outside." The deputy tugged on Jethro's arm until the man stood, albeit unsteadily. When he had a secure footing, the deputy guided him from the room, shutting the door behind them.

"Again, Marsha, I know we already went over this, but I need it for the record."

"I was sleeping with Kenny Mitchell in my room. He was with me from about midnight until you started pounding on my door early in the morning." She lifted her chin proudly and tried to prevent the embarrassment seeping into her cheeks, but one look at Dalian and the facade cracked. She lowered her head in shame.

"Thank you, Marsha," the sheriff whispered, sympathetic to her humiliation. He reached up and switched off the recorder, and then stood from behind his desk and went to retrieve Jethro.

"Damn it all to hell," Canton snapped when the sheriff asked him to return to the office, "I just sat down."

"Well, now you can get back up," Jonathan said, and then moved to settle back behind his desk. He waited for Jethro to shuffle back to his previous seat before speaking again.

"There is just one more thing that we need to get straightened out before I let you two leave today. Of course, your answers determine whether you actually get to leave today; that, and the result of the voice analysis," the sheriff stated, flipping the recorder back on. "Yesterday afternoon, the bartender in town paid me a visit." The sheriff watched the pair carefully and saw by their widening gazes that they had an inkling as to where this conversation was headed. "He heard about the assault on Dalian and his guest, and informed me that you, Jethro, had been making threats against Dalian, and bragging up a storm over how you were going to get hold of his land – one way or another."

"I didn't attack Dalian. I swear by God Almighty. Didn't you just say that I was innocent?" Canton squealed.

"You are, of assault, but not of making public threats."

Marsha was shaking her lowered head. The sheriff could see tears falling and hear her soft sniffles. "Let me approach this from a different angle. Marsha, did your dad push you at Dalian with the intent of producing an heir and/or ever mention plans for acquiring his land in a less-than-legal manner?"

Marsha covered her face in her hands, her shoulders shaking as her tears turned to full-fledged blubbering.

"You let her be, sheriff! I'll tell you what I done, but you let her be."

"I'm all ears, and before you speak, know that I did a very thorough background check on you and discovered you are mentioned in over a dozen fraud, coercion, and blackmail cases. Had I checked more thoroughly two years ago when you were a suspect in Carolyn

Rivers' murder, I would have done what I could to dissuade you remaining in my town. Now, speak."

Canton glared at the sheriff, but a quick glance at Dalian and he quickly changed his expression from open hostility to just above passive aggressive. "I get what you're saying, and I admit that I pushed Marsha at Dalian, ok? Hoped she'd catch his eye because I'd taken a liking to his spread and thought that I could get to share it if he married my daughter. Felt like we'd be co-owners of the property, especially if Marsha was to give him a son."

"And?" The sheriff prompted, when he fell silent.

"And, I may have made some stupid comments when inebriated, that I can't quite recollect right now, but I ain't ever carried out those threats. Wouldn't have done so either. I'm all talk. Marsha can tell you that."

"If you were all talk, how did you manage to get a rap sheet longer than my arm related to this very thing – swindling people out of their property?"

"My wife was the brains behind all of that," Jethro said quietly, and Marsha's head snapped up. She stared at her dad through tear- blurred gaze, as if seeing him for the first time.

"Dad?"

Jethro kept his gaze averted from his daughter and slumped further into his chair. "Your mom was the brains, okay? I said it."

The sheriff stopped talking, content to allow Jethro to cleanse his conscious, as long as the voice analyzer continued relaying that he was speaking the truth, that is. As far as he figured it, it was time that his daughter heard the truth about her old man, straight from the horse's mouth.

"She planned all of the blackmails. She enticed all those men to sleep with her and then blackmailed them out of their property; then she turned around and sold it back to them for a nice tidy profit. Your mom planned it all. I was just the cameraman. I set up the equipment at the motels, and then mailed it to the marks with instructions."

"I don't understand," Marsha whispered, shaking her head in a confused daze.

"Well, your mom, you see, she had a knack for picking those who'd be too lily-livered to turn us in; too afraid of losing their wives or families; too proud to have their names slandered in the media. We'd quick deed the land into our names as payment – hush money – and then offer to sell it back to the mark quiet like. We didn't want the land. Not really. But we sure knew that the men would want it back. Most times, the families of the marks didn't even know their lands had been sold–"

"That doesn't make any sense. Why not just blackmail for cash? Why land?"

"A sell of property is legit. No questions about the legality. No waiting to cash out bonds or stocks, or for the bank to open." Canton shrugged his shoulders. "That's what my wife said anyhow. "Ask a man for money," she used to say, "and they get all sorts of squeamish, complaining about how they can't come up with a certain sum fast enough, but ask for a quick deed to their land, it's a matter of acquiring their signature. No muss, no fuss." And she was right too. When it came to the land, they could provide whatever sort of excuse they wanted to their wives and families about its loss, but we'd be in the clear. The next day, we'd offer to sell it back, and nine times out of ten, the mark suddenly found all sorts of ways to get their hands on the required money – anything to keep their families from knowing they'd sold it to begin with."

"What about those who decided not to buy it back?" the sheriff asked, his curiosity over this scheme piqued.

"Well, if for whatever reason, they really didn't have the money to buy it back, or decided it wasn't worth parting with their money over, then we had something of value to sell to someone else. Had my wife been here with me today, Dalian wouldn't have known what hit him. She'd have bamboozled him out of his land and he'd have thanked her for it."

Dalian sucked in an offended breath over that final remark, "I ain't a lily-livered coward, and that doesn't change the facts. You were here, and you wanted my land, not my money, and Carolyn stood in the way of your getting it," Dalian hissed, unable to stop from bringing the subject back around to the death of his wife. "I don't give a damn what that judge said, you killed my wife. I was standing right there and saw you do it. So either you're the worst shot in the world or you–"

"I am," Canton interrupted. "I am the worst shot in the world," he said, lifting his gaze to Dalian's, and for the first time felt confident in his belief of innocence. "And the judge taking away my firearm license was the smartest thing he could've done. And I'll tell you something else; her death is the reason why my best friend became Jim Beam. The alcohol didn't judge me, condemn me, or laugh at my ineptness with a rifle. Yeah, I talk a big talk now – when I'm drunk – but I'm a coward and a lousy shot with a rifle. I should never have been firing after that cougar. Should never have let that cat anger me so that I couldn't see straight; should never have been chasing after it in the first place when all I'd had to drink for dinner was bourbon – but as God is my witness, I didn't see your wife. Didn't know I'd killed her, until I was arrested for it. If I could, I'd turn back the clock and take it all back." Canton stopped talking, his eyes filling with tears, and he shook his head at his own stupidity. "I'm just a coward that talks big," he whispered after another minute, swiping at his eyes. "Hell, I've even threatened my own kid here, when drunk. Hinted that if she didn't get you to marry her, then I'd have to resort to a plan B. Hell, I didn't even have a plan B. I just figured that, as pretty as she is, you'd be interested. That she was capable of taking up where her mom left off, when her mom left me..." He stopped talking again, wiping his eyes and nose with the back of his sleeves. No one moved or talked again for five more minutes, as if they each needed that time to absorb everything said. Marsha and Dalian sat staring at Canton with a mixture of pity and disgust, but each believed what he said, and the sheriff confirmed his sincerity.

"I've only had this voice analyzer installed on the system for about a year and a half," the sheriff stated softly, "but its accuracy has never been off, and its results never disputed. He's telling the truth." Dalian closed his eyes and lowered his head into his hands, and Jethro flopped back into his chair, relief nearly overwhelming him. Marsha, however, could not relax. She could not take her eyes off this man, whom she'd called dad for so long. No longer did she fear his wrath, rather felt empowered by the pitiable weakness he exuded.

After a few minutes more, Sheriff Masters reached up and switched off the recorder, took a deep breath, and began to speak, his tone official.

"You both have been officially cleared of any wrongdoing in the attack on Dalian Rivers and Kathryn McMurray, but I want you to take what I'm about to say to heart. I highly recommend you leave Wind River just as fast as you can sell your spread, or better still – before then. You aren't welcome in my town any longer."

Jethro's face reddened in anger and Marsha's in humiliation. Canton was about to argue, but one look at Dalian and he decided against it. He stood rapidly, swaying as blood rushed to his head. Marsha leapt up and clasped hold of his arm. Together they walked from the building and straight to their car. Marsha didn't stop driving until they'd left Wind River more than a hundred miles in their rearview mirror.

CHAPTER TWENTY-SEVEN

"You could have warned me," Dalian said, as soon as the Canton's left the office.

"If I had you wouldn't have come." The sheriff stood and detached the cable from his computer and then set about storing the digital recorder away. When it was locked inside the cabinet, he returned to the computer and depressed the necessary key that would automatically transmit the recorded information to the county courthouse, where a clerk would officially enter it into the records and store it on their own system. After he did that, he converted the file to one he could store on his own laptop and then pulled the recordings into a file labeled "Cantons' Interviews," which was inside a primary folder with the latest case file number assigned to Dalian Rivers. The only other evidence inside that computer folder was toxicology reports on all parties involved, the interview with the bartender, and medical reports on Dalian and Kat. Nothing had been finalized with the arson investigators yet, and now that the Canton's had been cleared, he didn't have any viable suspects to include in the suspects subfolder.

As if just realizing that the suspect subfolder was empty, Jonathan stopped fiddling with his computer and turned to face Dalian, a look of concern etched on his face, "Where's your girlfriend?"

Dalian's brow knitted, "At the house, why?"

"We don't have any suspects in custody."

Dalian's eyes widened as realization dawned. Kat was alone and the assailant was still at large. Both men leapt from their chairs and dashed out the front door.

"Follow me. My siren will ensure no one stops us or gets in our way," Jonathan shouted, as both men raced to their respective vehicles. The sheriff's siren sounded even before his Jeep began moving.

Without slowing to check for on-coming traffic, both men darted onto the main road and sped toward Dalian's ranch near Wind River Canyon.

Dalian threw his Jeep into park seconds before the sheriff threw his own Jeep into park. Both men quickly exited their vehicles and dashed up the front steps and into the house.

"Kat," Dalian called, taking the stairs two at a time. He pushed into Kat's room and came to a quick halt, bending at the knees to catch his runaway breath; tears pricking at the corner of his eyes. He stood after a minute and looked at the sheriff who entered behind him. "She's safe," he whispered, swiping the tears from his eyes. "Just sleeping."

The sheriff nodded and motioned with his head for Dalian to follow him from the room. Both men entered the hallway and were immediately met by Harvey and Mrs. Guthrie.

"She's sleeping soundly because I gave her something. She was too agitated to rest otherwise, with your being gone," Mrs. Guthrie said immediately, addressing Dalian. "I was just telling Harvey what happened yesterday morning, when we heard you tear into the house."

"So, now that you're back from your meeting, mind telling me what's been going on since I left?" Harvey demanded. Dalian placed a finger on his lips, pulling the door closed behind him.

He took a deep breath to calm his nerves and then seemed to realize suddenly that he was a ranch owner who had guests still to contend with, "Who do you have looking after the guests?" Dalian asked, making his way toward the study.

"I have Achak doing that," Harvey said, "not that anybody seems eager to do much right now. Since breakfast, they've all just been puttering around like lost sheep. It might be best if you and the sheriff fill them in. And we might consider sending them all home early."

"We won't be doing that," the sheriff interjected. "Has anybody attempted to pack up and leave?"

Harvey looked at both men and his brow knitted in concern and confusion, "Not that I'm aware of, but I just got back early this morning. Mrs. Guthrie?" The housekeeper shook her head. Harvey turned his attention back to Dalian and the sheriff, "Either of you planning on telling me what's going on?"

"Yeah," the sheriff replied, "we'll fill you in, but let's do it when we fill in the guests. Ok? That way I'm not repeating myself."

Harvey looked to Dalian who nodded in agreement with the sheriff, "Gather up the guests for me will you Harvey? Mrs. Guthrie, have the breakfast dishes been cleared away?" Mrs. Guthrie nodded. "Thank you. Harvey, have them meet in the dining room."

Half-hour later, a group of concerned vacationers filled the same room they'd only just departed from breakfast an hour earlier.

"Before I turn this meeting over to Sheriff Masters, I just wanted everyone to know that Kat is doing fine, and will make a full recovery, as will I – obviously." Dalian rubbed the back of his head softly and winced; and genuine smiles replaced looks of concern. Dalian wanted to say more, wanted to warn his patrons that there was a potential murderer still at large – possibly someone seated next to them – but decided it was best to let the sheriff handle that part of the news. "For more information related to all of this, I'll turn the floor over to the sheriff Jonathan Masters."

"Thanks Dalian." The sheriff stood in front of the small number of people seated around and cleared his throat. "As you all know, there was an attempt made on Dalian's life early yesterday morning, and possibly on the life of one of the other guest's here, Kathryn McMurray." Hands shot up to ask questions, as if at a lecture. The

165

sheriff waved all hands down. "Please let me speak. If you still have questions that aren't answered, I'll do my best to answer them when I'm done." Everyone lowered his or her hands and the sheriff cleared his throat again. "We thought we had two suspects in custody, but the alibis provided for each person proved solid. That means I have to assume that someone hereabouts still has a strong desire to bring harm to either Mr. Rivers or Miss McMurray. I can say that I don't think any of you are in danger, but as we can't be certain as to the identity of the assailant and/or to that person's intended target, I need everyone to be alert. Never go anywhere without a partner. I will also be imposing a curfew and a bed check until this matter is resolved."

Hands shot up again, and the sheriff sighed loudly. "Okay, I'll answer a few questions now." He pointed to Cal Withers, seated to the front of the others.

"You said that Kat is okay? I saw an ambulance transport her to the hospital, while we were all outside this morning. Will you allow us to go to the hospital to see her? Check on her well-being?"

"That won't be necessary, Cal," Dalian interjected. "I brought Kat home this morning, because the doctor gave her a clean bill of health. She's upstairs sleeping right now. As soon as she's feeling up to it, I'll permit guests to go up to talk to her. Jason?" Dalian pointed to another guest whose hand shot up the minute he finished speaking.

"Why can't we just pack up and go home? If we're not in any danger?"

The sheriff looked at Dalian and sighed before turning back to answer the question, "Because, my office has to clear you all as suspects," The sheriff concluded, and the room erupted into cries of outrage and distress. Only one person maintained her calm and raised a hand to ask another question. The sheriff whistled shrilly to silence the chatter, and then called on Chloe to speak after everyone fell silent.

"Miss, you have a question?"

Chloe nodded, "The two suspects that you cleared. Was it Marsha Canton and her father? If not, I would definitely consider them as suspects before any of us since Marsha was serious about catching Dalian, and I heard that her father..."

"They were cleared, yes," the sheriff interjected, and Chloe's calm facade cracked a little, her brow knitting in apprehension.

"That means—," she started, but the sheriff interrupted again.

"There's a possibility that someone in this room is responsible; or one of Mr. River's ranch hands, or a complete stranger – a transient passing through the region. Until we know who that someone is, we'll all be staying. The ranch hands are being sequestered in the bunkhouse until they are interviewed and fingerprinted; so rest assured you are not the only people being detained. Furthermore, I have a call into the state police. Members of their force and my deputies will be along within the next hour. Throughout the remainder of the morning, they will circulate the room, asking questions and acquiring your fingerprints. You needn't be concerned that your comfort will be overlooked during this time. After we finish with fingerprinting, you are free to roam about the ranch, but again, do not go anywhere alone, and please, do not try to leave. If anyone here wishes to contact an attorney prior to the start of this procedure, I highly recommend you contact them immediately."

The sheriff had no sooner finished that last statement, than people began yanking their cell phones from their pockets. A few people asked to be excused to go retrieve their Skype-enabled iPads from their rooms. With the flurry of activity from such a small number of people, the sheriff decided it best to cover his own ass. He stepped onto the front porch, pulled out his own cell phone, and dialed Wind River's county judge. He would get the permission he needed now for taking fingerprints so none of the attorneys could cry foul. He saw his deputy sheriff approaching and waved him over.

When he concluded the call, he turned to his deputy, "Judge Sanders is getting the paperwork together that we need to legally hold and fingerprint the people staying here at the ranch. I want you to get Nichols to pick it up and return it to the office. Have him give it to Deputy Mallory, with instructions she can fax it to attorneys if they demand to know how we're not tramping on their clients' legal rights. Tell her to expect the switchboard to be flooded, if all fifteen guests are contacting attorneys. She knows the song and dance. Finally, get in touch with the crime lab. Tell them to expect to be working nonstop until all persons fingerprints are run through the system. They should expect to get about thirty-five sets – that includes the vacationers and the ranch hands. I'll inform patrons that they will be free to leave once they are cleared from our suspect list."

"Whew. I can't remember the last time we had a crime of this magnitude here in Wind River."

"I can," the sheriff muttered.

"Oh yeah, that's right," the deputy murmured. "I guess this just seems so much bigger since there are so many more suspects. God, almighty! This is the second time something like this has happened to Dalian too."

"Yeah. People sure do seem to take a dislike to the man."

"I can't see why. He's a great guy, a hard worker, an honest businessman..."

"Maybe it isn't about him, personally."

"Then what in Hell could it all be about?"

"I don't know, but that's what we're here to find out. Go take care of that stuff, ok?"

"Sure thing."

The sheriff returned to the dining room only to have one of his deputies inform him that someone contacted the media instead of calling an attorney.

"How can you be certain of that?"

"Because Mallory called and said that reporters were starting to flood the switchboard at the office. On top of that and the calls from attorneys, she's got her hands full," the deputy stated.

"Okay, you head back and help Mallory field the calls. On your way out, have Matthews start confiscating all cell phones."

The outrage that followed the sheriff's order was borderline mob madness. He quickly reassured everyone that they would be allowed time to speak with their attorneys using the home's landline, as needed – and under close supervision.

An hour later, the state police arrived, followed by a horde of reporters.

CHAPTER TWENTY-EIGHT

It was an easy matter to resolve. How could you have screwed up so badly!

"It wasn't easy, and I thought it was done!"

Had it been done, it would have been done wrong. I never said 'double homicide' you moron.

"Well if you'd given more than vague directions and been there to stop me messing up, it would have been done. But you're always conveniently absent when it's time to get hands dirty. I was barely even awake at that hour. How did you even know they were going to be out there?"

Because I know everything. And now, because you are a first-rate screw up, the two patsies I'd chosen to take the rap, have air tight alibis, which means the cops are going to turn their focus on everyone else – including you.

"If you knew everything, you'd have known the two patsies would have alibis and had me wait until they didn't." The voice fell silent, and for the first time in twenty years, a sense of empowerment swelled within. Perhaps age and knowledge made bravery achievable, making it possible to see the voice clearly for the first time – not as an all-knowing presence, rather as an impish, demanding child that had to have its own way or would pitch a hissy fit. Then what it said registered and fear and uncertainty returned.

"Do you think they will see me as a suspect?" The tone whispered was reminiscent of the teenager twenty years ago – unsure and cowardly.

Apologize. The voice inside his head said sullenly, *and then we'll discuss what's to be done.*

"For what?"

For being stupid and stupidly arguing with me. I'm the one in control here, not you. And if you don't apologize, I will make certain that you're blamed.

Fear swelled again, "Not if you don't let them. You've always made certain that I'm never a person of interest."

You're worse than a moron; you're imbecilic. Didn't I just say that the reason you've never been looked at as a person of interest is because I always had pre-selected pawns on which to pin the murders? Now, there is no one and no way I can prevent them looking at you.

"How do you do that anyway? How do you always know that there will be someone that we can steer the blame towards?"

There is always someone, somewhere, whose life is seriously screwed up. Someone who'll make a good suspect for a police inquiry. It's just a matter of keeping eyes and ears open to find them. And find them I did; but now the cops know that they're innocent. On top of that, I gave you specific instructions to follow and had you done so successfully, we'd be ready to move in on our latest conquest.

"Yeah, well, I wouldn't be in this mess if it weren't for you!"

If it weren't for me, your life wouldn't be worth jack! You better not forget that!

"Right now, I can't forget that the cops are fingerprinting everyone. How do I know the police won't–?"

Dunce is your middle name, not mine. I've been more than careful. They may find your juvie record, but unless they dig deep, they'll be hard-pressed to connect you to any of the other deaths.

"I hope you're right, because if I get caught now, it'll be your fault."

Oh, make no mistake, if you get caught, it will all be on you. But just so you know how partners work, I'll be there the next time to help see it done, but time is getting short, so if I can't make it, you'll have to step up to the plate and hit more than a foul ball. You know you can't screw it up again.

"I won't, but the cops are suspicious. Another attempt—"

Better not fail! And this time, make certain you get rid of the right person. Now apologize, and stop thinking for yourself, or I'll make you stop.

"Sorry," came the reply, but it was lacking sincerity, rather was delivered in the manner in which it was felt – tired and reluctant.

CHAPTER TWENTY-NINE

It was no small feat keeping the reporters outside the ranch's main gates, but his deputies managed successfully. That was one load off of the sheriff's mind, since the main gate was so far from the main house. That meant nosy reporters with over-eager camera operators couldn't interfere with his investigation; that the most they could do for their viewing audience, was speculate as to the flurry of activity, and about the flock of police officers who came and went – and speculate they did. Dalian and the sheriff watched the afternoon news and shook their heads as the reporter for their local media station confidently stated that, "While police refuse to comment on what has transpired here today, our sources reveal that tragedy has once more struck one of Wind River's most affluent residents, Dalian Rivers."

Dalian reached for the remote and switched off the television, "They can be relentless, and just plain dumb. 'Our sources reveal that tragedy has struck yet again'? More like they put two-and-two together since the cops are at my house – again."

"They have to feed the masses," the sheriff snorted. "Speaking of the masses, I better go check on the progress being made. Everything appears to be progressing nicely, so I anticipate being out of your hair before lunch time."

"That's all well and good, Sheriff, but what am I to do then? Somehow, I have to convince my guests to return to business as usual while we await fingerprint results; guests that are probably holding onto to their sanities by a thread. That's a hard thing for me to focus on right now, when my only concern is protecting Kat and myself. That may be selfishness talking, but that's the truth of the matter."

"Let me worry about the guests, Dalian," Harvey said, stepping into the room. "You're right that your primary concern should be looking after Kat, and watching your own back. Besides, I'm the one who generally takes care of the guests during this time of year anyway, while you manage the ranch, so now that I'm back, I can do my job."

"I'll let you two hammer out those details," the sheriff said, moving toward the door. "My worry is catching a potential murderer, not keeping the guests happy. I will try to hurry things along though, to try to get things back to normal around here as quick as possible. There will be a couple of extra guests for you to be looking after, Harvey – wearing uniforms. They'll be here to make certain no one tries to leave, and also to help Dalian with keeping Kat and himself safe."

"Thanks Jonathan," Dalian replied.

"Mighty welcome."

When the sheriff left, Dalian turned back to Harvey, "How was the funeral? How's your Mom holding up?"

"She's a strong woman with a positive outlook on life, so losing Dad, while hard, wasn't an end-all. He'd been sick for a long time too, so she'd been preparing for this day for over a year."

"What about you? You okay?"

"Yeah. I'm good. I'll miss the old man, but I was prepared too." Harvey settled into a chair and looked up at his friend, "Have any theories?"

"About?"

"You damned well know what about."

"My theory was shot to Hell as soon as the sheriff cleared the Cantons. I can't even begin to fathom who would want to hurt Kat and me. Where's the motive? She's been here less than three weeks. We've only just come to an understanding this past week."

"So I see," Harvey grinned. "About time you got back into the game."

Dalian grinned, "Yeah, well, I was the one running all the moves and making all the passes, so it wasn't an easy understanding, I can tell you that! But she's a special lady, and I can't even tell you why."

"There's just something about her that called to you; whispered to your heart."

Dalian nodded. "Yeah, just like with me and Carolyn, and you and Scarlett. Think anyone will whisper to your heart again, old man?"

"My heart's too old, but I keep its ears free of wax, just in case some pretty lady starts talking."

Dalian laughed, "I think we've done beaten that analogy to death, so change of subject. How are you planning to keep our guests entertained when the police are roaming the place and all anyone can think about is a possible killer wandering free? If it were up to me, I'd refund their money and send them all packing, but as that doesn't appear to be an option."

"Well, as you said, it may not be business as usual, but maybe I can consult with them. See what they want to do about it all. With a little persuasion, they might just decide the distraction of a daily routine is preferable to sitting about frettin'. I know I'd find it preferable."

"Sounds good. So, while they're hole up in the dining room, why don't you go and speak to them. I've got something I want to take care of in here and then I'm going to check on Kat.

Harvey slapped at his thigh and stood, "Sounds like a plan, and I'm looking forward to seeing the little lady up and about before too much longer.

"You and me both, and thanks Harvey."

"For?"

"For doing everything possible to help me out; for helping me keep my head on straight, and for helping me with the guests."

"Not a problem. Oh, and I sent a deputy to sit outside Kat's door until you can get up there to protect her yourself."

"Damn, I should have thought of that."

"It's been a hell of a day. Cut yourself some slack."

Dalian nodded. When Harvey left him alone, Dalian reached for the phone and dialed Directory Assistance for Covington, Georgia, "I need the number for Janet Ackers, please. Thank you."

CHAPTER THIRTY

Dalian hung up the phone after a longer conversation than he intended, and then left his office. The dining room was on a direct line of sight to the staircase, so he veered off to watch his guests milling about, whispering among themselves. Some were seated with a police officer, answering questions and some were seated before the portable fingerprinting machine, which would digitally transport their information to the lab for identification. He shook his head in wonder, thinking that the next step in technological advancements would provide instantaneous results. Scan the prints, wait five minutes, and have a person's rap sheet pop up on the screen.

He spotted Chloe, the only woman in a room full of men, sitting and speaking with one of the state police officers. He felt for her. Partly because of the current circumstances, and partly because she wasn't garnering the attention she was used to. Her interviewer was completely professional, Chloe's beauty wholly unobserved. He wondered whether the knit in her brow was to do with that, or simply at having to be interrogated like a common criminal. He made a mental note to say something to her later; comment on how pretty she was looking. Lift her spirits a bit. Then he sighed and headed for the stairs.

He hoped this latest disaster to strike at him didn't affect the future of his ranch. He would need to make an appearance shortly to reassure his guests after checking on Kat. Despite his unease at having his guests stay disrupted, his primary concern was the woman who'd slept through the better part of the mayhem. Besides, he trusted that his friend and foreman would do his best to deter negative feelings and threats of lawsuits.

He knocked softly on Kat's door and was pleased when that charming lilt of a southern accent bade him enter. He pushed the door open and smiled widely. Kat was sitting up in bed and Mrs. Guthrie was beside her, coaxing her into eating some soup. "Mind if I intrude?"

Both women smiled and shook their heads, "We were just finishing up a bite to eat," Mrs. Guthrie said. She stood and collected the dishes and headed for the door. "Don't tax her overly much," she advised Dalian. "She's recovering nicely from her ordeal, but I'm not certain any stress right now would be good for her."

"I'll take good care of her, Mrs. Guthrie. I promise."

With a knowing grin, Mrs. Guthrie stepped into the foyer. "I'll see to it you're not disturbed," she said, pulling the door closed. Dalian saw the hue in Kat's cheeks brighten and laughed. He would never tire at how easily she blushed. He liked it.

Kat lowered her gaze and then a moment later looked back at Dalian, invitation in her eyes. Dalian's grin widened and he closed the distance rapidly. He sat down on the side of the bed, scooped Kat onto his lap, and kissed her thoroughly. When he broke the kiss, he started to say something, changed his mind, and resumed kissing her.

Kat's breathing was coming in gasps when he finally allowed her up for air the second time, "Wow! You certainly know how to take a woman's breath away."

"I could say the same about you taking a man's breath away, but," he said with a devilish arch of his brow, "I'm far from finished with you. I intend to leave you panting a good long while, woman."

"I take it that I'm in a whole heap of trouble?" She giggled.

"Damn straight!"

Kat grinned and lowered her gaze; however, unlike before, she wasn't afraid. She was through running, was ready to love again. To be loved. She ran her hand along the nape of Dalian's neck, her fingers fanning through his thick black hair. She gently tugged his face to hers and for the first time in her life, initiated a kiss.

Dalian placed his hands beneath her knees and stood, without removing his lips from hers. He turned toward the bed, lowering Kat to its center, his body following until they were lying in each other's embrace. Slowly, with near-reverence, his hand traversed along the side of Kat's body, sliding across her breast and then down to her hip. Her body arched into his caress, her own hands beginning an exploration of the muscles rippling along his back.

On the return trip from her hip, Dalian's hand found the edge of Kat's nightshirt and slowly edged beneath, his hand stopping when it encountered the warm flesh of her side. He broke the kiss and looked questioningly at her.

"I'm ready," she whispered.

"You are my heart," Dalian replied.

Kat lowered her hand to his, and slid it upward, pressing it against her chest, just above her breast, "And you're mine."

Dalian felt the rapid beat beneath his palm and looked at where the material had slid up, uncovering one of her breasts. He lowered his head and placed a tender kiss on it, and then skillfully shed their clothing and claimed her for his own.

CHAPTER THIRTY-ONE

You saw him standing there at the door; knew that he was headed upstairs to check on Kat; and you just sat here talking to this cop.

There was no way to counter the harsh reprimand; to object, speak – say anything in response, but the cop was saying something, posing more questions. Why did he have to pry; why be so thorough? Secrets weren't meant to be revealed. Tread softly, answer the inane questions, and then go take care of business!

"Okay. We've established your whereabouts, now just one more question, and then I'll send you along to the fingerprint officer for a quick read, and you'll be free to roam about unimpeded. Sound good?"

"Yes."

Sounds peachy! Unimpeded, my eye! Someone is going to be watching your every move. You'll have to be stealthy. No one can know that the culprit is you. They can't know your motivations.

"Is there anything in your past that we need to know about now that may show up in our records? Anything that you may want to reveal? Even if it's just an overdue parking ticket."

You're in the clear. Nothing can be tied to you, and no one is allowed access to your juvenile records. Just say 'no'.

"No."

"Very good then. Take a seat next to the man over there. You should be finished shortly. Next!"

Knees knocking, he stood and headed to the designated chair, but at least the hard part was over.

I hate questions! Why is someone always asking questions!

"Please be quiet!"

"I haven't said anything," the man in the next chair said.

"Sorry. I was talking to myself."

The man quirked a brow, then returned his attention to his iPad. He slipped on a pair of headphones, turning his back slightly.

As soon as you've done fingerprinting, slip off to the bathroom, and find a way to get upstairs undetected. I'm here now, so we'll take care of this together.

"What if they're together?" The reply was barely audible, but the worry of being overhead still great.

Separate them. We don't want them both harmed. We need the one alive, remember?

"Can't we just find someone else? Why this particular one?"

Because I said so, that's why, and I always get what I'm after. You should know that by now.

"Yeah, you've been getting what you want for over twenty years, can't I have a say for once?"

No, and lower your voice.

The sigh that followed was one of defeat. Never getting what was wanted was beginning to wear thin; so was hoping for a longer-term relationship. A break was in order. The police officer summoned, and instructions issued on the steps required for obtaining fingerprints. "Just slip your hand flat on this screen and remain very still. We'll repeat with the other hand, and you'll be all done for the day."

About time.

"Next hand." The machine whirred for another minute and then, "All done."

Nonchalant, he stood, slipped from the room, and ducked into the powder room downstairs.

"Now what?" The person asked his reflection in the mirror, which would have raised the eyebrows of any onlooker; however, it had become a common occurrence for the person staring at the reflection; a reflection from whom there was seemingly no escape.

Time to head upstairs and finish what we started, and try not to let anyone see you.

CHAPTER THIRTY-TWO

Kat lay nestled in Dalian's embrace, feeling drowsy and sated. She smiled at the small ache in her abdomen, as she lifted her leg and laid it over his; snuggling closer. Her hand slid from his chest, down by his side, and she hugged him slightly, a sigh of contentment escaping. Dalian instinctively drew her nearer, nuzzling his chin on top of her head. He placed a kiss on her hair and released his own sigh.

"Think anyone would mind if we didn't make an appearance until tomorrow? I'm beat," Dalian said, and Kat laughed.

"It may take me that long to be able to walk again," she admitted sheepishly.

Dalian laughed and hugged her tight, then relaxed his grip and kissed her hair again.

"Dalian?"

"Yes, darling."

Kat closed her eyes and savored the endearment, even more reluctant to broach the topic of their assailant. She felt compelled to know what was transpiring; yet, at the same time, wanted to keep that part of the world shut out of their bedroom and their world forever. Wishful thinking, she knew.

"I know it may not seem the best time to talk about this, but I won't be truly satisfied until I know what's going on with the sheriff's investigation. Do they have any leads?"

"I meant to talk to you about it earlier, but you were too inviting by far, and I completely lost my senses." Dalian shifted to a sitting position, and Kat reached over to grab her nightshirt from the floor. He sighed, "You don't have to get dressed, you know."

"I do if we're going to have a conversation, and you put a shirt on too. Talk about a distraction," she declared, gazing lustfully at his bare chest.

Dalian laughed, "Fine, we'll get dressed first. I suppose it does seem absurd to have a serious conversation in the nude." Kat laughed and shimmied into her nightclothes, watching with increasing desire a naked Dalian slowly don his own attire. She smiled and then shook the lustful thoughts away. She had a lifetime to lust over her man, she mused, and then the smile vanished altogether when reality intruded. She could only hope right now that they would have a lifetime together. Until the sheriff apprehended the assailant, there were no certainties.

When they were clothed, they repositioned themselves against the headboard and Dalian filled her in on his visit to the sheriff's office early that morning.

"So, you and the sheriff are now one-hundred-percent convinced that the Cantons had nothing to do with the assault on us. So now what?" Kat asked, trying to keep the worry from her tone.

"Well, while we've been busy up here, about a dozen officers have been busy downstairs, questioning and fingerprinting my guests and my ranch hands."

"Oh my stars! Could it really be someone that we've spent the better part of three weeks with?"

Dalian shook his head, "There's really no way to know. A disgruntled former employee could be hanging about the place unseen; or a current employee could have a beef to grind. I can only speculate, which is not a good thing to do if I want peace of mind. The best thing we can do is let the sheriff do his job and never go anywhere unattended. If I can't be with you, one of the sheriff's men should be." Dalian sighed heavily.

"We'll get through this, Dalian," Kat assured, placing her hand on his.

"Damn straight," Dalian said quietly, "and when we do, I'm marrying you."

Kat looked into Dalian's gaze, startled. He grinned, and leaned forward until his face was mere inches from hers, "That's what I said. Any objection?"

Kat shook her head, barely perceptible, and Dalian placed a kiss on her lips.

"Sorry it wasn't the most romantic of proposals, but there doesn't seem to be much normal about our entire time together, up to now."

Kat laughed shortly and had to agree. From the time she arrived at his ranch, life had been a whirlwind of activity, good and bad, so for him to bend formally on one knee to propose marriage seemed contrary somehow; and if she were honest with herself, she was just thrilled that he proposed. She was a novelist who lived and breathed romance; so to her, his proposing the way he did was more significant than the romantic accoutrements of a fairytale proposal. But it did give her an idea.

"Once we get through this, I think I'm going to turn our story into a novel," she said, smiling widely. "I mean, if you think about it, what's been happening to us sounds like it came straight from a book anyway, doesn't it?"

Dalian grinned and nodded, "It sure doesn't sound real life. Hey! Can I name it?"

"The book? I haven't even written it yet." Kat laughed at his enthusiasm; felt a deep sense of pride that he wanted to be a part of her world, as she wanted to be a part of his.

"I know, but if you're going to write about our time together, I think I have the perfect title."

"Okay. Tell me this perfect title."

"Whispers of the Heart," Dalian said softly, placing her hand on his chest.

Kat's eyes glistened with tears and she smiled softly. "I get it, and it is perfect."

"I love you, Kat." Dalian leaned over to kiss her when a knock sounded at the door. "Well, that's poor timing."

Kat laughed, and gave him a quick peck, "Come in," she called.

CHAPTER THIRTY-THREE

"Did you have to invite them in?" Dalian whispered, as the doorknob turned. "I had plans to ravish you again." Kat laughed as the door swung open.

"Good to see someone's having a nice time," Harvey said, stepping into the room, followed closely by the sheriff, Chloe, Mrs. Guthrie, and Cal Withers.

Dalian saw them file in. He brushed their intrusion aside, his brow knitted in concern. He was suddenly glad they'd determined to converse clothed, as it would have been embarrassing to be caught in a compromising position.

"Something happen?" He asked, addressing the sheriff. When no one replied immediately, Dalian snapped, "Why are you all standing in our bedroom if nothing is wrong?"

They looked at each other and then shrugged simultaneously. "Nothing really wrong," Harvey replied. "We just encountered each other heading in this direction, so thought we'd come see you all together."

Chloe stepped from the pack and headed over to the bedside. She sat down beside Kat, "How are you feeling?" She asked softly. "I feel horribly guilty that I couldn't come see you sooner."

"That's okay, Chloe, I was...um...preoccupied earlier," Kat's ears tinted pink, and Dalian laughed.

"Completely my fault, Miss Chloe, I assure you. So, what's up everybody? Cal? I guess I should ask you first, since you're a guest here. Then again, so are you, Chloe. Unless you came up here for another reason other than to check on Kat?"

"No, no other reason," Chloe said and settled into a chair next to the bed. Dalian turned his attention back to Cal.

Cal's face was flushed and Kat could tell it was taking a monumental effort to keep his temper in check at seeing her and Dalian in bed together. At least she read his demeanor, and his expression, that way. He was also avoiding eye contact – a sure sign of discomfort. When he finally spoke, it was in a barely polite and completely insincere tone of voice. "I'm sorry to intrude, Dalian, but I didn't really come up here to see you or Kat. I just happen to see the sheriff headed this way and wanted to ask his permission to leave."

"I'm sorry sir, but I can't allow anyone–"

"I don't mean to return home," Cal interrupted. "I just mean to take a motel room in town, until this blows over. I'd be mighty grateful, since the thought of staying under the same roof as a killer . . . well, it just doesn't sit well with me. In fact, it's making me downright nauseous," he concluded with a quick glance at the bed.

Dalian looked at the sheriff and then at his foreman. He missed the contempt aimed in Kat's and his direction, because his mind was on the potential fallout to his ranch. This was just the concern he had earlier – that people would try to bolt out of fear and the reputation of his ranch would suffer. Still, while he was doing everything possible to resume and maintain some sort of normalcy, that didn't mean his guests were willing to do the same.

"I can't allow anyone to leave until cleared. Even if cleared, there may still be questions I need to ask, so it isn't likely anyone will be free to return to their homes for a few days at least. Have you had your fingerprints taken?" The sheriff asked.

"Yes."

"Okay. Good. We should know something before tomorrow

afternoon. If we don't find anything that implicates you in this attack, I'll let you leave, but only in so far as I'll permit you to take a motel room in town. That's the best I can do."

"Understood. Thank you, sheriff, and again, I wish I wasn't the squeamish sort. Kind of a turn off to the women, let me tell ya."

Dalian nodded, not understanding at all. Still, it wasn't his job to judge people and their proclivities. "I'll prorate your payment and try to have it to you before you leave – tomorrow?"

"Yeah, probably tomorrow afternoon," the sheriff concurred.

" Ordinarily, I would say keep the money, since I'm not really hard up for cash, but since this is a business and my vacation has been interrupted because someone apparently holds hatred for the owner of this business, I'd say a refund would definitely be in order."

"Completely understood," Dalian replied in as concerned tone as possible, but this man's comments, tone, and demeanor was making civility a challenge. "I only hope that you can come to realize that I am not responsible for the actions of a madman. Still, collaterally, this person has inconvenienced all of my guests severely. Kat included."

Cal nodded, but didn't reply. He appeared to lack empathy completely for anyone else's circumstances.

"Harvey will drive you to a motel in town..."

"I'd rather he rent a car for me. I may decide to tool around here a bit before returning to the airport. After all, I still have several weeks of vacation time left. Might go to Yellowstone."

"We can't rent the car *for* you, but as we only have the one rental agency in town, it shouldn't be too difficult for you to procure a car to have brought around tomorrow evening, after the sheriff clears you for departing. Of course, there's always the option of staying and our shuttle will return you to the airport . . ."

"This vacation has been very inconvenient," Cal griped, interrupting, "anything but the fun I expected to have, so, no, I'd not prefer to hang around any longer than need be."

"We're very sorry that things turned out the way they did," Harvey replied.

"You and me both," Cal said and then turned to leave.

"Oh and Cal," Dalian called, stalling his departure, "I do have one request."

Cal turned and quirked a brow as if any request would add yet another inconvenience to his life. Still he nodded his acquiescence.

"When you do leave tomorrow, try to do so quietly. Don't let the other guests see you go. I don't want to start a stampede for the doors. As you said, this is a business, and I don't want the remainder of my guests unduly agitated. I'm sure you understand."

Cal nodded again, and then, as if suddenly realizing that his manners had been atrocious, turned to address Kat, "I should have said something to you first, Kat. I guess I just let my fears overshadow my manners. I just want you to know that I'm happy that you weren't hurt – too badly, that is. I haven't known you long, but I can tell you're a special lady – which I'm certain Dalian will agree with. Anyway, you take extra care of yourself, and if you ever tire of this particular ranch owner, I wouldn't be overly upset if you decided to look my way."

His expressionless delivery left Kat confounded, so that all she could do was nod. Cal turned and left the room. Dalian looked at Kat, "Well, that was interesting," he said, and then shook off the feeling of menace lingering in the room. He affected a positive demeanor and then turned to the sheriff, "I feel like the King of England, holding court."

The sheriff laughed. "Well, I'll keep my visit brief. I just wanted to let you know that our job here is done, so I'm headed back to town. The lab is already providing information, so I should know something by this evening as to whether someone has a criminal background."

"I thought you said it would be tomorrow evening before you knew anything?"

"It still could be, but information is coming in faster than I first anticipated. It could still very well be another day before I can grant anyone permission to leave the premises, since I don't know how long it'll take for me to get through all the backgrounds. I couldn't give Mr. Withers leave because I don't know if a report has been generated for his prints yet. I'm not rushing through this process. I want to be extremely thorough – this time."

"Thank you, sheriff."

"No problem. Anyway, as soon as I know something, I'll give you a call, so keep your cell phone handy. I'm leaving two deputies, as I said earlier, so if there's trouble you'll have backup."

"If there's trouble, I'm prepared to handle it," Dalian said, nodding to his firearms sitting on the dresser.

"I can't condone your taking the law into your own hands, Dalian, but at least you know the law is on your side, but only if an assailant enters your house. It's important you make that distinction. I don't want to arrest you over this. It'll make me feel real bad."

"I promise not to fire my weapon anywhere but in my house," Dalian replied in his best oath-taking voice.

"Good to know. Well, I'll head on over to the office and get to work. Ladies." He tipped an imaginary hat toward Kat and Chloe and then departed.

"Next?" Dalian said with a grin. "What's up, Mrs. Guthrie?"

"Well, I have the guests settled in for lunch and thought perhaps you could use a bite, since I know you haven't eaten since before sunup."

Dalian's stomach chose that moment to growl, and he grinned at Kat, whose face flushed at the implication it was she responsible. She laughed, "Go eat, Dalian. I can't have you passing out from lack of nourishment; and I've already had my soup."

"Mrs. Guthrie, would you mind putting something aside for me? I'll be down in a bit to eat."

"Not at all, Dalian. Can I put something aside for you too, Kat?"

"No thank you, Mrs. Guthrie. Your marvelously delicious soup earlier was very filling."

Mrs. Guthrie blushed, and then turned and left the room. Dalian turned his attention to his foreman. "Well, that just leaves you, old man." Dalian pointed to a seat near the bed and Harvey moved to sit down. "What gives?"

"I talked to the guests. You already know where Cal stands, but I guess the sheriff handled it well enough that none of the others felt their civil rights were trampled on, so I don't foresee any lawsuits in our future. What about you, Miss Chloe? Plan to sue over this little nightmare?"

Chloe laughed softly, "It *would* mean I wouldn't have to try to snare a rich rancher."

"Hmm, good point. Her, we may have to bribe," Harvey said, cocking his head at Chloe.

Dalian grinned, "I guess the biggest concern, besides paying Miss Chloe hush money, is whether the guests feel safe now. Did any express a desire to leave? Request a refund? Other than Cal?"

"Nope, not even Miss Chloe over there."

"You willing to hang around a bit longer, Chloe?" Dalian asked.

"There isn't anyone trying to do away with me, that I'm aware of, so I can't see why I should be concerned about staying. Of course, since Kat managed to snare the only eligible rancher in this county, I may pack up as soon as I'm cleared and head on to the next county. See what sort of men they have over there."

"Hey, hey, hey, what am I, chopped liver?" Harvey retorted playfully.

Kat laughed, "She didn't mean offense, Harvey, but she really meant it when she said she's out to snare a rich rancher, and a rancher owner you aren't," Kat explained and Chloe nodded.

"Well, I run a ranch," Harvey sighed dramatically. "That should count for something. Still, I get it, but you don't know what you're missing out on young lady."

It was Dalian's turn to laugh. "Alright, think we can bring this conversation back on track? Our primary concern should be getting our other guests interested in resuming their vacations. Move forward as though none of this ever happened?"

"That was the other reason I stepped in. I managed to persuade every last one of them of the benefits of keeping preoccupied, while reminding them that no one was going to be left alone to be causing any mischief from this day until the case is solved."

"Thanks Harvey. I certainly couldn't have managed without you."

"That I already knew," Harvey said, and then turned to address Kat. "Like Cal, my manners seem to be lacking today, and I can only blame the hubbub. So, I'll extend my heartfelt commiseration over what happened to you and just say that I'm mighty happy to see you doing much better."

Kat smiled, "Thank you, Harvey, and I completely understand. I'm just glad that everything is turning out for the best; however, the only thing that could truly return things to normal is catching whoever is responsible for this."

"Everybody is definitely working on that. Well, I'd best be seeing to my own lunch. Care to join me, Miss Chloe?"

Chloe appeared reluctant, eyeing Kat with concern. "Want me to leave you alone?"

"Um, Miss Chloe. I'm here, remember?" Dalian laughed at Chloe's look of embarrassment. "She's in safe hands. I promise."

Chloe laughed nervously, and then stood to leave with Harvey.

"I'll check on you later, ok?"

"Thanks, Chloe."

"Try to get some rest," she replied, eyeing Dalian with a 'stop bothering her' look.

When the two left, Kat looked at Dalian, "You know, despite the fact that she gave up on hopes of snaring you, I think she's still a tiny bit jealous that you and I got together."

"She was seriously trying to snare me?" Dalian asked. "Wow, a looker like that! Had I only been more aware...oof...hey...watch where you land those punches, woman!"

"Then watch what you say, mister!"

"I knew she was interested, Kat," Dalian said, scooting to wrap his arms around her. "My radar's not broken, remember? I also have absolutely zero interest."

"I know. She said as much – after a few days of trying to catch your eye. In fact, she was the one that had to point out to me that I was the object of your attention."

"Wow, I knew you'd erected a rather high wall around yourself, but didn't realize it was so high that you couldn't tell I was pursuing you without someone telling you I was."

"I guess after Robert and the kids died, I never thought I'd ever want to find someone again."

"That's how I felt when I lost Carolyn and our baby. But, as I told you a few days ago, I really do believe that time heals the heart. We're entitled to fall in love more than once in our lives. If we weren't, we'd all be miserable and lonely when loss occurred."

"True enough. I'm glad too. Oh, and I really do like the title you came up with for my future book."

"Really?"

"Yeah, very appropriate. Of course, you more like yelled at my heart, than whispered, but . . . hey, at least it listened – finally."

"I wasn't yelling, I was whispering with blaring determination," Dalian growled playfully, grabbing at Kat. "Now, come here. I want to do that ravishing I was denied earlier, before someone else comes knocking on our door. Oh, wait!"

"Where are you going?" Kat asked when Dalian leapt off the bed.

"Putting a 'Do Not Disturb' sign on the door.

CHAPTER THIRTY-FOUR

Dalian slipped from beneath the covers, after both awoke from a leisurely nap. Each had been justifiably exhausted from both the activities of the day and the activities beneath the sheets. He slowly donned his clothes and then tucked the sheet snug around her shoulders, placing a kiss on her smiling mouth.

"I'll have Harvey come up and keep an eye on you while I see about placating the other guests. He may have convinced them not to sue, but it wouldn't do me any harm to show them I care about more than just your wellbeing."

"Well, you just tell Harvey to stay outside of the bedroom, will you, because I fully intend getting out of this bed and taking a nice, long, relaxing shower; then I plan to resume my vacation. I agree with you, though, that it's important to maintain some sort of normalcy while the sheriff conducts his investigation."

Dalian nodded, "We can't let this person get to us. We do, and he wins."

"I'm glad you're here with me. I'm not certain I could face this alone."

"Same here, sweetheart. I'll let Harvey know what you said. I'll be in my office, when you come down, so meet me there. I want you near me at all times. Especially while our attacker is still out there somewhere; and if I don't happen to be available, stick close to Harvey. I may want things to seem normal, but that doesn't mean I want you wandering about alone."

"You don't have to twist my arm."

Dalian stole another quick kiss, and then moved to collect his weapons from the dresser.

"You look more like a cowboy when you're wearing a holstered gun," Kat commented admiringly.

"Think I look serious enough to keep anyone from trying another stunt like they did in the barn?" To lighten the impact of the reminder, Dalian turned and assumed a broadened stance, his fingers twitching at his sides as if he were readying for a showdown at high noon. It had the desired effect. Kat laughed.

"Oh my, I certainly wouldn't want you calling me out for a face-off," Kat said in a more pronounced southern drawl, which made Dalian laugh.

He made for the door, then turned again, "Remember, be certain that you don't go anywhere unescorted, okay?"

"I give you my word," Kat said softly, and then sighed when Dalian left, pulling the door closed behind him. She felt brave when he was near, but the moment he left her side, vulnerability stole into her heart. She didn't like feeling unsafe. She pulled the blanket to her chin and lie there breathing slow and deep, forcing all negative thoughts from her mind. It was a calming technique she employed whenever panic threatened to overtake her.

A light rap sounded at the door, startling her. "Come in," she called, then wanted to retract the invitation. She'd managed to calm her nerves sufficiently from Dalian leaving that it didn't register that the killer could be the one knocking, and she was still lying in bed naked.

The door opened and Achak stuck his head around, "Just wanted to let you know I'm right outside, okay? Harvey was tied up and couldn't get up here. Hope I'll do?"

Kat smiled nervously and sighed in relief. She must have been lying there breathing longer than she realized if Dalian already sent someone up to stand guard at her door. She gave a quick glance at the clock on the nightstand. Ten minutes had passed, leaving her to wonder if she hadn't actually breathed herself back to sleep. She realized that the ranch hand was still standing there watching her, waiting for her to acknowledge him, "Um, I'm sorry; I never can remember your name. It's so unique."

"Yeah, my mom really wanted to go for broke with the Native American theme. I'm Achak Broadwater, and it's nice to meet you again."

"Well, Achak, I appreciate you keeping watch over me. More than you know."

"It's my pleasure. When you're set to head downstairs, I'll escort you to Dalian."

Kat nodded, "I'd like to shower first, if that's not going to keep your from your regular duties."

"My duty is to ensure your safety until I can get you back to Dalian. I'll just be right out here." Achak closed the door behind him. She quickly slid from the bed, moved to the dresser, removed a set of clothes from the top drawer, and laid them on the chair.

She didn't realize the extent of her fears and concerns until she stood beneath the warm spray of water, and the tremors began, intensifying to a ferocity that made her bones clatter. She slid to the floor of the tub and wrapped her arms about her knees. She tried to slow the panic setting in with her breathing, but it wasn't working now, so she let the tears fall unchecked. During this emotional upheaval, awareness surfaced that she had relied upon Dalian's confidence and his strength during this ordeal, when before now, she'd only herself to rely on. She lifted her head and let the water caress her face, as her mind continued its ruminations. How would she have managed to cope had he died in the barn? Would she have had the mental fortitude to continue as if all was well, as she'd been doing when in Dalian's company? She began unspoken supplication, asking the Lord to forgive her weakness of mind and requesting the strength to continue each day unencumbered by fear. Her next thought breached unbidden and she held her breath at the unwelcomed allegation that she'd survived the death of her husband and children with little more than a couple of years sleepless nights and several weeks of shed tears. Why had she felt more capable of dealing with the trauma of that loss than she did now at just the proposition of loss?

Without faltering, an answer found its way into the forefront of her mind. An answer that left her feeling guilty yet simultaneously comforted. She had not been present when that driver killed her family, so felt detached from the tragedy. Moreover, while she loved her children with every fiber of her being, Robert had been more a friend and she did not suffer his loss as she would Dalian's loss. Her children, on the other hand, was a loss she felt deeply and daily. Thinking of them, even a flicker of a moment, made her heart ache painfully with longing for the years she would never have with them and brought tears to her eyes for the times she would never get to shed them in happiness. She lie her head back down on her knees and wept, until her tears were exhausted.

When she was certain she'd regained enough of her composure, she swiped at the tears and stood on legs, shaky from lamentation. She'd have to be stronger if she were going to get through this psychologically whole. Now that she knew how much Dalian really meant to her, she would also be as alert as he in regards to their safety.

CHAPTER THIRTY-FIVE

Why is it that you can't do anything right?

"Oh, yeah, like I deliberately charmed them into following me into Kat's bedroom. You should be saying 'bravo' for giving a credible performance as to why I was there in the first place. You know, sometimes I wish you'd just get out of my head and stay gone."

The voice remained silent, and a sigh escaped; hope flooding throughout that perhaps, for the first time since puberty, individualism would come back. It was too big a hope to have, because a moment after the thought emerged, the voice retorted, tone laced with reprisal and derision. *If I stayed gone, how would you survive, how would you get what you wanted? Your life would be devoid of fun without me, and you certainly wouldn't have the charisma to snare all of those rich spouses.*

"For far less time than I should have, and spouses that you had killed, remember?"

You mean spouses who were getting ready to cut you out of their will because they'd discovered our deceit. They needed to die before we let that happen. If it weren't for me, you'd likely have screwed everything up long ago and ended up sitting in a jail cell for fraud.

"Yeah, well that's better than being on death row for murder."

No one will ever find out what we did, so relax. We can do better for you anyway. We stayed in the wills because of me, and you inherited a nice tidy sum each time.

"Why can't things have been different? Maybe had we stayed with just one, we could have been persuasive enough to stop the changes to the will. I just can't comprehend how killing them was a better option."

That's because you're a dolt. I'm the brains; you're the body. Besides, the people we married didn't appreciate the way we spend money. One was even considering putting you on an allowance. Can you imagine us on an allowance? Where's the fun in that? The one we're after now is plenty wealthy, and if we can get 'em to turn eyes in your direction . . . well, who knows, this may be the one you live with for the remainder of your life. You'd like that wouldn't you?

"Why don't you leave me be now? Now that we botched our plans here, can't we just move on? There are plenty of wealthy people out there looking for a spouse to wed. This one isn't even on the market anymore."

You botched our plans, and since I fancy this one, you'll have to find a way to unbotch it. Besides, have you even seen the person we're interested in? How many people look that good and have money as icing on the cake?

"I just think you're being stubborn now. You know we could probably find someone equally suitable. You just don't like that their attention is focused elsewhere. It's become a challenge for you; so you think it's smart to get rid of that challenge. What if it doesn't work? What if you eliminate the threat and their grief is too great to become interested in you?"

Have you looked at us in the mirror lately? No one in his or her right mind could pass us over.

"And yet we did get overlooked, and that's what's stuck in your craw. That's why you're determined to stay where it's no longer safe; pursuing someone who isn't interested. Maybe if you'd been more assertive and let your attraction show, we wouldn't be in this mess, but no – you had to play it cool; had to think that your looks and your natural allure would be a winning combination unable to be ignored..."

Maybe you're right. We've never had to do more than be in the same room with a potential target to be noticed. This time was different though. The one I was interested in didn't seem to be interested in anyone, and by the time I realized my mistake . . . well, I won't make that same mistake twice.

"You mean you won't let me make that same mistake twice."

Well, I think maybe once the competition is eliminated, we'll have a shot.

"And if we don't?"

No one I've set my sights on has ever turned us down. And neither will this one, or there may very well be a double homicide before we move on.

"I would rather just move on. I'm getting too old for these games anymore. If you'd looked in the mirror with me lately, instead of just shouting at me from it, you'd have noticed that too. It won't be long before we're no longer appealing to the opposite sex; and I'd rather find someone before I'm old and gray, if you don't mind."

Once you're happily wed, I'll see about moving out of the sphere you call a brain. You're getting too argumentative for me anyway. Takes the fun out of my amusing pursuits.

"Fine. What do I need to do to see that happen?" The prospect of getting rid of the voice had a euphoric effect, which made the question more enthusiastic than intended. The voice didn't miss it.

Don't let your eagerness to be rid of me spoil my plans again or I may decide it more beneficial to rid myself of you instead; and while you may be tiring of me, I'm not yet done with you.

"I understand."

Good. Then let's see about getting those two separated, shall we?

"Actually, they already are, remember? I heard that Kat is still in her room and Dalian is downstairs in his study. If you are going to act – I mean, if we are going to act – now is the perfect time. Also, I heard Dalian say that he's going to ride out to check on the cattle soon. It won't be easy to execute, but if your plan is as good as the ones in the past, we have a perfect window of opportunity now."

Glad to see you're back in the game. I was beginning to think you'd gone wishy-washy on me, but I just realized that now is a little too soon to implement what I have in mind. First, I need to find another patsy. I already have someone I think may suit. Still, now would be a good time to take advantage of that excuse you gave earlier for being in their bedroom when you bungled my other plan. It may have been a blunder before, but now that I can use it to our advantage, I'll give you that 'good job' you were panting after a few minutes ago.

CHAPTER THIRTY-SIX

"Ah, there you are, and looking as fresh as a spring daisy, if not a bit red and puffy around the eyes. Are you ok?" Dalian quickly signed off of his chat session, shut down Firefox, and closed the lid on the laptop. He walked over and met Kat halfway with an affectionate embrace.

"Just needed to rid myself of a bit of anxiety," Kat replied, planting a quick kiss on his lips.

"Thank you for keeping an eye on her, Achak."

"No worries, boss. I'll get back to work now. Ma'am," he tipped his hat at Kat and then ducked out of the office.

"You know, Kat, if you ever feel uneasy or sad, or just need to talk, I'm here." Kat nodded and Dalian smiled, then bent to give her a kiss meant to offer comfort and to drive away any remaining anxiety. He broke away only when he heard Harvey clear his throat loudly.

Dalian grinned at Harvey and winked at Kat, "Sorry Harvey, but ever since I managed to break through Kat's wall I can't seem to keep my hands off of her."

"Can't say as I blame you, but if you plan to maul your woman outside your bedroom, you might consider shutting the door first. Anyone could just stroll in here and interrupt you two."

"Like you?" Dalian laughed.

"Yep. Anyhoo, since I'm back now, I can go about tending to the guests, and you can focus on the ranch. Think you can focus on the ranch?" Harvey quipped.

"It won't be easy..."

"I'll keep him on the straight and narrow," Kat interjected and Dalian laughed.

"Already planning to hen-peck me?"

"Only if you get to misbehaving too much."

"Okay you two, let's get back to focusing on something besides each other. Did you have a chance to check in on the guests, Dalian? Everyone still willing to make a go of their remaining time here?"

"Last I heard. The only one ready to bail, as you know, is Cal Withers."

"I was just pondering over that very guest. I expected Chloe to want to leave sooner than Cal Withers bolting. His cowardice shocked me a bit."

"I was thinking along those same lines. Fear making him nauseous? Really? You'd think a man built like that shouldn't fear much of anything."

"Come on, you two," Kat interjected. "Certainly you know that size doesn't equate to courage."

"Maybe not, but it's a rare man that's built like a bull that acts like a sissy and loudly announces that spinelessness to all who'll listen. Most men would rather act strong than admit they ain't."

"And you're as tiny as they come, Kat, and as courageous as five of Cal Withers," Dalian added, causing Kat to blush profusely.

"Ok, ok, before you two start smooching on each other again, I came in to see if you still planning on riding out to check on the cattle?"

"Headed that way now," Dalian said. "I was just waiting on Kat to finish showering to see if she wanted to join me."

Kat smiled, "You bet I do. Can we take a picnic dinner with us?" As with Dalian's enthusiastic greeting, Kat's exuberance had more to do with wanting to feel normal, and wanting to stay near Dalian, than at the actual prospect of having a picnic. Not that the idea of riding with Dalian and spending some time alone . . . Kat's face paled and she swayed slightly.

"Whoa, sweetheart. What's wrong?" Dalian asked, grasping Kat's upper arms firmly.

Kat shook her head and smiled shamefaced, "Sorry, Dalian. I just . . . it's just that I realized we would be alone if we went on a picnic, and I guess the thought jarred me a little."

Dalian moved to a nearby chair, pulling Kat along with him. He lowered into the seat and gently tugged Kat onto his lap, hugging her tight against his chest. After a few moments, he spoke softly, his breath brushing the hair on top of her head, "We are both anxious over what happened, and I think you and I are thinking along the same lines in that we are trying to remain in control of our minds and emotions during this time – which is a good thing. We just have to lean on each other and our friends and have confidence that the sheriff will do everything within his power to catch whoever is trying to harm you or me.

"I am and I do," Kat whispered, "but sometimes the memory of what happened sneaks in and . . . well, I give it the boot as quick as possible."

"I promised to keep you safe, right?" Kat nodded, and Dalian kissed the top of her head. "If I thought I couldn't defend us, I wouldn't take you out with me today. You trust that I will?" Kat nodded again.

"If it helps any," Harvey interjected from across the room, "Dalian's a deadly accurate shot with a firearm."

Kat smiled, sucked in a deep breath, and released it with a whoosh, "I'm okay now. And the thought of a picnic does sound lovely."

"Yes it does," Dalian concurred. "Want to go help Mrs. Guthrie get something ready for us?"

"Yes."

"Good." Kat planted a kiss on Dalian's mouth, and then slid from his lap. "Sure you're okay?" Kat nodded and headed for the kitchen. "Straight to the kitchen, Kat!" Dalian called after her, only realizing that he'd sent her running off unescorted. He turned when one of his ranch hands walked in. "Can you go after Kat?" He asked without preamble. "I would rather she not wander about unaccompanied and I need to have a word with Harvey."

"Sure thing," the ranch hand said, "just wanted to let you know that word has spread about the barn burning, and our neighbors are already spreading word for a barn raising this weekend. If you think that'll work for you. I know we have a lot on our plate right now..."

"No, this weekend sounds great. That will give our guests another aspect of ranch life to try out; another way to keep them all distracted. Thanks, Mitch, and relay my agreement and thanks to our neighbors after I relieve you of watching over Kat. She's in the kitchen."

Mitch nodded and took off for the kitchen. Dalian turned back to Harvey and quirked his brow at the look in his foreman's eyes. "What's on your mind, old man?"

"We could have gone after her, you know."

"I know. I am just trying for a sense of routine here, Harvey. I hover over her too much, and it'll likely drive her nuts. I want her to feel at home here, not as if she's trapped in a prison. God, all I want is our lives back."

"She looks like she's holding it together pretty good. A lot of women would have gone into full meltdown and stayed a puddle of goo until their attacker was safely behind bars. You're a lucky man, Dalian."

Dalian nodded, "Yeah, but right now I feel like I've got luck on one side and ill-fortune on the other."

"You shouldn't think like that."

Dalian moved to settle behind his desk, running his hands through his hair. He was tired and worried, although he did his utmost to hide it. He couldn't hide it from Harvey though.

"Everything will be right as rain before too much longer, Dalian. You know the sheriff is going to do everything humanly possible to see your attacker brought to justice."

"I know. If I didn't believe it, I wouldn't have told Kat that.

"Still, despite what I said about being a good shot, I can't say as I think traipsing about with Kat after the cattle and having a leisurely picnic is the safest course of action for you to be taking right now. Kat had every reason to be worried."

"It goes back to being as normal as possible. The more I focus on routine, the less anxious I'm likely to be over everything that's transpired."

"The less you focus on what's happening, the less you'll be on your toes and able to head off another attack. Still, if you want to head out on the range, why not take someone along to act as protection. Someone who isn't likely to keep their eyes solely on Kat."

"I'll have my rifle with me."

"Yeah, but your focus won't be on potential danger."

Dalian's face reddened beneath his tan and he smiled wryly, "You make a good point, old man, but what I plan to do with Kat out on the range, I don't want no ranch hand getting a peek at."

It was Harvey's turn to turn crimson, and he laughed, "Good point. Just keep that rifle handy so that you can get at it quick-like if needed."

"That's my intent."

Harvey nodded. "I'll see your horses saddled, and then get the guests engaged in some sort of activity."

"Thanks again for everything, Harvey."

"Not a problem. Just be safe out there."

CHAPTER THIRTY-SEVEN

"Is this what your life is like all the time?" Kat asked, as they rode from the house and headed out toward what Dalian called 'the range'.

"Minus people trying to kill me, yeah," Dalian grinned, and Kat laughed. "Think you can live with that?"

"Minus the people trying to kill us, yeah."

"Well, that and knowing there will be many a days where I'll be gone for hours at a time, tending to the cattle; and that I'll be gone for upwards of two months when it's time to drive them to market?"

Kat smiled. Love swelled throughout her at this simplest of conversations; knowing that Dalian and she were truly planning a life together gave her hope for a future that she hadn't felt in over two years. "Well, if you can live with the fact that I'll stay burrowed in a room pecking away at a computer for hours on end, then I can handle you being gone for hours on end. I'd miss you when you're gone, but I'll have plenty with which to keep myself preoccupied."

Dalian pulled on the reins and halted his horse, turning it around so that his stallion stood in close proximity to her mare, "Does that mean you're really willing to marry me, Kat? That you're willing to uproot to way out here and be my wife?"

"Well, this is about as far from civilization as I ever imagined being. A lot different from Covington, that's for sure. Still, I watched my hometown turn from a small community into a booming little metropolis over a few decades and have to confess I was tiring of it pretty quickly. I find this preferable somehow. I kind of said all of that to say that, yes, I would be more than willing."

"Glad to hear it." Dalian flung his leg over his horse's rump and dismounted, moving to Kat's side to assist her in dismounting. "Is this

211

where we're having our picnic?" Kat slid from her horse into Dalian's embrace. "We didn't get very far from the house, and we haven't even checked on the cattle yet."

"No, we have a ways to ride before we stop for dinner, and yes, we have to check on the cattle before we eat, but this is what I consider a perfect place for this." Dalian reached into his pocket and then bent onto one knee. Kat's eyes widened and tears welled in her eyes. She immediately knew what he was planning, but never imagined he would propose so formally, especially not after his less-than-formal declaration in bed the day before.

Dalian reached for her hand and kissed the palm softly before looking up at her, "Thank you for coming into my life, Kathryn McMurray. For proving to me that there can be love after tragedy; and for showing me that hope does spring eternal. I guessed already that you've consented to being my wife, but I have to ask just the same. Will—"

"Yes!" Kat dropped to her knees and wrapped her arms around Dalian's neck, hugging him tightly. She pulled him down until his lips met hers and gave him a yes to remember.

Dalian laughed when he finally broke the kiss, "You didn't even let me get around to asking the actual question. What if I was going to say, 'will you consider shacking up with me for the next...oof...hey, watch where you land those punches, woman."

Kat laughed and hugged him again, "Were you going to ask me to shack up with you?" She whispered near his ear.

"I wouldn't in a million years insult you in such a manner." He pulled back so he could look into her eyes. "Think I could put this ring on your finger now?"

"I get a ring too?"

"Ha ha. Cute." He picked up her hand and slid a simple-setting diamond and sapphire ring onto her ring finger.

"Sapphires are my favorite stone. My birthstone too. How did you know?"

Dalian grinned, "I actually got in touch with your publisher. You haven't mentioned her much, but you did say she was your best friend too. If anyone would know what type of ring you preferred, I figured she would. She's a pistol, but was thrilled to hear that you'd finally found someone new. Of course, the exact phrase she used was 'got yourself laid'...hey, I didn't say it, she did." Dalian rubbed his arm from where Kat landed yet another smack.

"Yes, but you repeated it," Kat grinned. "I'm glad she's happy for me. I should have thought to contact her myself, but there's been so much happening. I think I was a bit worried too that she'd be worried about my moving so far away."

"Actually, there was a rather extended monologue about having to cancel tour dates and reschedule out here and about maybe you telling her of your plans in advance before she makes plans. Then she got around to actually conversing. Asked whether I planned to let you keep writing, and wanted to know the reliability of our internet access out here in the boonies, despite my having been in touch with her via that very internet."

Kat laughed. "That sounds like Janet. Hey! When did you get this ring? When have you had time? We've had so much happening this past week–"

"Janet helped there too," Dalian replied sheepishly.

"You've lost me."

"Well, like I said, I've been in daily touch with her. She's been ring

213

hunting since the day I brought you home from the hospital...says she's happy that you're okay, by the way. Of course, her exact words there were that she didn't want to have to 'come out here and open up a can of whoop ass on somebody'. You Southerners do have a way of expressing yourselves, don't you?"

"Got that straight!"

"Anyway, once we found a ring we thought you'd like, she overnighted it to me. It arrived this morning. She said to keep her apprised of the wedding plans and she'll make certain she makes it out here on time."

"Oh Dalian, thank you for this. For everything. I know we've been going through Hell this past week, but you have a way of making me feel safe despite it all."

"Well, you know how that old country favorite goes, don't you?"

"There are quite a few old country favorites, goose."

Dalian laughed, stood, and reached down to help her up. "The one by Rodney Atkins."

"Wow, there's a singer who goes back about a dozen decades. I know him though. Which song were you talking about?"

Dalian grinned, and then, in a surprisingly good singing voice, broke into song while helping her mount, "If you're going through Hell, keep on going, don't slow down, if you're scared don't show it, you might get out 'fore the devil even knows you're there...[2]

Kat laughed, but then decided to join in; and soon the sound of their voices echoed across the grassland as they rode along to check on

_____

[2] *If you're going through Hell*, Rodney Atkins. Curb Records 2006.

the cattle.

CHAPTER THIRTY-EIGHT

"How do you keep up with where your cattle are? Didn't you say once that you have over two hundred acres of land? Yet you somehow managed to bring us straight to them – almost anyway."

"No big secret. I radioed ahead and one of my men gave the approximate location of each herd. If you look over yonder a bit, you'll see a couple of my men keeping watch over this herd." Dalian lifted his hand and waved, and Kat saw in the far distance a return wave.

"That's impressive, but you still have two hundred acres . . . I guess what I'm asking is, how do you know precisely where we are? When you radioed ahead, did your employee say 'look for the lone tree next to the short snow-covered peak'?"

Dalian laughed. "Not quite. Harvey and I sectioned off the land into eight twenty-five acre plots. Each one of those is broken down into coordinates so that we can easily maneuver around as needed. So, we have two herds. We rotate them between those sections, giving the grass and plants in each alternate section plenty of time to revivify and flourish. At any given time, several of my men are out here keeping an eye on them – tending to injuries, corralling strays, assisting in deliveries in the spring, and warding off predators – the two greatest of which are wolves and bears. If I need to find them, they just tell me the approximate coordinates in whichever plot the cattle are occupying."

"Wow, I have to admit it's all very impressive. It must keep you very busy indeed."

"Takes up a considerable part of my days, yes. Still willing to marry me?"

"I'll think about it," Kat quipped. "If this takes up so much of your time, why run a dude ranch during the spring and summer? I'd think that would be a big hassle."

"I've been running this ranch for some years now. I can't imagine doing anything else. Unfortunately, there are times when caring for the cattle costs more than my herd can fetch at market; a market that fluctuates based on the eating habits of the populace in a given year. Remember back in 2035, there was a big push to eliminate beef from the American diet altogether? I nearly lost the ranch that year. If it weren't for the dude ranch business and governmental subsidies, we wouldn't be here now. Thank the good Lord above people's eating habits are as changing as the weather. You aren't a vegetarian, are you?" Dalian's question was asked with a nose crinkled in mock antipathy and Kat laughed.

"Not on your life! I'll take a tender Ribeye any day of the week, but I like a flaky Tilapia filet just as often. I guess balance is the key."

"And you certainly are well balanced." The tone of Dalian's voice and the sweep of his gaze appreciatively over her body, made Kat flush. Dalian grinned and then gave Swift a firm 'whoa'.

"We're nearly there, but I just thought we'd stop down below at the river and let the horses get a drink," He said, and Kat's focus shifted from thoughts of Dalian's lovemaking to the breathtaking scenery surrounding her. Dalian had ridden from the valley into a section of Wind River Canyon. The dissimilarity between the valley in which his ranch lie situated and where they sat atop their horses now, was stunning. To their right was a small crystal-clear river snaking its way through a ravine of virtually sheer canyon walls. On either side of the river, wild grasses grew amidst boulders half the size of her previously-owned Honda Fit Hybrid.

"I love nature." Kat's tone held an awe, which made Dalian glance about. He had lived here for so long, he sometimes failed to realize the impact its splendor had on others. "There isn't anything like this back where I'm from. Growing up, if we ever wanted to see impressive canyons like this, we always assumed we'd have to take a road trip to

Arizona. Oh, but don't get me wrong, we have some really amazing places back east, like Stone Mountain, the Appalachians, and if we want to head north a short spell, there's the Great Smokies, and Ruby Falls, but...wow, nothing like this. It's gorgeous."

"No, sweetheart. This is majestic. You're gorgeous." Dalian laughed at her shy reaction, and then leaned over and planted a quick kiss on her mouth. "Come on. We're nearly there. Be careful wending your way through. Let the horse take the lead so we don't have to worry about surefootedness and you taking a tumble into the river. It's only April, so it will be months before that water rises above frigid."

Kat nodded and soon they were ascending to a small ridge on the top of which was a gully of emerald, springy grass. "Is this it? Where we're going to picnic?" Kat asked enthusiastically.

The moment Dalian said yes, Kat dismounted with eagerness and dashed over to the rock wall situated atop the ledge of the cliff face. With cautious exuberance, she leaned over the top and glanced down at the way in which they'd climbed. It hadn't been a steep or lengthy ascent, but the river below seemed much smaller than when they'd ridden beside it. The view from above was even more breathtaking to her than when she'd been down in the ravine. "Oh, Dalian, promise me we can come here a lot."

"As this is one of my favorite places to come, that shouldn't be too difficult a promise to make and keep. Most times though, the weather doesn't clear up here until June. We got lucky this year. Fair weather started early. I guess you brought the sunshine with you when you came. I know you brightened up my life." Dalian walked up behind Kat and wrapped his arms about her waist, pulling her flush against him. "Look up there." He pointed to a bald eagle soaring above the canyon.

Kat sighed, "I've never seen one so close before. Now that's majestic and gorgeous."

"Can't argue with that zeal," Dalian laughed, and turned Kat into his embrace. "I have a confession to make," He whispered, lowering his mouth to brush lightly against her lips. She felt the warmth of his breath as he whispered his confession. "When I brought you out here today, my intentions were anything but honorable."

"Is that a fact?" Kat breathed in reply.

Dalian grinned, "Yes ma'am. In fact, I'd say my thoughts right now are downright impure."

"That's okay. Mine aren't exactly wholesome. Make love to me, Dalian."

"A stampede couldn't stop me," Dalian whispered, and then claimed her mouth in a soul-searing kiss.

CHAPTER THIRTY-NINE

Cal Withers opportunely disregarded the sheriff's request to remain on the ranch just one more day, until fingerprint clearances came through. Dalian had instructed him to request the rental be dropped off in the evening, but he'd conveniently forgotten that detail, and asked that it be dropped off as early in the a.m. as was possible, which they did. If he'd rented a car at the airport, instead of using the shuttle service offered by the dude ranch, he would have been able to leave sooner; but they'd requested that people not drive in since parking was limited.

The rental agent from Enterprise had him look over the vehicle and then sign the documentation. As soon as that was tended to, he quickly packed up his clothing and supplies and began loading it into the trunk. One promise he was able to keep was that he'd leave unnoticed, but that was only because Harvey had the remaining guests out back assisting with clearing away the burned out barn in preparation of the barn raising the next day. *Some vacation activity that is,* he thought, tossing his last piece of luggage in the Dodge Charger.

After a quick inventory of his room, he loaded himself into the car, and then drove out of the main gate, a swarm of reporters attempting to stick microphones into the opening of his window. He would have pressed the accelerator and gunned it out of the drive in order to get past the annoying questions, but they surrounded his vehicle like an army of ants. When he persisted in inching forward, the mob finally parted, and Cal accelerated quickly, glad to put The Heart of the Mountain Dude Ranch in his rearview mirror.

About forty-five minutes later, he pulled onto 2nd Street in the ramshackle town of Shoshoni, parked his car, and walked straight into the Cactus Plains Motel. It was as rundown as the scarcely populated town surrounding it, but he wasn't planning to stay long. Despite his promise to the sheriff, he only had one purpose for leaving the dude ranch – minus getting some lunch.

A third tap on the bell sitting atop the peeling linoleum countertop brought an elderly woman from behind a closed door. "You would like a room?" She queried, her voice raspy from what could be age or a recent tracheotomy, a supposition supported by the bandage covering the area of her windpipe. Either way, her outward appearance was even less appealing than the stained carpet lining the foyer, which made him wonder why tourists ever bothered to stop in here on their way to Yellowstone. He wouldn't be here at all were it not out of necessity. Her next comment lent understanding to his unvoiced musings. "Most people do not stop here when motel row is just about 20 miles southwest from here. So what brings you?"

"Oh, I was actually heading for my motel when I realized that I was running real low on gas, so thought I would stop in and ask for directions to the nearest station."

The old woman quirked her brow, disbelief written on her features. She knew he was lying, but a shrug of her shoulders declared her disinterest, "If you came in on 26, you passed a few gas stations, and you will find more on your way out of Shoshoni." Her thick accent spoke of the purity of her native blood, but just as she was disinterested in his lies, he could care less about her heritage – or the fact that he could help her out quite a lot financially if he did choose to stay in that particular flea motel.

"I'll keep a better look out, but just for my edification, are there any decent places left in this town that serve a hearty meal?"

Her brow quirked again and she snorted, "You might want to wait until you get to your motel to find good food."

"Wait," Cal called, when she turned to leave, "what about a gun store? You have one around here, right?" Other than the Enterprise rental business, Cal had done some additional surfing online – first, to determine the gun laws in Wyoming, which were surprisingly lenient; also to find a gun store in a town that was more concerned with the dollar than his purpose for needing a weapon. He could have driven around until he located it, but he was far too lazy and in too big a hurry to waste his time.

The old woman's brow quirked again, but this time a knowing gleam lit the dark pupils in her eyes. She nodded slightly and cocked her head, indicating he go right, "If it is still in business, there is one on Pine Street, but I do not recall the name." She turned to leave again, but again Cal bade her wait.

"Um, I really hate to be a bother, but could you give me an idea where Pine Street is located? I'm afraid my GPS isn't functioning in my rental car."

"It run out of gas too?"

Cal blushed, but decided not to reply. The woman eyed him for a few minutes more before speaking again, "Turn right out of the parking lot. Stay on 2nd Street. You will see Pine Street a few miles down to your right. Take Pine until you are close to 5th Street. Are those good enough directions for you?"

"I appreciate your time, ma'am."

"Enough to pay for it?" The woman snorted again.

Cal pulled out his wallet and threw two fifties on the counter, "You have a nice day, ya hear?" He turned and walked from the building, leaving an old native woman standing there wondering who was going to die.

CHAPTER FORTY

"Good morning everyone," Dalian called as he strolled into the dining room early the next morning, his gait as light and cheery as his disposition. "I understand I owe each of you a debt of gratitude." Forks lowered at his declaration, and all gazes turned in his direction. "Harvey tells me that you folks spent the better part of yesterday clearing out the rumble, while I was out on the range tending to my...cattle." No one but Harvey caught the pause in that explanation, and he quirked a brow at his friend. Cattle my eye, he thought with a smirk. "Anyway, if you folks are able and willing to help a bit more, we'll be raising us a new barn this morning, with the help of my neighbors. That's one of the elements of my life I appreciate more than most – the willingness of a neighbor to help another. We have some mighty fine people living around here that you are going to have the pleasure of meeting and working with today. Now, bear in mind, that this isn't necessarily what you signed on for, so you aren't under any obligation to assist, but many of you came out here because you wanted to experience what this sort of life is genuinely like. Well, building and repairing our buildings is a daily part of living. And if you need incentive to work today, well our women folk get together to ensure that we men get fed a hearty meal that you can rest assured will be some mighty good eating. And there's bound to be some fresh-baked homemade pies for dessert." Murmurs of appreciation sounded at that announcement and Dalian grinned. *Yep,* he thought, *men everywhere are pretty much the same. Mention food, sex, or money and you can get them to do about anything.* "And before you go fretting, Miss Chloe, I'm not going to be asking you or Kat to pick up a hammer today, unless you want to; but you're mighty welcome to help Mrs. Guthrie and the neighbor women in the kitchen. That, too, is optional. That's what Kat said she's gonna do."

"That sounds more my speed, for certain," Chloe said, sighing in relief. "And Dalian, I know you and Harvey are doing everything humanly possible to keep our minds off of what happened to you and Kat, and we appreciate that, but has there been any further news from the sheriff's office? Weren't you supposed to hear something sometime today?"

"I expect to be hearing something from the sheriff this morning, or early afternoon at the latest, but what I don't expect is that he'll have anything negative to say about any of you. After all, I can't see that any of you have acted in a suspicious nature." Dalian heard murmurs of concurrence, and suddenly appreciated that his assertion comforted him also. Not one person seated in his dining room had been enraged at having their lives turned topsy turvy, had objected overly much at being named a person of interest; had, in fact, worked in concert with Dalian, Harvey, and the sheriff to see things returned to routine as quickly as possible. Each person could have demanded a refund and an end to their vacation, but not one had – except for Cal Withers. It gave him hope for humanity. In fact, he could not recall a time in recent history when turbulence and joy concurrently filled his life. The sense of serenity faded as his ponderings concluded with a 'yeah, but there is still someone out there who's determined to do you or Kat harm. And if not one of these people, then who?' thought.

He sighed and looked at Harvey, who quickly read the worry in Dalian's eyes. He stood, "Well, folks, if any of you are willing to get a little sweaty and dirty, we'll be starting on that barn in about an hour. In the meantime, eat up. You're gonna need your energy. If you simply wish to swim, or ride horses, we'll have a few men who'll be hanging back to assist with anything you need. Remember, you're never under any obligation to do anything you don't wish to do. This is, after all, your vacations."

As soon as everyone refocused on his or her meal, Harvey made his way over to Dalian, "You alright?"

"I don't know. At times, it's easy to forget what happened earlier in the week, and at other times, I feel as if there is a boogie man just in the shadows waiting to catch Kat or me unawares. It's no way to live, old man."

"I agree, and I certainly admire your attempts to keep things running as routine as possible while the sheriff conducts his investigation. Keeping busy is one of the better ways in which to keep thoughts from running amok, that's for certain. Why don't you give the sheriff a call and see if he has any comfort to give? I'm especially curious to know if he turned up anything on Mr. Cal Withers."

"I was considering giving him a call, but then decided to wait. He's got a lot of information to wade through and doesn't need me harping at him. So, what makes you say that about Cal?"

"Didn't notice Cal isn't among the guests this morning? Mrs. Guthrie said the rooster had only just signaled a start to the day when he was loading up his stuff and driving off. Apparently, the sheriff's request that he wait here until fingerprint clearance was issued didn't sink in deep enough. Makes a body wonder as to what secrets he's running from."

Dalian scanned the faces of his guests, but didn't spot Cal. For the second time in a twenty-four hour span, his curiosity over Cal's behavior was piqued. First, he acts contrary to a man of his dimensions, and then he bolts against the advice of law enforcement. Both, characteristics of a person with something to hide. "Could he be the assailant?" He asked Harvey. "But, if he is, what is his motivation?"

"I don't know whether he is or not, but his behavior is seriously contradictory."

"I can't argue that. Still, it could be simply that he's behind on child support or something like that. You know how I feel about jumping to conclusions."

"Yeah, a person jumping to conclusions is likely to jump into an unseen pile of dung."

225

"Yep, still, it might be best to inform the sheriff of his early departure. See what he has to say about it. Of course, I don't like to borrow trouble. Could be the man really is a coward in a body-builder's physique. Being physically fit doesn't automatically equate a person with bravery."

Harvey sighed, "True enough, and if I was to be honest about it, there didn't seem to be anything off about him. He seemed like a regular Joe Blow; a bit jealous over your relationship with Kat, but I can't say as I blame him for that. Being jealous doesn't mean being willing to kill. I mean, look at Marsha and Chloe. Both women would jump into bed with you with just a crook of your finger, but neither would kill another woman just to get there."

"True, maybe, not that we really know; although I still have my doubts about both women's mental stability. Just as I don't really know what Chloe and Marsha are capable of, I don't really know enough about Cal to make any sort of assessment. It does make you wonder though. I mean, being a regular Joe Blow doesn't preclude violent tendencies. Everyone probably said that David Berkowitz, Carroll Cole, Ted Bundy, Jeffrey Dahmer, and others like them, were just regular guys – and now I'm just psyching myself out."

"Yeah, you're psyching me out too with your eerie knowledge of so many serial killers. I've known you the better part of twenty years, and didn't realize you had that level of fascination with the macabre."

Dalian laughed, "There's a lot you don't know about me, old man."

"Obviously. So, you definitely planning to help with the barn today? Or do you and Kat have another picnic planned?" Harvey asked with a wink of the eye.

Dalian grinned, "I'd like nothing better than a repeat of yesterday, but no, I plan to help out with the barn, which means I'd better get some food in me before it's all gone. You eaten yet?"

"Nope, and I just realized that Kat isn't around. She isn't alone is she? She planning to eat breakfast?"

"I left her in the kitchen with Mrs. Guthrie. They're planning to eat while they bake. Apparently they anticipate feeding an army."

"Well, if past experience is any indicator, they probably will be," Harvey quipped.

"As soon as neighbors start arriving, there will be loads of additional help for her and Mrs. Guthrie. It'll be nice for Kat to get to meet the neighbors, since they'll be her neighbor too before much longer."

"Did I just hear you correct? You proposed?"

"Don't tell me that you missed that rock on her ring finger."

"Nah, I saw it. Just thought you might want to tell me instead of me just bringing it up, at meal time or some such."

The two men continued their amiable discussion as they piled food high atop their plates and settled in to eat.

CHAPTER FORTY-ONE

Cal slowed his speed as he approached the front gate of The Heart of the Mountain Dude Ranch, but his pulse refused to slow. As when he left, the horde of reporters converged on his car when each realized his destination was the ranch. He sighed heavily and pulled to a stop at the gate, delighted that law enforcement prohibited the nosy journalists sticking microphones in his window. He took a deep breath and affected a calm demeanor when the police officer approached.

"Mr. Withers, isn't it? We were under the impression you didn't intend to return."

"I wasn't planning to, but I left some personal items in my room in my haste to depart. I need to get them." In fact, he'd deliberately left a dirty shirt in the hamper and his razor on the counter. He knew his return might cast suspicion and needed a good reason should suspicion be aimed in his direction.

"Not a problem." The officer nodded at the other officer, manning the entrance to the main drive. With a return nod, the officer opened the immense gate and swung it open, just wide enough for Cal to slip past the wrought iron without scratching the gray paint on his rental car. He waited until he rounded the first bend in the drive, when he was certain he was out of sight of both the main gate and the main house, and then turned off onto one of the many paths used by both guests and maintenance vehicles. He hadn't thought much about these off roads on his first trek up this drive; however, when he'd spotted it on his way out – or rather when his constant mental companion noticed it – it became part of the plan. The objective at this point, was to wend around without a ranch hand or guest spotting him, and find a location in which to hide the car. A place that he could easily access for a quick escape, once he executed his cerebral collaborator's plan.

There! His mind shouted so loudly that he instinctively stomped on the brake.

"Would you mind not screaming inside my head like that? Especially when "there" doesn't do me a bit of good. Where is there?"

If you kept your eyes opened as well as I do, I wouldn't have to shout, and if you'd just turn your head to the right, you'll see the there to which I'm referring.

Cal saw the space between the shrub grasses, backed up a short bit, and then turned the wheel to the right. "I only hope the car doesn't get bogged down in something, or that we don't wind up in a ditch," He muttered beneath his breath. He winced as he heard the branches of bushes scratch at the car's surface. He imagined they were the tiny fingers of demons taunting him; waiting to haul him off to Hell for allowing his mind control over his actions. Of course, he'd allowed that control for the better part of twenty years, so why he suddenly felt apprehensive over his mind's actions was beyond his comprehension. "Maybe because you never played this sort of game before. Pitting your charm and looks against another. Having to commit murder to get a person's interest."

No, you just committed murder when it was time to move on to another target. Now stop mewling like a banshee and man up.

"I wish you'd stop talking as if I were the only one to kill those people–"

You were.

"Yeah but you're the one that decided it was time to kill them."

It was. Stop here.

Cal obeyed as he'd done his entire life – with a sigh of resignation, growing agitation, and renewed desire for a return of individualism. If he had any courage at all, he would kick the voice out of his head, but he knew it was more than just a lack of bravery, it also had to do with a lack of knowledge, and, admittedly, a small measure of gratification. He neither knew how to get rid of the voice in his head, nor knew how to live a life without it. The voice was right, without it, his life would have been ho-hum, lacking excitement and wealth. Or would it? Did he only believe that because the voice made him believe it?

You seem to have forgotten that I can hear your thoughts. The voice said in a contemptuous manner. *You are beginning to doubt the benefit of our symbiosis. Perhaps I'll just leave now and let you explain your way out of all of this yourself. Explain why you left against the sheriff's dictate, why you are carrying a gun in the car, why you're creeping about in the bushes . . .*

"No! Stop! I'll curb my thoughts."

Without me, you're nothing. You'd have nothing. Say it!

"My life would be nothing without you."

And you best not forget again, that the only thoughts you're permitted are those that I give you.

"I understand."

Good. Get out of the car, collect the gun, and let's get into position. I'll be damned if I'm going to let someone take what I want.

CHAPTER FORTY-TWO

It was noon, and Dalian felt a sense of gratitude sweep across his mind – for the progress made on the barn, for the breeze that kept the late April air fresh and cool, and for the hard work of neighbor and guest. Many of his guests had never wielded a hammer or saw, but that didn't stop them seeking assistance and applying direction with fervency. One guest even commented in passing that he felt like a bona fide member of Dalian's ranch.

With so much assistance, the barn's frame had been erected and the roof was well underway by the time that Mrs. Guthrie announced lunchtime via the bell hanging on the porch. Dalian grinned as each person immediately dropped his tools and made a mad dash over to where two lengthy tables had been set up, each laden with mounds of food, dessert, and freshly brewed iced tea. He glanced at the faces of each, as he settled with a plate at the head of the table. Enthusiasm shone in their gazes and zeal in their mannerisms, but he knew full well that, come nightfall, each would collapse into bed with exhaustion his only companion.

He pulled his cell from his pocket, only just realizing that he'd not heard from the sheriff, because he'd forgotten to turn the ringer up on the phone. The sheriff had called an hour earlier. Dalian dialed his voice mail and listened to the message. He spied Kat exiting the back door, with a tray full of ham steak, and smiled at her disheveled appearance. Tendrils of hair had fallen free from the loosely piled mass atop her head; moreover, flour coated the front of her apron and a streak smeared her forehead. She looked adorable.

She placed the tray on the remaining empty spot on the table and then made her way over to where Dalian sat.

"Would you like a piece of ham steak, before it's all gone?" She asked, and then realized he had the phone to his ear. "Oh, sorry," she whispered, and then settled on the bench next to him. After a moment, he lowered the phone, and leaned over and planted a kiss on her lips.

"Everything okay?" She asked immediately.

"That was a message from the sheriff. He didn't say much. Only that he was finalizing the last of the reports and would be driving out here . . . well, he should be here shortly."

"I hope he has some good news to impart."

"You and me both, sweetheart. Now, what was it you asked before you sat down?"

"Oh, um, I just wanted to know if you're set for food, or if you wanted a slice of the ham steak I just brought out?"

"Nah, this vulture descended on the beef steak first thing, so I'm set. Um, sweetheart, I don't want you to take offense if my attention is less on you and more on my stomach right now. I'm famished."

Kat grinned, "No offense taken. I'm rather hungry myself." With a grin of appreciation, Dalian stabbed at his mashed potatoes and gravy and gave a long drawn out moan of satisfaction as he savored that first bite. Kat laughed, "I'd better go retrieve a plate. You're moans are making me famished."

She stood and grabbed a plate of food and then settled back down next to Dalian. With deliberate drama, she took a bite of her baked chicken breast and mimicked Dalian's satiated reaction. He laughed at her dramatic delivery, and nearly choked on his second bit of mashed potatoes.

"Sorry, baby, I didn't mean to make you choke. Are you okay?"

"Wrong pipe," Dalian wheezed and after several effective coughs, dislodged the food from his windpipe.

"You alright down there?" Harvey called from the other end of the table.

Dalian nodded, lifted his cup in a salute, and then downed half the glass.

When Kat was satisfied that Dalian wouldn't choke to death, she returned to her meal, and deftly consumed every bite. She wiped the crumbs of the biscuit off her fingers and took a sip of her tea before turning to converse with Dalian again, "I never realized that cooking for so many was such a chore. I know it isn't as difficult as raising a barn, but it definitely ranks a close second in exhaustive undertakings."

"I don't doubt it, and you ladies outdid yourselves, for certain. The food is delicious."

"Thank you kindly."

"You're mighty welcome."

"So how much longer do you think it will take to finish the barn?"

Dalian swallowed his food and downed a gulp of tea before responding, "With the way everyone is moving, we should be done before dinner." Dalian saw the look of relief pass over her features and laughed, "Worried you'll have to make another substantial meal so soon?"

Kat grinned sheepishly, "A little, but if it'll help in not having to, I'll gladly pick up a hammer and start helping."

"Don't worry sweetheart. We'll have it completed early enough, and if anyone is hungry afterward, there is bound to be a few leftovers to eat."

Kat looked at the dwindling supply of food dubiously. "I don't know about that. Everyone seems mighty hungry."

"No worries. Harvey will prevent going back for seconds–"

"Folks!" Harvey called, standing to address the group and Dalian quirked a "told you so" look at Kat. "I hope everyone got enough to fill their bellies. I know that you probably could eat until you drop, but if you did that, you wouldn't be fit for finishing up the barn today. Rest assured that the food isn't going anywhere, so as soon as we put the last plank in place, we can all return to the table and eat our fill. However, right now, we all need to finish up what's on our plates and head back on over to the barn to continue working. Take your time though. We want you to finish up the food in front of you, and I know that not everyone has a vacuum for a mouth like me."

"Amen to that!" Dalian shouted, and everyone laughed.

"You do too," Harvey rejoined, "so you hardly have room to mock."

"Touché, my friend." Dalian lifted his glass of tea in a salute, and then stood. "In fact, I'm probably as ready as you are to head back to work."

Harvey picked up his plate so everyone could see how clean it was, and grinned, color seeping into his cheeks from the laughs, "Hardly anyone can out eat me, or eat as fast – except maybe you."

"Can't argue with that," Dalian agreed, lifting his own clean plate to the amusement of everyone seated, "but as Harvey said, take your time. Just make your way over as you finish. There are trash bins set out near the side of the house that you can deposit your plates into, so please take advantage of them."

Everyone returned to their meals and Dalian returned his attention to Kat, "I'm going to get back to it, okay?"

"Anything I can do to speed things along?"

"You ladies have done your part, so you relax and let us finish the barn. I don't want to alarm you, but you'll have plenty to keep yourselves preoccupied with when we finish."

Kat's gaze widened, "You may not have meant to alarm me, but when you start a sentence like that..."

Dalian laughed, "It's just that...well, now that the cooking is done, you ladies get to tackle the cleanup."

"Eww, yuck." Kat looked at all of the dishes lining the table, some still half full of food, and winced. It should have registered when they were cooking and baking that there would be a ton of dishes to wash, but it hadn't; however, now it did, and she wasn't looking forward to it.

Dalian laughed again, this time at the mortified expression on Kat's face, "Oh my! I can't do it!"

"Do what?"

"Tease you about this. It just so happens that I bought Mrs. Guthrie a brand new 2057 Hobart CZ970 industrial-size dishwashing unit a few years back to prevent her having to wash so many dishes during times like this, when the ranch is swarming with people. Clean up will take you ladies less than half hour, tops."

"Oh, that was a cold-hearted thing to do, Dalian Rivers," Kat growled in mock displeasure. "Just for that, I may decide to withhold that slice of cherry pie you've been eyeballing since you sat down at the table – and don't try to deny it! It wasn't your steak that was distracting you from me, it was dessert."

Dalian swept Kat into his embrace and gave her a thorough kiss, and then whispered sincerely, "There isn't a dessert on this planet that is as sweet as you, or one I would rather eat."

Kat was about to respond, when she suddenly stiffened and cried out in pain. Everyone, but the embracing couple, reacted swiftly to the discharge of gunfire. It wasn't until Kat swayed into Dalian, her gaze wide-eyed and filled with disbelief, than the two lovers realized what had happened. Harvey shouted for someone to find a police officer and to call the paramedics, but to Kat and Dalian, his pleas sounded far away and muffled. Kat slowly drifted to the ground, a stunned and disbelieving Dalian clasping her tightly in his embrace.

CHAPTER FORTY-THREE

We're done!

That one short phrase, uttered with such urgency, and dripping with revulsion, should have spurred Cal into motion, but it didn't. Instead, he sat stunned that he'd not only failed again, but that he'd again injured the wrong person. "To my credit," he muttered dejectedly, "I did try to tell you that it was simply too far a shot for this caliber weapon."

Get up, you imbecile! It won't take them long to determine the trajectory of the bullet and to descend on our location.

"You sound scared," Cal taunted. "Why would you be scared? You always have a plan, don't you?"

A plan that you continually mess up, and that you're about to botch again. Now get up. We have to get to the house.

Cal laughed, "You're mad. That's like stepping into a viper's nest."

We need to plant this gun in Chloe's room. She's been after Dalian, so the assault on Kat will give the sheriff the motive, and we'll provide the means. Once we've slipped the gun in among her possessions, we'll dash out the front door, as if we heard the shots fired and are coming to check. If anyone asks about why you're back, the police officer at the front gate will substantiate your statement about forgetting some things. Since suspicion will be deflected away from you again, we'll ride out the investigation and leave with the rest of the group; however, my plan will fail and you'll be caught if you don't get up and move now.

"First I want to know what you meant when you said 'we're done'. Did you mean that we'd leave and forget all about this woman? Find someone else to target?"

Sure. That's precisely what 'we're done' meant, and yes, I mean it. There were

237

too many errors this time around. You're slipping up too often.

"I told you that I'm getting too old," Cal muttered. He slid the gun into his trouser pocket, shifted to hands and knees, and instinctively began crawling down the path to the car. He muttered curses beneath his breath as twigs stabbed at his hands and branches tore at his clothing.

Stop whining like a banshee, his brain snapped, in response to the tacit complaints. *If you stand up, the people scurrying about in the yard below will see you. We've got to get out of their line of sight fast. Once you get to the car, floor it. This path is bound to lead back to the house. As soon as you get there, make a mad dash into the back door and up to Chloe's room then back downstairs equally fast — and you'd better not tell me you're too old to run.*

"Don't worry. I can run."

I've done nothing but worry ever since we got here. Now, though, we have the chance to get out of here without a shred of suspicion tainting our life.

Cal jumped behind the wheel of his car and sped along the path, ignoring the damage the potholes were causing to its struts and shock absorbers. He stopped short of the tree line and peered out of the dirt-caked windshield, trying to catch sight of anyone running around near the back door of the house. There was no one. Everyone was near the barn or searching the area he'd only moments before vacated. He accelerated cautiously and eased from the trees, and then parked along the back of the house, next to the other work vehicles and ATVs. He slipped from the car and immediately ducked, peering over the hood of the car to see if he was still in the clear.

Looks like we're going to make it. Get inside so that we can get our alibi sewed up tighter than a lady's corset.

CHAPTER FORTY-FOUR

"Dalian," Harvey said gently, kneeling next to his distraught friend, "she's just fainted from shock. The paramedics are en route, and the deputies stationed here are out scouring the grounds for the shooter, along with everyone else. The sheriff arrived and already called in backup. There are so many people searching that there is no way in Hell this person will escape the dragnet this time. We'll catch him."

Dalian didn't respond. He just sat with Kat's head on his lap, the flurry of activity around him disregarded. The shooter hadn't severely injured Kat, for which he was grateful; in fact, the bullet had penetrated the fleshy part of her upper arm and exited out the rear. His apathy stemmed not from fear over her well-being rather at the knowledge that he truly could not protect her, as he promised her he'd do. They had been in a yard full of people, but that hadn't prevented the shooter making another attempt on their lives. It meant that the killer was far bolder than he'd first imagined, which indicated they were in greater danger than he'd surmised.

"Dalian?"

"We have to catch whoever's responsible, Harvey," Dalian whispered finally. "Nothing more can happen to Kat. She's suffered so much in so short a time. It isn't right that someone so gentle hearted should be the target of someone with a vengeful spirit. What could she possibly have done in the time she's been here, to generate animosity?"

"You're assuming that she is the target," Harvey replied. "You were embracing, so that bullet could have been intended for either of you – or both of you," he concluded softly. "Kind of makes you wonder, especially since you both could have easily died in the fire also. And don't forget that it was you that got walloped on the head in that attack."

"So you're proposing that we've pissed off someone so badly that we've both got bullseyes on our backs?

"Well, someone is holding some serious resentment against one or both of you, there's no doubting that," Sheriff Masters said, moving to kneel next to Kat. "How is she?"

"I think she'll be okay. The paramedics are on the way – again." Dalian was about to comment further, but before he could launch into his list of growing concerns, the sheriff continued speaking.

"We've got ourselves a real mystery here, because not one of your guests or ranch hands has any kind of a record to speak of. An outstanding parking ticket here and there, but nothing serious. There are two guests with a half dozen marriages under their belts – Chloe Harper and Cal Withers. All of Chloe's marriages ended in divorce, with the exception of one; but Cal is another matter altogether. He was a person of interest in the death of his wives – all three of them – because of the amount of the life insurance policies; however, in each of those cases, the police apprehended a suspect who a jury subsequently tried and convicted. Whoever is making these attempts, we have to assume that he or she is, one – fearless; two – a decent shot; and three – completely bonkers."

"I'd have to agree with that assessment," Dalian said with a sarcastic snort.

"Anyway, I brought some extra men with me to help in the search. Has anyone found anything yet, Harvey?"

"Not that I've been made aware of. Now that you're here though, I'm going to join in the hunt. It's time we ran this fox to ground."

"I agree. I'll stay and talk to Dalian until the paramedics arrive and then I'll join up with everybody. We won't leave a shrub unsearched."

Harvey nodded, clasped Dalian's shoulder reassuringly, and then headed toward the area that he was certain the shot originated. He didn't know who was trying to harm his dearest friend, but whomever it was better pray he didn't meet up with him before the police made an arrest; or he would be going to jail with some freshly inflicted bodily injuries.

Kat stirred and her eyelids fluttered opened. Dalian smiled encouragingly, but the smile refused to erase the concern in his eyes. "Well, it looks as if I find myself once again lying injured on the ground in your embrace," Kat quipped in a whisper, trying to assuage Dalian's fears. Her armed ached painfully but the fact that she woke up and was still breathing relieved her mind a great deal. Now she needed to relieve Dalian's mind. If the pained look in his gaze was any indicator, he somehow blamed himself for this latest assault. "This wasn't your fault."

"I gave you my word..."

"And you couldn't have guessed that this person would be as audacious as to fire into a crowd of people," Kat countered quickly. "Oh my, no one else was injured, were they?"

"Just you," the sheriff answered, and tears misted Dalian's eyes.

"I'll be okay, Dalian. It could have been far worse, as we both know. I will happily carry a scar over dying and never seeing you again." Dalian pulled Kat tighter into his embrace and then the tears started to fall.

"I hear the paramedics approaching," the sheriff said softly, and then stood to leave.

"Sheriff," Kat whispered, continuing to stroke Dalian's hair in comfort, "did you catch the guy responsible?"

The sheriff lowered his gaze, his face flushed with humiliating anger. He wished he could ease her concerns, tell her that the person responsible was on the way to jail, but he couldn't. "I'm sorry," he whispered, "we haven't caught whoever's responsible yet, but there were a lot of people out searching just after the shot was fired, so whoever it is couldn't be too far off getting caught."

Kat nodded and then refocused on Dalian, as the sheriff walked away. He lifted his head and swiped the tears from his eyes, "I'm so sorry, Kat."

"And I'm mad as a hornet," Kat said, her tone sharp. That brought a small smile to Dalian's lips.

"You are, are you?" He whispered, placing a light kiss on her lips.

"You bet your ass I am. I hope to high heaven they catch this person and when they do, they should hang him by his toenails during his trial. See how he likes enduring excruciating pain."

"Hurt a lot?" Dalian whispered, stroking her arm gently below the wound.

"Like Hell, if you want the truth."

Jake, the same paramedic that took care of Kat last time, approached, cutting off Dalian's response. His brow quirked in puzzlement, "What happened this time?" He asked, instinctively searching for another burned down building.

"Someone took a pot shot at us. Injured Kat." Dalian began to assist Kat to a seated position, but Jake stopped him.

"Let's let her stay where she is until I have a look, okay?"

Dalian nodded and Kat relaxed her head the best she could against his thighs. She winced when the paramedic made to lift her elbow-length shirt over the injury, "Okay," he said, stopping in mid-lift when she hissed loudly, "the blood is starting to congeal, which is good; however, the drying blood is attaching the clothing to the skin. The doctor will be able to get to the wound easier than I can right now. All I needed to do was make certain it isn't life threatening. We'll get you to the hospital. The doctor will need to clean the fibers from the shirt out of the wound. Once he's ascertained that there is no risk of infection, he'll probably release you to return home rather quickly.

"She'll be staying at the hospital under guard for a few days," the sheriff said approaching again. "This is Deputy Will Remer. He'll be escorting you to the hospital. He'll stay posted outside your door until I determine it's safe for you to return. You'll be staying in the room with her, Dalian. I want you both out of this guy's line of sight for a few days. And before you argue, Dalian, that you want to be a part of this search – the answer is an emphatic no. We don't know where this guy is, or who his intended target is. I can't risk you tramping about on the range."

"I wasn't going to argue, Sheriff," Dalian said, helping Kat to stand. "I agree that Kat and I are in danger, and I don't plan to leave her side or do anything that would put us at further risk," and then added, "see? I can be amenable," when the sheriff quirked a brow in his direction.

"So you can. Go with the deputy, and pack some supplies for you and Kat while Jake and I get Kat into the ambulance.

Before any of them could move, a shout sounded from across the yard. "Over here! We've found something!" It was Chloe. She was standing near a hill at the edge of the yard, waving her arms frantically. Dalian was about to move in her direction, but the sheriff placed a restraining hand on his arm, "You're out of this, remember?"

Dalian closed his eyes and counted to ten, but then nodded. He was truthful when he told the sheriff that he planned to stay out of it and let law enforcement do their job, but hearing there was a break in the case nearly made him forget. He sighed heavily, and wrapped his arm around Kat's shoulders as he watched the sheriff and everyone else converge on Chloe's location.

"You want to go too, don't you Deputy?" Dalian asked, his tone empathetic.

Will inhaled sharply and nodded, but responded diplomatically, "Keeping you and Kat safe are equally important." A theory borne out by the gun he'd pulled from his holster rapidly when Chloe began shouting at them. He kept the barrel pointed at the ground, but his stance made it clear he was ready to take aim and shoot if it came to that.

"What do you think they've found?" Kat asked in a near-whisper, hope pounding through her veins.

"Whatever it is, it must be important or Chloe wouldn't have been dancing around like she was auditioning for Dancing with the Stars.

Kat laughed and Jake and Will snorted. The humor helped relieve a small measure of the tension swirling around in all four of them. It also snapped them out of their current mesmerizing stances. Each wanted to remain there waiting for some word, but Jake knew it wasn't good for Kat to stay standing with a bullet wound in her arm. As if just realizing his professionalism had slipped, he turned and reached for Kat's good arm, "Let's get you on the gurney. You don't need to be standing up right now, and your increased pulse rate has caused your wound to start seeping. Let me see if I can't help with that while Dalian and Will go to pack up some supplies as the sheriff instructed. The sooner we get her to the hospital," Jake continued, turning to address Dalian, "the better it will be for her."

"Let's just go on to the hospital. I'll come back and collect some things as soon as the doctor sees to Kat and she gets settled into our room."

"Fair enough," Jake said, gently lowering Kat on the gurney. "You'll take this trip lying down, Miss. Rules are rules." He smiled and carefully strapped Kat onto the stretcher. "Dalian, help me lift her up?"

The two men hefted the gurney and slid it into the back of the ambulance. Kat winced when the legs bumped and collapsed beneath her, but kept her discomfort quiet. She didn't need Dalian worrying any more than he already was, and other than some pain in her arm, she knew she was going to survive this latest assault; a knowledge that boosted her spirits – and her temper – considerably. She didn't know who was responsible for these attacks against her and Dalian, but she hadn't come on vacation to suffer through all of this drama; although she did have to admit, it would add an exciting element to the story she planned to write about her and Dalian when all of this was over. She sighed at where her thoughts automatically directed – writing. Still, she was an author and her story ideas did originate from life. This particular story would just happen to stem from her own life.

Her thoughts ceased when Dalian and Jake climbed in on either side of her. Jake immediately got to the business of being a paramedic, retaking her blood pressure, and hooking her up to an IV drip, while Dalian gave her a gentle kiss.

"Will and I are going to follow along behind the ambulance in our cars. That way I can get back here when I need to. Are you okay with that? I know it won't be a picnic riding back here on your own."

Kat wanted to beg him to ride with her, but instead she tamped down on her fears and smiled bravely, "It isn't too far a ride, and just knowing you are coming with me is enough to keep me from falling to pieces."

"You're braver than any woman I've ever known. I love you, Kat." Dalian kissed her again, and then moved to jump down from the ambulance. Jake was right behind him. "We're headed out now, Kat." Jake smiled encouragingly and then closed her in the back of the ambulance, her thoughts and fears her only companion.

CHAPTER FORTY-FIVE

"What have you found?" The sheriff asked, his breathing coming in short gasps as he came to a halt near one of the junior state patrol officers.

"Over here. We haven't touched anything, since we're waiting for the forensic team to get here to lock down the scene. I took the liberty of radioing it in and also in ordering a continued search for our suspect."

"That's great, thanks..."

"The name's Trooper Mitchell Brown. I was in the area when I heard the call go out."

"Much appreciated Mitchell, and nice job. Show me what we've got."

Mitchell turned and walked a few feet down the main trail, and then turned and headed down a much narrower path. "It's over here. We won't know until forensics gets done on whether this is related to this case, but if I were a betting man, I'd say we've got ourselves a mighty big break."

The sheriff stopped and looked down at the path, a giant grin spreading across his thin lips, "And I would be placing a bet right alongside you. I think we may have a shot at solving this case."

"Yes, sir."

The sheriff stepped gingerly around the evidence lying on the pathway and made his way over to the edge of the hill. He peered over and saw Chloe headed toward the main house, conversing with Kenny, the ranch hand who'd given Marsha her much-needed alibi. *Didn't take Kenny long to get over Marsha,* the sheriff thought with a grin and then shifted his gaze. He panned around until his gaze located the ambulance. Dalian, Kat, Jake, and Will were standing there facing his direction. He could only imagine what was going through their minds, but he definitely knew what was going through his – that very thought he'd voiced aloud just prior to making a mad dash across the yard, "He's bonkers," he whispered the thought aloud.

"Sir?" Mitchell asked, moving to stand beside the sheriff.

"Our shooter. He's bonkers, and apparently fearless, or he wouldn't have taken a shot from this distance into a crowd of people."

"Your point, sir?"

"I'm not sure, but I do want extra men manning this evidence until it's bagged and tagged. If he's as crazy as I'm presuming, he may attempt to retrieve it, and one man alone up here may not stand a chance at stopping him. Dispatch five men to this spot – good shots – and tell them they are to remain on high alert. Let's get back out to the main trail. If he left evidence like this lying about, then he may have been careless enough to leave other evidence."

The trooper quickly radioed in the given orders and then trotted to catch up with Sheriff Masters. "There are a lot of tire tracks out here, any of which could be our shooter's – or none at all."

"Tracks," the sheriff whispered thoughtfully.

"Yes sir. My brother owns a ranch. Trails like these are what the hands use to get around the range in the vehicles, when it necessitates.

"Understood, and we may not be able to discern which tracks are our perps – if any at all – but we may be able to deduce direction."

"Sir?"

"Find me a ranch hand that knows these trails like the back of his hand, and get back on the horn. Tell central I want a helicopter airborne in less than fifteen minutes. If our assailant is still mobile – whether in a car or on foot – and unfamiliar with the range, he may be sticking to the trails.

"If he's mobile, isn't there a good chance he's already hightailed it out of here?"

The sheriff shook his head, "The guard would have informed us had anyone left the ranch, especially anyone attempting to do so right after the shooting. No, I have to believe that this guy is still out here somewhere, and we're going to find him. Since he didn't hightail it out the front gate, there's a two-hundred acre spread for him to try to get lost on.

CHAPTER FORTY-SIX

"I just want to change and put on a better pair of shoes before I continue traipsing around in the woods some more," Chloe was saying to Kenny as she made her way toward the front door of the house.

"I'm not certain you should be traipsing around after anyone, ma'am. I wouldn't exactly think it safe. What if you are out there and you happen to be the one who comes across him?"

"I'll charm him into surrendering," Chloe quipped and then grew serious. "Kat is a good person. She doesn't deserve what's happening to her, and if I can help find the man responsible, then I'm damn well gonna try. I certainly am not going to sit back on my fanny and do nothing.

"Well, maybe you can ride along with Miss Kat to the hospital. I'm sure she would like your company and..." Kenny stopped talking as the ambulance drove past, closely followed by Dalian's Jeep and the deputy's patrol car.

"Looks like that idea just passed me by," Chloe said, heading up the front steps. "Perhaps I can join you in the search, Kenny. Unless you think I'd get in your way," she batted her eyelashes, and Kenny's heart thumped against his chest. He didn't know if she'd get in the way or not, but he could think of a dozen cozy little caves he could use to keep her out of harm's way. He smiled at the thought, and Chloe grinned, "I'll only be a moment. You wait down here for me, okay?"

Kenny nodded. The vapid grin Chloe had been wearing when conversing with Kenny slipped and in its stead, a worried crease formed along her brow, as she headed up the staircase. She didn't really want to go traipsing along after Kenny, despite her brave words to the contrary, but the thought of hanging about in a nearly empty house with a potential killer at large was far more unsettling.

Unfortunately, her sundress and flip flips had proven ill-suited for traipsing about in the bushes, as she'd quickly discovered when they all heard the gunfire. Without thought, she immediately ran after the hoard of men, and then proceeded to slip and slide her way up the hillside in an attempt at not being left alone.

The same with now. She simply didn't want to be alone in the yard; although in hindsight she probably could have stayed by Kat's side – as Kenny suggested – as she did when the barn burned down around the poor woman's ears; however, in her estimation, to do so would have proved far too dangerous, since someone was firing a gun at Kat. To her self-centered way of thinking, it was safer being in a group of angry men trudging about the brush, than next to the intended target.

Unfortunately, the men began to scatter immediately after reaching the top of the hill, and she was unprepared to dash after them, so she hung nearby the junior state trooper, Mitchell Brown, who seemed content to traipse along the main trail, literally sniffing out clues. She tagged behind him, silent, and unnoticed for the most part, until Mitchell located that single piece of damning evidence. Then he noticed her enough to shout at her to go find the sheriff. She turned quickly without thinking, and ran back in the direction she'd come. She slipped repeatedly on her way down the hill and determined then and there that she wasn't going to take another step through the brush until she was suitably dressed. Before she could do that, however, she had to find the sheriff, and since she wasn't going to go gallivanting around the yard, alone, in search of him, she did the next best thing – she started waving her arms and screaming like a banshee.

She felt pleased that she'd been there to greet the converging hoard, but once they heard the news, they started heading up the hill en masse, leaving her to stand there gawking after them. All but Kenny. He seemed to sense her distress and stayed to talk to her, comfort her.

And now, he was going to allow her to tag along with him – all because she'd been too cowardly to stay next to her friend's side during this crisis. She only hoped that once they got out on the range, Kenny would skillfully keep her out of harm's way. She sighed and pushed open the door to her bedroom, and immediately pulled her soiled sundress over the top of her head, followed quickly by her torn panties. "Damnable hill. I liked these panties," she sighed, tossing them toward the wastebasket near the dresser.

As if just realizing that she'd stripped naked with her door still open, she lifted her foot, kicked off her flip-flop, and then kicked the door closed. She was just about to kick off her other flip-flop when the sight of Cal Withers cowering against the wall near the door stopped her in her tracks. She squealed, and would have ran from the room had she been less full of common sense at that moment. Although his intrusion unnerved her, her mind reminded her that she knew him; that he wasn't a dangerous stranger – and that she was butt naked. Her skin flushed pink and she slowly moved toward the wardrobe.

Cal chose that moment to raise his head from his knees and spear her with a daunting maniacal glower, "How could I have been so stupid? He's going to make me pay for my mistake now, and I won't be able to stop it. You know how I know he's going to make me pay? Because he isn't shouting at me for making that enormous blunder, that's how. He's silent. Oh God, he's completely silent."

Chloe's gaze widened in alarm when Cal clasped the sides of his head and began to squeeze tight, as if trying to squash the disturbing thoughts from his mind. Then he returned to muttering nonsensically. At least it sounded like nonsense to Chloe, whose greater concern was to get dressed and then go to find help – for her or Cal she had yet to determine.

"I can't believe I didn't know."

"Didn't know what, Cal?" Chloe asked calmly and quietly, as she reached into the armoire to retrieve another sundress from inside.

He looked at her again, tears glistening in his gaze, but it didn't appear as if he truly noticed her standing there. "I didn't know that the gun had fallen from my pocket. Why didn't *he* know? He supposedly knows everything. Why didn't he make me stop and pick it up? Whenever I make a mistake, he always stops me. He could have said, 'hey moron, pick up the gun!' or anything, but he didn't. He let me blunder, and now, oh God, he's going to make me pay."

"Um, Cal, I'm sure that whatever's happened, everything will be okay. If you tell me who he is, I'll make certain that the sheriff apprehends him and then you'll be able to make a case for coercion or something, surely," Chloe said in an attempt to calm his ever-increasing agitation, but Cal wasn't listening. He just kept muttering in a self-derisive tone.

"He warned me that I'd been making too many blunders this time around, but I figured he would step up and fix everything. He's always fixing everything. But now . . . oh God, he's silent. Usually, when he goes quiet, it's only for a few minutes, never this long. Never this long! He never stops talking. Talk, damn you!"

Chloe stopped her movements again, alarm registering on her face, when Cal began slapping at the side of his head. Not the type of slap when an idea forms, but a hard, skull-rattling slap, as if trying to knock the brain out the other side.

Oh my God, he's lost it! She thought, and then another thought registered. He said something about a gun. Her heart started thudding hard inside her chest when she realized she was standing naked in the room with Kat's assailant; that it had been Cal who dropped the gun that the state patrol trooper found on the hill earlier. Tears glistened in her own eyes then, as fear raged and her flight response kicked in. She took a deep calming breath and slowly slipped the sundress over her head. When Cal remained unaware, still slapping at his head, she felt less fearful and more confident that she might be able to escape the confines of this room and go get help – for herself, she now realized.

She sidled along the wall, careful to keep her movements slow and precise, nothing that would draw Cal's attention back in her direction. *Almost there!* She encouraged herself.

Cal chose that moment to look up. She froze.

Like a scene from a horror movie, Cal's head turned slowly until he was staring directly at her, only Chloe sensed that Cal was no longer present. The gaze was different now – steady and confident, commanding and cocky. "Going somewhere?" The voice purred, and Chloe felt the hairs on her body stand erect, as if an electric current slid throughout. She shivered, and then made a leap for the doorknob. Cal was far quicker. He stood and blocked the doorway, his gaze boring into her own.

"What do you want?" Chloe asked, knowing she sounded like a character from a B-rated movie.

"As tired as I am of cleaning up after Cal, I can't just let him get caught. He gets caught, I get caught," the voice continued. Cal took a step toward her and Chloe took a step back. Cal took another step toward her and Chloe took another backward.

"I like to have fun," the voice continued speaking, while Cal's gaze continued raking over her appreciatively. "Too bad I don't have time to appreciate you the way I know you like to be appreciated. The worst thing that should have happened to you is that you spend the rest of your life in prison for trying to kill Dalian; but since Cal kept bungling that and no longer has the gun to plant on you . . ." Cal shrugged, and he cocked his head, looking at her with intrigue. Then with the speed of a snake, his hand lashed out and snagged Chloe's wrist.

Chloe opened her mouth to scream, but Cal quickly raised a hand and covered her mouth, pulling a jagged knife from his coat pocket, "I would be quiet if I were you. I need to think on how to get out of this unscathed, and you're going to help. Willing or not."

CHAPTER FORTY-SEVEN

"Sheriff Masters?"

He pulled the radio from his belt and depressed the talk button, "This is the sheriff."

This is Phil over at the lab. I was already running the fingerprints your deputy scanned from the gun when your deputy called and asked me to run it against a specific guest – Cal Withers.

"That's right. What did you find?"

Cal Withers' prints were the only ones on both the gun and the bullets. I think you've found your shooter, Sheriff.

The sheriff nodded, "Thank you, Phil." He pressed the off button and returned the radio to its pouch on his belt. "Didn't someone mention that Cal Withers departed the ranch . . ."

"Yeah, but the deputy at the gate said he returned. About half hour before the shooting started."

The sheriff sucked in a deep breath, "Anyone seen him since?"

The deputy shook his head, "He who we're looking for?"

The sheriff nodded, "He's our guy. Confirmed. He probably won't make it easy to find him, so ensure that we turn over every stone."

The deputy got on the radio and issued the instructions, then started off on his own search. The sheriff sat down on the hood of his car and rubbed his jaw, "I knew he was strange, but how I overlooked the potential for him to be the perp . . . maybe it's time to hand the reins over to someone younger." He sighed loudly, and then headed off to help with the search.

CHAPTER FORTY-EIGHT

"Please, I can't write that!" Chloe protested quietly.

"Oh, but you will," Cal threatened, placing the knife against her throat. "Now, do it!"

Chloe closed her eyes, terror coursing through her body against the option of dying or complying. She wanted to scream, but the knife against her throat was a sharp reminder of what would happen to her if she did. She liked life too much, so chose to comply; penning the words Cal dictated to her, careful to follow his instructions and that she not allow her nervousness to translate into shaky writing.

A knock on the door startled them both, and for a moment the pressure of the knife against her throat increased and Chloe thought Cal would slit her throat right then. She glanced up when she saw him lean over her, his finger pressed against his lips. He pressed the knife a little firmer to ensure she knew the consequences should she call out. She nodded as best she could. He tilted his head, signaling she should rise and move toward the door.

"Are you still in there, Chloe?" A voice called from the other side. "We really need to get back out there to help with the search."

Cal leaned in and whispered next to her ear, "You've decided to sit it out. Stay in your room where you feel safe." He grinned widely at that irony, "And remember, I'll kill you if you give anything away, and then I'll kill him."

Chloe swallowed hard and then leaned against the door, "I'm so sorry for behaving so callously. I should have let you know. I'm going to shower and stay in my room. I just don't feel safe traipsing about outside where there's a . . . ." she tripped over the next word, but quickly recovered, ". . .killer," She finished, tears starting to stream down her face.

"That's a good idea; and keep your door locked. I'll check in on you later," Kenny called from the other side of the door.

"I look forward to hearing that you've captured the guy," Chloe replied.

"I'll inform you ASAP."

Cal tilted his head and listened as the receding sounds of footfall.

"You're a fair liar," Cal murmured appreciatively. "Now, let us return to our work, shall we?" He guided her back to the table and pushed her down onto the seat.

"Now, you'll write that you simply couldn't bear what you'd done. That you're sorry for all the pain you caused. Pick up the pen please."

Chloe picked up the pen and finished up the letter, "How am I supposed to get this to the sheriff? If this is my confession, why can't I just tell him in person?"

"Ah now, do you really think you'd spill your guts if I let you walk out of here and turn yourself in? Tsk tsk. I thought you took me as being smarter than that. If there's a note, written in your hand, then it'll go a lot faster in convincing the good sheriff of your guilt." He watched her put the finishing touches on the letter, "Now, sign it please."

Chloe signed the note and laid the pen down, "Now what?" She asked, sniffing loudly.

He slid the chair back, "Stand up."

Chloe's knees were knocking so hard that it took her two tries to stand without falling over. She made to turn, to face Cal, but he put a hand on her shoulder.

"I'm going to hand you my knife," he whispered against her ear.

"A chance to defend yourself." Chloe couldn't see his actions while she stood and waited for him to seal her fate.

Chloe closed her eyes and the tears grew in intensity, "I can't . . ."

". . . defeat me?" Cal concluded for her. "You're right," he whispered, reaching around and clasping her wrist. He placed the knife in her hand and she gripped it instinctually.

"Don't drop it," he ordered, when he saw her fingers begin to unclasp. "You may not be able to defeat me, but it's only sporting of me to give you the chance, so you may want to grip that knife as if your life depends on it – because it does."

Chloe closed her fingers around the hilt as tightly as she could.

"Good," Cal purred. "Doesn't it feel good to have a modicum of control returned? And if by some miracle you do happen to stab me, you'll be free to tear up that note I made you write. Sounds fair?"

Chloe nodded.

"I thought it might," he whispered, running his hand along hers and up her bare arm. Chloe had never felt so vulnerable or exposed as she did, standing there while a psychopath caressed her. He slid his hand back down and clasped her hand with the knife. "Now, a quick lesson in knife fighting. I want to make certain that, when I let you turn on me, you know precisely where to strike. So you see, I want you to have that fighting chance."

Chloe was having a hard time breathing. She'd never faced this kind of insanity before and didn't know what to expect, or how she was going to survive the encounter. She only knew that she wanted to live, so she forced herself to breathe and relax as much as she was able.

Cal turned the knife toward her abdomen, pressing the tip at a place just below her ribs, "Right here," he purred, his lips sliding along her hair next to her ear. "Here is where you want to strike. You have to thrust hard. You can't thrust like a girl," he continued, his tone silky, like a lovers caress. "Understand?"

Chloe nodded her understanding.

"Good. Are you ready? You have to be relaxed. Breathe normally. Otherwise, you'll not have a hope of defeating me," Cal continued. "Can you do that?"

Chloe nodded again.

"Good, good. I'm ready when you are. If you need a moment more to compose yourself, I'll wait," Cal whispered, thoroughly enjoying himself.

Chloe shook her head and sniffed loudly. Cal grinned wider.

"This is quite exhilarating, wouldn't you agree?" He asked rhetorically. "The most fun I've had in a while. You want me dead, don't you?"

Chloe nodded.

"Well then, let's not postpone this any longer," he murmured, gripping her hand and thrusting the knife into her abdomen, pushing it higher, forcing her hand into a twisting motion; ensuring her fingers remained firmly attached to the hilt.

Chloe was so stunned that she could utter no more than a squeak. She bent over as the pain shot though her abdomen and throughout her body. Cal gave the knife a final thrust and twist, and then released his grip. Chloe however, held to the knife firmly in shock, toppling to the floor and onto her side. Her gaze was wide with stunned disbelief and agony.

Cal stood over her, watching as the blood slowly seeped onto the carpet below. He stepped back, to prevent the blood oozing along the carpet and staining his shoes. He'd planned this carefully and didn't want any more hiccups.

He could hear the insipid Cal inside his head, screaming his disgust and displeasure over the brutality of Chloe's assault, but he could scream all he wanted. The wishy-washy weakling had been in charge of their lives too long, it was time for the stronger to take the reins. He walked to the bathroom and washed his hands, careful to ensure no blood would be detected. He then returned to Chloe's side. He'd brought a wet cloth from the bathroom and stepped gingerly up to her body; then used the cloth to wipe down her wrist and arms, so that there would be no signs that he'd assisted in her suicide.

He left the room, then went to his room and collected the few things he'd deliberately "forgotten" and departed the house through the back; headed for the area where he'd parked his car. He knew he wouldn't get far; not if they'd located the gun and found his prints on it, but he was ready for them. He was always ready.

CHAPTER FORTY-NINE

"Cal Withers, put your hands on your head and get down on your knees!" An officer yelled before Cal made it halfway across the yard. He dropped the few items he was carrying and complied immediately.

"I don't understand," Cal cried, mimicking his weaker counterpart. "What have I done?"

The officer ran over and set to cuffing Cal, quoting his Miranda rights, "Do you understand these rights as I've explained them to you?"

"What I don't understand is why you're arresting me? What have I done?"

"I'm arresting you for assault, and two counts of attempted murder," the police officer droned, leading him toward the house.

"No, no, no," Cal cried. "You've got the wrong man. I didn't do those things. I would never try to hurt anybody. I couldn't. I didn't."

The police officer ignored the pleas. He guided Cal with one hand and then pressed his radio with the other, "Sheriff, I've taken Cal Withers into custody. I'll meet you at the house."

CHAPTER FIFTY

It took less than fifteen minutes for everyone to reassemble at the house. The sheriff asked everyone to gather in the dining area until further notice.

"It won't take long to close this up folks," he said reassuringly, "then we'll let you get back to enjoying your vacation – again. While it does seem that there's been an inordinate amount of chaos and violence of late, I can only assure you that this isn't commonplace for our little community and hope it won't deter you from returning at some time in the future. I also want to commend each and every one of you on your assistance in every aspect of this investigation. You all are the epitome of what humanity should entail and you should give yourselves a hearty pat on the back."

There was an outburst of applause. The sheriff applauded back and then turned to speak to the officer who'd brought in Withers and was standing guard next to the powder room door where he'd stashed him.

"He say anything?" The sheriff asked.

The officer nodded, "Said he was clueless on why we are pointing the finger at him; and sheriff, I have to admit, his surprise and concern seem sincerely genuine. He didn't act suspicious in the least. Far from it."

The sheriff furrowed his brow. He'd never heard one of his officers go to such lengths to all but defend a suspect before. It surprised him; however, his assertions were nowhere near as vehement as Cal's were, when he opened the door to the powder room.

"Why am I being arrested," he wailed, tears pooled in his eyes. "I haven't done anything." His protestations continued as the sheriff led him down the hallway to Dalian's office.

"We'll talk in here. Be more comfortable that way."

"The officer said you were arresting me for . . . for . . ." he sputtered, as if not certain.

"Assault on Dalian and the attempted murder, twice, for Kat . . ."

"Kat! I'd never hurt Kat. She's the most precious woman I've ever met. Dear sweet Jesus . . . and what do you mean, twice? Is Kat okay?"

The sheriff watched Cal intently and was beginning to agree with his officer. Something wasn't right. This man seemed genuinely distraught. He'd dealt with some serious psychopaths in his years on the force, but never had they been able to maintain a ruse of innocence for too long. Something always tipped them into revealing themselves for what they really were. He continued watching Cal closely, waiting for that slip up to occur.

"Kat will be fine."

Cal closed his eyes and sighed heavily, "I'm very glad to hear that. What happened to her?"

"She was shot."

Cal's eyes bugged a bit and he sucked in a deep breath, "That's . . . who?"

"You."

"Wait . . . no . . . no . . . why would you . . ."

"Well, let's go over everything that I have so far, and you won't be able to conclude anything other than what I have. First, you were jealous of Dalian's burgeoning relationship with Kat."

Cal nodded.

No denial, the sheriff thought, his eyes narrowing, "Next, you were the only one to leave the area after being told not to . . ."

"I told you . . ."

"And then," the sheriff interrupted, "you return just half hour prior to the shooting of Kathryn McMurray." *Let's see you explain that one away*, the sheriff thought smugly, but was surprised when Cal just sat there shaking his head. He lowered it, whispering the word 'no' repeatedly. Psychopaths generally had an answer to everything. Cal wasn't behaving the way he anticipated, and it bothered him. *Well, he won't be able to get around the gun.*

"Finally, there's the gun.

Cal sat as if he didn't hear, continuing to mutter 'no' beneath his breath.

"Did you hear what I said, Cal? We found the weapon where you dropped . . ." The sheriff stopped speaking, suddenly on edge. *If he's the shooter and knew his prints would be all over the weapon, why leave it to be found? Did he expect to be gone before being arrested? Surely he'd know we'd put an APB out for his arrest. Things weren't adding up and it was making the sheriff even angrier.* "Cal?"

Cal raised his head, the look in his eyes dejected, "I didn't shoot anyone. I swear, I didn't," he whispered, then lowered his head again.

"Then how do you explain your prints on the weapon?"

Cal shook his head, "What weapon?" He implored.

"We found a 9mm Beretta with your prints all over the bullets and the gun."

Cal looked up, puzzled, and then blinked rapidly.

The sheriff narrowed his gaze again, "You look like a man with something to say," he stated.

"I handled a gun before I left," Cal murmured, "but I don't know what kind it was, or if it's the gun you're talking about. I was just helping . . . I swear I didn't . . . I can't even step on an ant without feeling terrible about it. The thought of hurting anyone makes me physically ill . . ."

"Yet you have three dead wives to your name," the sheriff jabbed, knowing that if anything was going to break this man's façade, it would be the truth of his past acts being found out. To the sheriff's dismay, the tactic didn't work.

"No, my wives were killed...not by me. Never me," Cal declared passionately.

"I know you were never charged, but the number of bodies in your wake is too coincidental for me to overlook, don't you think?"

"No . . . no . . . not guilty . . . no . . . only touched the gun to help . . . I'd never hurt anyone," Cal cried, lowering his head into his hands.

The sheriff felt sick to his stomach – both at the man's cowardliness and at the sinking sensation swirling about in his gut that they may have the wrong man in custody after all; but surely the timing of his return from town couldn't be overlooked; couldn't possibly be coincidental.

A scream rent the air and the sheriff nearly fell out of his chair. He raced to the door and yanked it open, just as Mrs. Guthrie came running along the upper landing, shrieking like a banshee.

CHAPTER FIFTY-ONE

"Guard him," the sheriff commanded to a nearby officer and he immediately went to stand guard at the office door. "Tell the people in the dining room that Mrs. Guthrie is beyond petrified of spiders and that she just overreacted to a really big one in the upstairs bathroom. Go!"

The officer ran over to the dining hall where those assembled were beginning to move over to the doorway, distress lining their faces. The officer immediately filled them in using the sheriff's lie, and they instantly relaxed; some laughing, some sighing in relief. The officer didn't know what was going on, but he did comprehend the sheriff's reasoning. The last thing these people needed was another reason to fret or panic.

The sheriff met Mrs. Guthrie halfway up the stairway and immediately set to calming her, "I need you to quiet down now, Mrs. Guthrie, and try to explain what's going on, okay? It's in everyone's best interest not to stir up another hornets nest with hysteria. Understand?" Mrs. Guthrie continued crying, but nodded her understanding, "Good. Is this something you can vocalize or do you need to show me?"

Mrs. Guthrie shook her head violently and then turned and headed back up the stairs, wiping at her face and nose with her apron. She stopped halfway down the hallway and pointed, "I can't . . . go . . . back" she gasped tearfully.

"Which room?"

Mrs. Guthrie just pointed, shaking her finger violently, her breathing ragged.

"Okay, one of those," the sheriff stated. "I'm going to ask that you go to the kitchen and stay there; and please, Mrs. Guthrie, do whatever it takes to compose yourself. I don't know what you've seen, and I know whatever it is has upset you aplenty, but right now I need you to calm yourself so we don't incite more mayhem. Agreed?" Mrs. Guthrie nodded. "Good," the sheriff sighed and kissed her on the cheek. "Go. I'll check in on you as soon as I'm able."

Mrs. Guthrie was on her way to the kitchen when Dalian returned from the hospital. He saw her state of distress and dashed over, "Mrs. Guthrie, what's happened? Are you okay?"

She started crying heavily again and could do no more than nod and point up the stairs. Dalian didn't know all that had transpired, but he knew that whatever it was had shaken Mrs. Guthrie to the core, and that was not something easily done. He took the stairs two at a time and spotted the sheriff leaving one of the bedrooms, "Sheriff?"

The sheriff turned, shaking off the sense of eeriness that had settled over him – first during his interview with Cal Withers and now with this unknown horror that had distressed Mrs. Guthrie so greatly, "Dalian."

"I just ran into Mrs. Guthrie. What's happened?"

"I don't know. I just know that something down here scared the living wits out of that woman. In one of the guest rooms. She couldn't be precise as to which. I had the guests informed that it was no more than a spider that sent her screaming in terror. I didn't want any more stress circulating than already has been. How's Kat?"

"Resting. That's why I came back to collect some things."

The sheriff nodded, "You think you can help search the rooms? I can't say for certain what we'll find."

Dalian nodded.

"Took Cal Withers into custody for the attacks on you and Kat," the sheriff stated casually as they moved room to room.

Dalian turned, stunned, "I knew he wasn't thrilled over Kat and me, but I never took him for anything other than a scaredy-cat."

"Yeah, me either, although there seems to be a boatload of evidence piling up against him," the sheriff stated, but something in his tone gave Dalian pause.

"What are you thinking?"

"Something's hinky, and I haven't yet been able to put my finger on it," the sheriff muttered, as he stepped in to Chloe's room, "but I'll bet a year's wages that this holds part of the answers." He drew in a deep breath through his nostrils and stepped inside, allowing Dalian to follow suit.

"Son of a bitch," he declared, and started to move to where Chloe lie, but the sheriff stopped him.

"Might want to stay over here, Dalian. I need the coroner to have a clean scene to work with," the sheriff said professionally, but inside, he felt like vomiting. Chloe lie on her side, blood pooled all around her abdomen, her skin pale from exsanguination. He got on his radio and requested a call be made to the medical examiner's office, "And tell him I said to get here quick and silent."

"Silent?" Dalian asked, tearing his gaze from the body.

"No sirens. I need to confirm Chloe's death is a suicide, since I see a note over there on the table next to the body. I'll let the coroner retrieve it though, to confirm. Don't want to trample all over the scene."

"Why would Chloe kill herself?" Dalian whispered.

"We'll know when we get that letter. I'm not liking the timing though. Something isn't right. I can feel it in my gut."

"What do we do now?"

"We wait," the sheriff stated. "Can't do much else until then."

"What about Cal Withers?"

"I've interviewed him to my satisfaction for the time being. If this proves to be a suicide, I'll book him for the other charges."

"*If* this proves to be suicide?"

"If it's murder, then Withers is either guilty of this too or we've got someone else to worry over."

CHAPTER FIFTY-TWO

"Right now, upon a cursory exam, it appears death by a self-inflicted stab into the upper abdominal cavity," the M.E. stated. "Knife still impaled. Victim still holding the hilt. I'll dust for secondary prints, but the method of entry and the way the victim is holding the knife says suicide; and then there's this." The M.E. handed over the letter. "Found it on the table. Didn't read it, of course, but generally a letter found next to an apparent suicide . . . well, I'll let you know more after my full examination."

"Thanks, Mick," the sheriff said quietly. He watched two orderlies lift Chloe's body onto a stretcher. "Take her out the back way," he stated as they passed. As soon as the room cleared, he moved out to the hallway. Dalian was there waiting.

"So, here's the note that was on the table," the sheriff said, lifting the letter.

"Suicide note?" Dalian asked, perplexed.

"I haven't read it yet," the sheriff admitted.

"I've not known you to ever get squeamish over a crime scene," Dalian stated, feeling suddenly tense. "Want me to read it?"

The sheriff nodded, handing the note over, the knots in his stomach refusing to loosen. He had the best, most reasonable suspect downstairs, but if this was a suicide note, and it was directly related to the goings on of late . . . he hated monkey wrenches being tossed into his work, and the minute Dalian started reading, he knew that's what was happening.

I can't do this any longer. I'm at fault for it all. I planted the gun for the officers to find because I wasn't ready to get caught.

But knowing that I shot Kat and nearly killed her instead of Dalian . . .

I asked Cal Withers to show me how to load and shoot a gun because he seemed like the perfect patsy for my crimes; but now, I know I was so wrong. I allowed myself to be clouded by anger and hate and . . . I can't let an innocent man take the blame for my actions. I just can't, nor can I live with what I've done. I'm so very sorry. Please forgive me.

"She signed it," Dalian whispered. He shook his head in disbelief. "This is insane," he muttered.

The sheriff nodded, "It would explain Cal Wither's perplexity when I mentioned the gun though. It would explain his behavior quite a bit – with the exception of why he left and why he came back."

"He left and came back?"

"Yeah," the sheriff said. "Found that out from the officer at the gate when we started our search for Withers, when his prints came back as being on the gun. Apparently, he came back just half hour before the shooting. Said he forgot some things in his room . . ."

"Could be that's why Chloe waited. When Cal left suddenly, she didn't have him as a fall guy anymore," Dalian supplied. "When he came back, she could have easily decided it would be a good time to . . . well, you know."

"Sounds logical," the sheriff mumbled. "Can anyone account for Chloe's whereabouts at the time of the shooting? I know she was the one who alerted us to the gun's whereabouts."

"We can ask around, but you know as well as I do that with so many people traipsing about, no one is going to be keeping up with someone else's whereabouts. Normally a beautiful woman like that would stand out, but there were a hell of lot of woman here for the barn raising, and they aren't nothing to sneeze at either," Dalian sighed heavily. "What are you going to do with Cal Withers now that he's not looking good for any of it?" Dalian asked.

"If we can find something to compare the handwriting to, we can determine if she actually wrote this."

"Or if it was Cal Withers? I have both their writing and signature on file," Dalian stated, heading toward his office. The sheriff followed. "Guests fill out questionnaires and sign waivers." When they entered Dalian's office, Cal Withers sat precisely as the sheriff had left him – with his head lowered and shaking slowly. The sheriff looked at Dalian, who looked at Cal with brow knitted, then looked at the sheriff with a 'he's isn't acting like a killer' look.

The sheriff cocked a brow in agreement, then turned and whispered to the officer that had been standing guard outside the office, "Take Cal to the front porch. Have him wait for us out there."

The officer nodded and moved to clasp a non-resisting Cal by the upper arm. It wasn't until he shuffled past the sheriff and Dalian that he seemed to find reason to speak, "I didn't . . . I couldn't . . ." he muttered, his gaze pleading with them to believe him.

The sheriff nodded at the officer to keep moving, then Dalian approached the desk where he kept files on the guests. He flipped through and found the one for Chloe first. He placed it, and the letter, on the desktop and scanned the writing on Chloe's forms and the suicide note carefully, shaking his head in disbelief repeatedly.

"I can't see any discrepancies," he stated finally. "I can't see how Withers could have wrote this. The writing and the signature are too much like hers. There's no doubt she wrote this."

"I'm having a tremendous amount of difficulty equating that sweet, soft-spoken woman with attempted murder. Did she say or do anything . . ."

"She was upset that I didn't find her attractive," Dalian admitted. "I knew how she felt and she made no bones about it to Kat. Even said she'd come here to marry herself a rich rancher. Would failing to snare me drive her over the edge? God, I don't know. I didn't know her well enough to know what she was capable of doing if rejected," Dalian sighed heavily. "Still, she just didn't seem unbalanced in that way."

"Most killers don't," the sheriff replied softly.

"Seeing this, what are you going to do about Cal now?

"Cut him loose," the sheriff said with a shake of his head. He slapped his hands on his thighs, stood, and headed to the front porch. "I haven't got anything to hold him on, except the gun, and…Christ! That's been explained away. If forensics turns up anything over the next few days, I can always detain him at a later date."

CHAPTER FIFTY-THREE

Cal drove down the drive, keeping one eye on the road and one on the rearview mirror. The sheriff had cleared him of all wrong-doing, but he wasn't taking any chances of him changing his mind. He wanted out of their fast. Said as much when the sheriff said he was free to go. For his closing curtain, he finalized the performance of his lifetime.

"Mr. Withers, you're free to leave," the sheriff stated simply, watching a final time for any tale-tell sign that he should detain this suspect further.

Cal's head shot up and he appeared genuinely stunned, "You mean . . . but you said . . . you found . . . you know what," he said, jumping up rapidly, "I don't care. I'm getting out of here before you find some other crime to accuse me off," he snapped, and bolted down the front steps, calling over his shoulder, "and if I never see any of you again, it'll be too soon."

"What about the stuff you came back for?" The sheriff called after him.

"Keep it!" He shouted. He picked up speed until he was literally running for his car, grinning like the proverbial Cheshire cat.

Now, as the gate to freedom approached, he was all but laughing, "You kept saying I didn't have the guts to do the real dirty work," he told his alter-ego smugly, "but I did more to save our skins this time than I ever did prior, so from now on, I think I'll lead this two-man band. You can keep your sniveling little whiny behind tucked away. I'm in charge now!"

CHAPTER FIFTY-FOUR

"How is it," the sheriff asked when Dalian came out onto the porch, "that I can be so damned certain of something and yet so uncertain at the same time?" They both watched Cal's car peel up the driveway, his hurry to leave more than clear.

"It's a feeling in your gut that won't dissipate," Dalian murmured. "A stone that sits there day in and day out, reminding you."

The sheriff looked over at Dalian, "The stone in your gut . . ."

". . . tells me every day that Jethro Canton shot my wife with deliberate intent, to keep me from having a child that would inherit my land. I know it as certain as I'm standing here talking to you; but he was cleared because he was the perfect psychopath . . ."

". . . able to fool even the most seasoned of professionals, and the latest in technological advancements?" The sheriff concluded, and Dalian nodded.

"Developing a stone of your own?" Dalian asked softly.

The sheriff nodded, "Yep. The only evidence tying Cal to anything was the prints on that gun, but . . ."

". . . Chloe's letter clearly explains that away."

The sheriff nodded again, "And would make it difficult for a jury to convict Cal of a crime. Reasonable doubt, and all that shit; but my gut's shouting at me that I just let a murderer go free, and I can't do a damned thing about it."

"It hurts, I know," Dalian said quietly, placing a hand on his friend's shoulder. "And it always will."

"Not for him, it won't," the sheriff muttered, then turned and headed inside. It was time to release Dalian's clients so they could resume their vacation and start working on his report. He didn't know how long it would take for Dalian and Kat to get over everything that had happened in the span of less than a month, but he hoped that they'd find peace now, and manage to live a happy life.

For him, things would never be the same. He'd let a good man down – a good friend – twice. Had been outwitted twice by two cunning psychopaths, and had released those psychopaths out on the world to harm again. If he were any other man, he'd hunt those two men down and kill them – if only to spare their future victims; but he wasn't capable of that, and he knew it. Instead, he'd live with that stone in his gut, like Dalian – and retire. He would never be able to face another criminal and not be able to perceive their guilt or innocence. It was hard enough carrying the guilt of these two tragedies. He looked over at where Dalian stood in quiet conversation with his foreman and wondered how the man could even look him in the eye and call him friend. He sighed heavily and wiped his face with his hand.

Dalian walked over, "I've going to go check on Kat. If the doctor clears her, I'll bring her home. We certainly don't need to hide out at the hospital anymore. Harvey is going to get the guests situated in their rooms. He's been told to keep Chloe's door closed. I'll hire a clean-up crew as soon as you, or your forensic team, give me clearance to do so. You okay?"

The sheriff shook his head, "Not really, no, but I will be. I'm going to head into town and type up my report."

"Thank you, Johnathan."

"For what? Didn't do anything."

"Cal's gone and the person that tried to kill us committed suicide. I feel safer right now that at any time during this week. That's thanks enough."

The sheriff didn't reply, merely collected his hat and headed to his car.

"Think he'll be okay?"

"No, I don't," Dalian replied softly, "but I can't carry his burdens for him, not and carry mine too. He'll have to sort his demons out himself."

"Rise above 'em, right?"

"Rise above," Dalian agreed. "I'm going to go to the hospital."

EPILOGUE

October 2061
Wind River, Wyoming

"Want me to leave you alone, Mrs. Novelist?" Dalian bent and kissed Kat on the neck.

"Hmm, that's lovely," Kat purred, and then took a deep breath to regain her equilibrium. She needed to write, or Janet was likely to stop publishing her books. Writing had never been difficult for her before, but so much changed for her since arriving at Dalian's ranch, and she was simply a different person. That meant new experiences from which to draw upon for her writing. "No, sweetie, you don't need to leave me alone."

Dalian pulled his chair from in front of his computer and settled next to Kat. "What are you working on?"

"I thought I'd start our story now, especially since there's so much snow on the ground that any other activities are on hold." She smiled, but something in her gaze made Dalian's brow quirk.

"Something's bothering you?" He asked.

"I want to start our story, but there's so much that happened, I simply don't know where to start, and with everything a jumble in my brain, I'm having a difficult time sorting it all out."

"Well, you've definitely got a story worth telling. Not that anyone would believe our story to be true. You'll be changing our names right?"

"Oh, definitely. You know, I still get the shivers from time-to-time, thinking about Chloe."

"Actually, that's why I came in here. I just got off the phone with the sheriff. Apparently, the medical examiner concluded it wasn't suicide," Dalian said, settling in a chair next to her.

"What? You mean—

"Chloe wasn't the guilty party. Cal was, after all."

"Okay, now I'm completely confused…"

"There was a print on the hilt. Belonged to Cal. The M.E. got suspicious when he determined the knife had been twisted. He'd never known a suicide victim go to those extremes," Dalian sighed.

"Dalian, that means that Cal is still—

"The sheriff has an APB out for his arrest. He'll be apprehended. Until then, there will be a deputy stationed outside our gate day and night. Kat, we have to try not to let this get to us. Something in my gut tells me that Cal is done with us. He failed twice to kill us, and now that he knows we can't be gotten rid of as easy as he hoped…"

"He'll leave us alone?" Kat concluded, hope filling her tone. "At least the sheriff can feel vindicated, knowing that his gut was right all along."

"Yeah, that's one stone he'll be able to pass," Dalian quipped.

"Wow, Dalian. Really?"

"We'll be okay. You know that, right?"

Kat nodded, "I know, I just wish my brain agreed and would transmit that message to my fingers," she said, placing her fingertips on the keyboard. "My writing is usually therapeutic."

"Usually?"

"This story is different. It's our story. I'm questioning whether to write this book, because it'll dredge up all of those negative things again. At the same time, I've always found writing my experiences – even if in a work of fiction – to be cathartic, as I said, a way to release it all so it doesn't weigh me down."

"I can see that proving beneficial," Dalian concurred. "I say go for it."

"Thank you for the support, but like I said, I'm having difficulty finding a starting point. I know that I can make sufficient changes so that no one recognizes our lives – spice it up here and there, tone it down; although I doubt anyone of our acquaintance would read a romance – but where to begin?"

"I can't think of a better place to start than at the beginning. Are you still going to use the one I suggested?"

Kat smiled, "Absolutely. It's perfect for the essence of the book. You know, you may end up being an invaluable asset to my career, if you continue feeding me such marvelous ideas."

"Just trying to help, ma'am." Dalian tipped an imaginary hat and then stood, returning his chair to his computer desk. "Something tells me that the biggest help I can give you right now is to get out of your hair and let you write."

Kat laughed, "You're probably right. I promised Janet that I wouldn't let my move out here inhibit my work; and since I owe her a new book before the end of this year, I'd best make some form of a start as soon as possible. After all, a chapter a day a best seller makes, right?"

"I wouldn't have the first clue, but sounds reasonable to me. Have fun, baby." Dalian gave Kat another kiss and then turned to leave. "Want me to close the door?"

"Nah, it's not necessary. Once I get into a zone, it's hard for noises to distract me."

Dalian smiled, then headed for the door. He turned before exiting, "Just remember, Kat. We can't allow others to dictate how we live our lives. For our sanity's sake, we have to go on as if Cal is already behind bars."

"Understood, and I'll do my best." Kat waited until his footfalls receded and then turned to face the computer again. "Start at the beginning. Just change the names," she whispered. She lifted her fingers and placed them on the keyboard, then closed her eyes for a moment, composed her thoughts, placed herself back in the bedroom in Covington, and began typing.

CHAPTER ONE

March 2059
Covington, Georgia

"I'm coming," Adrianna murmured and then rolled over, nuzzled further beneath the quilt, and drifted back to sleep. A few moments later, the chimes sounded again, twice in succession, and Adrianna opened her eyes, rubbing the fatigue away. She started to poke her husband, in hopes he would crawl out of bed on this chilly morning, but her elbow met empty space. She glanced over at where he generally slept, and then at the clock on the nightstand. Seven o'clock, the bright red digital display read. *Odd*, she thought, as she threw the quilt back and slid to a seated position, *Stephen is usually home from work by now.*

www.ingramcontent.com/pod-product-compliance
Lightning Source LLC
Chambersburg PA
CBHW071459110726
47908CB00003B/666